MW00643757

PRAISE FOR SOMETHING BETTER

"If you are looking to get lost in a story about forgiveness, where the characters' genuine humanity makes you laugh, cry and open your heart to all things hopeful, you will not be able to put down *Something Better*. In her amazing debut novel, Diane Parrish beautifully constructs a world where things left unsaid create a pathway to redemption."

—Susan Aronson, writer and
Emmy Award-winning producer

"*Something Better* explores all facets of love, faith, and forgiveness while maintaining a propulsive plot and unexpected turns and resolutions."

—Liz Matthews, author and program director,
Westport Writers Workshop

"Diane Parrish's debut novel is breathtaking. It is a stunning reflection of the human spirit and the complexities that bind our lives together. A reminder of how deeply we are tethered to one another in loss and grief, love and passion, and the hope of forgiveness and redemption. The intricately crafted story is so absorbing and the characters so authentic that I still expect to bump into one of them at the grocery store. *Something Better* is a must-read that will live with you long beyond its reading."

—Caroline C. Barney, award-winning author
of *The Trebor Tales*

"In her debut novel, Diane Parrish takes us on roller coaster ride when it comes to our closest bonds and what forgiveness means. Readers will be captivated by the three narrators of *Something Better*—Ruth, Annabeth, and David—turning the pages to know the outcome of their personal, entwined journeys."

> —Susannah Marren, author of *A Palm Beach Wife*, *A Palm Beach Scandal*, and *Maribelle's Shadow*

"*Something Better* gently explores grief in its many forms Infused with keen insight, empathy for our human foibles, and wisdom about grace and forgiveness, Diane Parrish's deft prose offers a timely reminder that it's never too late to heal, if only we can take the first step."

> —Kristin Koval, author of *Penitence*

"With compassion and honesty, *Something Better* takes readers on a journey through the country of grief and the messy aftermath of love and disaster. Parrish's clear-eyed writing dives into the question of forgiveness: can we forgive the ones we love when they are the ones who hurt us the most? And can such radical forgiveness be life-changing? This tender story cheered me, moved me, and made me want to linger with its characters for long afterward. A novel with deep wells of heart and oceans of uplift waiting in its pages."

> —Blair Hurley, author of *Minor Prophets* and *The Devoted*

SOMETHING BETTER

SOMETHING BETTER

DIANE PARRISH

MERIDIAN EDITIONS

MERIDIAN | EDITIONS

Published by Meridian Editions

ISBN (paperback): 978-1-959170-13-6
ISBN (hardcover): 978-1-959170-14-3
ISBN (ebook): 978-1-959170-15-0

Book design by John Lotte
Front cover design by Kendall Farris

Manufactured in the United States of America

TO STEVEN

It is very easy to forgive others their mistakes; it takes more grit and gumption to forgive them for having witnessed your own.

—Jessamyn West

BEFORE

February 2009

THE HOUSE SITS INSIDE A SNOW GLOBE. The man and the woman catch glimpses through the swirling flakes of the party glittering within, a scene of warmth and light and laughter, confirmation they'd been right to risk the storm. They pick their way along the ice-covered walk toward the front door. She clutches his arm until he can guide her safely into the welcoming embrace of their hosts. The door closes behind them and the storm ceases to exist. This is a real party, not some faculty chips-and-beer affair. There are bartenders and servers, passed canapés, drinks in crystal glasses. Somewhere a piano plays. The guests are well-dressed, preparing to make a night of it because it's beastly out there and in here is all they need.

He gravitates toward a lively group of fellow professors by the fire. She wanders until she reaches the library where a handful of guests are quietly chatting from the comfort of large leather chairs. They've found their people. Whenever he replenishes his drink or revisits the buffet, he peeks into the room where she sits, lifting his glass or raising his eyebrow. She smiles, nods yes or no. He sees to her, then moves on to charm another group. They roar at his stories, beg him for more. By night's end, he will have collected a dozen new acquaintances, and she will have made a new friend. A perfect evening.

When it starts to get late, she finds him, catches his eye, and touches the watch on her wrist. She stands by the door, waits for him to shake hands with every lingering guest. By midnight, they are the last ones in the foyer. It's all—thank you, goodbye, maybe you should stay, it's so awful out there, but no, we'll be okay. Stepping into a furious wind, she asks if she should drive, but he assures her he's fine. He fires up the heater, scrapes the windows, then takes the driver's seat, full of news to share about his version of the night. "Of course, I'll be careful, but listen to this . . ."

At first, he seems up to the task. "Not too fast," she reminds him. For the most part he keeps his eyes on the road, and they skid just a little now and then. But on this winter night, the wind is fierce, the road is winding, and the driver is distracted.

He's still talking and gesturing when they begin to slide sideways downhill. Only when the car starts to spin does silence descend and the laws of physics have their way. The car whirls in wider and wilder accelerating spirals until it leaves the road, careens through the woods, and smashes headfirst into a tree.

Snow falls all night, obscuring their tracks and the trail of broken limbs. It isn't until the next afternoon that a beam of sunlight glinting off a window catches the eye of the snow plow driver passing by. The location of the car makes retrieval difficult. The passage of many hours renders rescue impossible. The plow driver keeps vigil until the police arrive, then resumes his route and makes his way home to his wife. He walks in the door and describes what he's seen—who, how?

She asks, "What if you hadn't happened by?"

He asks, "But what if I'd been there sooner?"

PART ONE

June 2009

Chapter One

THE CONNECTICUT SUMMER ARRIVED in its usual way—belatedly, after everyone had given up on it and long past time when the cold, stubborn spring should have surrendered. One sunny morning in breezed June, warm and balmy and bright, David, surprised by the unexpected mildness of the day, shed his jacket on the way to his pickup. He tossed it on the passenger seat, hopped in, and started the engine. What a day! A day when he should be planting with his landscaping crew, but he'd promised to be elsewhere and so elsewhere he would be.

He lowered the windows and tuned the radio to the old-time country music that Ruth didn't like. The honky-tonk tunes provided an infusion of cheer he might well need for the coming day. He cranked up the volume. At the bottom of the drive, he heard Ruth calling for him to wait. He smiled as he watched her mince her barefoot way down the gravel driveway.

"Whoa there, cowboy!" she said, reaching his window.

"Ouch?" he asked, looking at her feet.

"Yeah, kinda. But I forgot to give you the scones I made. Do college girls consume carbs?"

David shrugged, no idea.

"They're whole wheat blueberry, very nutritious," she said as she passed the basket of pastries through the window.

"If she doesn't eat them, I sure will. Thanks, Ruth. Are you headed to the office?"

"Nope. Hannah and I are planning to tear up this town," she said.

He laughed. "Oh, right."

She smiled back at him. "We'll probably be out all day, or at least long enough for Sarah and Mark to finish the living room—three-year-olds and open cans of paint not exactly the interior design experience they are looking for."

"Only for the three-year-old. I'm not sure when I'll be back either, so I guess we'll catch up later. Give Hannah a hug for me and you two ladies have a wonderful day."

Ruth leaned in the window to kiss him, then said, "I hope your day goes well, too. It's a good thing, David, you're doing this."

"Better late than never, I guess."

He put the truck in reverse and waved to her before he backed into the street. A few minutes later he was at the Brady house. He'd only been there for dinner a time or two and hadn't seen the place in daylight. The gray clapboard house was old, not pre-Revolutionary War like so many in town, but probably built at least 150 years ago. It looked well-tended, and the shady lawn surrounding it was mowed. The fact that the property had been unoccupied for several months wasn't apparent. Maybe that was why Annabeth had accepted his offer of help without much interest. She might not need anything at all. But he was here now and willing to work for five minutes or five hours, whatever suited her.

He opened his door and discovered the Bradys' ancient, mixed-breed dog sitting next to the truck, wagging his tail. "You're quite the ferocious beast, aren't you?" he said as he scratched behind the dog's ears. "How you doing, buddy?"

The dog enjoyed the attention for a minute, then loped toward the backyard. David hesitated about whether to follow or take the walkway to the front door. The front seemed more appropriate, so he rang the bell and waited. After a second ring got no response, he traced the route the dog had taken. He noticed that although the lawn was mowed, there were weeds in all the beds and quite a few of last fall's leaves caught in the azaleas, both projects perfect for him. He rounded the corner and saw Annabeth sitting on the back porch, leaning against the old dog's side, her arm wrapped tightly around him. The dog sat tall and still, proud in his role as protector. Only the back of Annabeth's head was visible, her thick, curly hair caught up in a band hidden somewhere in the mass of it, the coppery-brown color so similar to the dog's fur that it was hard to tell whose was whose. Her face remained buried until the dog noticed David and began wagging its tail again.

"Oh, hey! I didn't hear you." She stood to greet him. "Chip and I were just hanging out, having some coffee. Well, only me, of course!" She laughed and rolled her eyes. "Uh, do you want some, too?" She gestured to her cup sitting on a table.

"Sure, thanks. My wife made some scones. Blueberry, I think." He handed her the basket.

"Thank you. Thank her! I'll be right back."

He sat down, giving Chip a pet while peering around the yard at the brightly colored perennials blooming here, there, and everywhere. Whoever planted this garden was big on color, scent, and chaos. Peony and lily, dianthus and iris in every available color were crowding each other in beds long overgrown. It was obvious why Jack Brady had asked him to redesign it, a shame Jack died before they got around to doing it. Maybe Jack's daughter would want to make a new garden as a tribute to her father? Even though David had only known Jack since the previous autumn and there was a twenty-five-year age difference between them, the two men had become fast friends. He missed Jack and their rambling conversations about everything from American history to plant propagation. Jack had been good company, a man who knew a little something about all kinds of things and quite a lot about more than a few things.

When Chip wandered off the porch, David adjusted his position to lean against the railing. He could see Annabeth in the kitchen, opening cabinets and drawers one after the other, apparently looking for something. He heard the microwave timer and saw her retrieve a mug, then open the refrigerator and rummage through its contents. She seemed so frazzled that he looked away, wondering if it was his visit that had thrown her off her game, or if maybe this was, in fact, her game. He hopped up to open the screen door when she approached carrying a tray with a mug of coffee, a small pitcher of milk, and a folded paper towel. No scones, he was disappointed to see. As she set down the tray, she said, "My dad taught me to drink coffee black, so I'm sorry, I don't have cream. Just skim milk. I never know how much, so I'll let you do that."

"Yeah, I remember." He added a generous splash of milk. "He gave me grief about my wimpy coffee-drinking ways."

They both smiled. David swirled the coffee, then sat across from her on the top step. For a few seconds, neither spoke. He was now the awkward one, contemplating how to raise the reason for his visit, when she spoke first.

"So, yeah, it's nice of you to come over."

"I meant to come sooner. I wasn't sure . . ." he paused, "I'm so sorry about your parents."

She just nodded at his words.

He took a breath and continued, "I miss Jack. I think about him, and . . . of course, the party . . . the accident . . . that terrible night. If . . . I wish . . ."

Annabeth held up her hand. "No. No need to talk about that, what happened. Just . . ." She shook her head.

He nodded too. It would be easier for both, and probably more helpful to her, if he got busy working. It always seemed to him that other than a sincere "I'm sorry," no words of comfort were ever comforting.

"So, what can I do for you today?" David asked, gesturing to the space around them. "Gosh, I'm sorry." She looked around, then made a sheepish face. "I don't have anything in mind. I feel bad you wasted a trip over here. Maybe I can make a list? For another day—if you have time and want to come back?"

"Sounds good. Think about it this week and I'll come back Saturday. Not a big deal at all, Annabeth."

Her face relaxed as she said, "Okay, great."

David left, feeling a guilty kind of relief that this dreaded condolence call turned out to require so little of him.

———

HANNAH TORE OUT OF THE HOUSE to greet her before Ruth had even reached the front door. Unable to contain herself, the little girl hopped up and down and chattered nonstop. Over her head, Ruth and Sarah tried to finalize the details for the day.

"She'll be worn out by four, o'clock, which should give us time to finish. Call me, though, if you need to bail sooner. We're grateful for any progress. Thank you!" Sarah called as Hannah pulled Ruth down the sidewalk.

Hannah's chirping continued for the duration of their walk to a nearby outdoor cafe. It was Hannah's favorite place because it sat alongside a waterfall that splashed into a well-populated duck pond. She loved feeding the baby ducks almost as much as she loved eating the chocolate-chip pancakes that were the restaurant's specialty. Ruth knew it often took some time for Hannah to express all that love, but with no other item on this day's to-do list, she gave herself over to her niece. A good portion of Hannah's breakfast went to the ducks, but even more of it ended up on her clothes, in her hair and, by the end of the meal, in Ruth's hair. On their way to the bathroom to deal with the chocolate, one older woman stopped them.

"Did you have a nice breakfast, honey?" she asked. Hannah nodded an enthusiastic yes.

"Your little girl is adorable!" the woman said to Ruth.

"Thank you. Yes, she's pretty great—but she's my niece, not my daughter."

"My! She looks just like you."

"I'll take that as a compliment, but if you saw my sister . . ."

"Then you three must look alike." The woman paused a moment. "I guess I should have known you weren't her mother, though. You were so . . . patient . . . about everything."

Ruth laughed. "Yes, I guess a mother would be teaching proper table manners. An aunt can just let mayhem reign."

"And I'm sure your sister is happy to return that favor with your own children."

"I'm sure she will be when she gets her chance," Ruth said. "For now she has to bide her time and plot her revenge."

"Don't wait too long. You don't want to give her too much time for scheming. Enjoy your weekend."

The woman waved as they left the dining room. Ruth kept her smile, as she always did when people said these things, but her heart sank as she thought, I am trying. If you only knew how hard I'm trying.

BY DAY'S END, Ruth was worn out and more than ready to order sushi and crash with David. She figured he would also be tired from working at the Brady house. Instead, she found him in the kitchen with dinner almost cooked and an open bottle of wine on the kitchen counter.

"I expected you to come limping home after dark with mulch in your hair," she said as she kissed him hello.

"And instead, it's you limping in with chocolate syrup in yours."

"Oh, I thought I got it all." She shrugged. "How was your day? How's Annabeth doing?"

"Okay. Distracted, disinterested. She didn't have anything for me to do, but I guess that's not surprising because I didn't have anything concrete to offer. I'm going back next week to redeem myself," he said without looking up from the cutting board.

She put her hand on his back and asked, "You good? You sound a little . . . something."

"Yeah, I'm okay."

He set down the knife and turned around. Ruth moved into his arms and rested her head on his chest. When she pulled away, she saw that her gooey hair had smeared chocolate across his shirt. David laughed, "Should we have some wine with our chocolate?"

She made a face. "Oh no! Sorry, I guess I'll just be popping off to the shower now."

She started to back away from him, but he caught her hand and pulled her closer.

"Nah, I don't care about the shirt." He wrapped his arms around her. "Just you." He held her tighter and rocked her gently from side to side. "Just you, Ruthie-belle."

Chapter Two

DAVID'S VISIT provided Annabeth with the first bit of motivation she'd had in a long time to do much of anything. Knowing now that he was going to return prompted her to focus on the space around her instead of drifting blindly from one room to the next. The place had been unoccupied for weeks, and so there must be tasks needing her attention, she supposed. Her parents had loved this old house and left Annabeth with enough insurance to keep it. She owed them the honor of tending to the place. For her father, she would have David help with the weeding and whatever needed to be done outside. The neighbor boy who mowed the lawn didn't know anything about gardening, and neither did Annabeth, but she guessed it must require a lot of work based on the amount of time her father had spent in the garden. For her mother, she would tackle spring cleaning and consider it a labor of love. She decided to devote the entire week to the inside of the house and spend Saturday outside working with David.

No time like the present, she thought. She opened the cabinet where her mother kept the cleaning supplies. She collected bottles and cloths, then looked around deciding where to begin, steeling herself against the memories the rooms might inflict upon her. It helped a little that this house, as lovely as it was, had never felt like her home. Although she moved here with her parents when her father took the new teaching job, she'd left to start college before they'd finished unpacking. She'd come back over breaks and stayed in the bedroom she and her mother had decorated together, which was charming, but devoid of memories. Coming here had never felt like coming home. Twice she'd gone back to Kansas to see her old friends, but that had been strange, too. They were all scattered to different colleges with mismatched vacation schedules, so they were never together as a group. She herself had no home base at all. Even though her friends were happy to have her, that meant living out of a suitcase and eating their favorite meals, not the ones she'd been craving. Once she asked a friend to drive past her old house. The new owners had already painted it a different color and torn out the vegetable garden her father had so patiently tended. It was a sight she didn't want to see again. In those dislocated days, Annabeth felt herself to be, if not quite a refugee, then maybe a nomad. Because Annabeth had spent so little time in this house, or maybe because she'd paid so little attention, she was now startled to realize that most of the furniture in the living room was new, pieces her mom must have bought just for this spot. When? No faded popsicle stains on this sofa. Its pristine condition was evidence of a fresh start for her empty-nested parents who'd embraced their new state and anticipated their daughter would do the same. But it hadn't worked out that way.

Her college campus was pretty, the students were smart and funny, but she'd chosen it mainly because she wanted to run for a competitive team and this school had a good one. Too good. The times that would have won conference races at her high school put her near the bottom of the pack on this team. She expected that her willingness to work hard would lift her to a scoring spot. Instead, she over-trained and developed one injury after another that kept her sidelined much of the time and impaired her performances when she did compete. Midway through the indoor winter season she decided she wouldn't run for the team anymore—a decision that felt like removing her right arm. She had planned to tell her parents in person that she'd quit, but never got a chance to have that conversation, which she now realized would have taken place on this showroom couch.

Annabeth moved from the sofa to the bookshelves. Some sections were still organized according to her mother's preferred Library-of-Congress system. Others were a mess, re-arranged by her father's preference for shelving books sideways wherever they happened to fit. Interspersed among the books were framed photographs, many of them pictures of Annabeth holding medals from races she'd won. Her tactful mom would have tucked those away if she'd been aware of Annabeth's heartbreak over leaving the team. Her mom, although not an athlete, understood how essential running was to Annabeth and always had been empathic to the ups and downs of her daughter's racing career. Those conversations did help, up to a point, but no amount of maternal support would have filled the pit in Annabeth's stomach every afternoon when she was not standing in the field house with the other girls, stretching and gossiping before they headed out in groups to run through the gathering darkness. Three o'clock became the most dreaded hour of her day.

She turned away from the track pictures and began to flip through the three-ring binders of family photos her mother had maintained since the first year of her marriage. Don't cry, you won't cry, she told herself as she pulled them off the shelf. She got a kick out of the oldest pictures—family vacations when she was a toddler, grade school class photos, pictures of overladen Christmas trees. The more recent albums were a different story. Her parents looked like themselves, the actual people she remembered and missed, not the twenty-something strangers in the early photos.

Rising from the floor, she left her cleaning supplies where they were and went into the kitchen to regroup. She drank a glass of water and sat down at the table, longing, not for the first time, for the company of her high-school teammates. They had all, every one of them, come to Connecticut for her parents' funeral. Her two best friends had arrived early and stayed late to help Annabeth through the ordeal. Months after their last meet together, the three of them still functioned as a team. Their sixth sense about each other's needs, built over years of training together, running in a pack to win as a team, turned out to be practice for this painful life event as well. Annabeth was the girl stuck in the woods, lost and aching, and there they were, running right beside her, elbows out, surrounding her with a shield of compassion. Dazed in those early days, she was grateful to exist inside the cocoon of their protection. After the funeral, Annabeth returned to school because she didn't know what else to do. Even her dearest friends had to get on with their own lives, so she went back to the place where very few people even knew what had happened. Some of her professors had been kind, inquiring after her and giving her extended deadlines, but only a few students and her roommate were aware of the accident. Oddly, the stark contrast between the loving support of her old friends and the uninformed indifference of the people on campus suited her. She spent almost all her time alone, in her room or hidden in some corner of the library, pretending to study. She sometimes sat for hours looking out the window or into open pages of a book, unable to read or even think coherently. Unbidden, a thought would come to her, so this is grieving. Once, she caught an unexpected glimpse of her ashen face reflected in a window and didn't recognize herself. As the semester progressed, she began to regain some of her footings, and by exam time, she was able to concentrate again for short spells. She managed to finish most of her classes, receiving the lowest grades she'd ever had. She didn't care. She wasn't sure she wanted to return to school, and if she did, she wasn't sure it would be to this one. "I'll decide over the summer," became her mantra. Every time she thought of something she needed to do, she'd tell herself, "I just need some time."

Here it was summer and the only thing she'd decided was where to spend it—in Connecticut, by herself. When the school year ended, her father's sister, Janet, insisted on bringing her back to Aunt Janet's house in Kansas. Annabeth resisted the idea of living even briefly with her very bossy aunt, but Janet kept Chip after the funeral and Annabeth missed him more than she dreaded Aunt Janet. The first few days were not too bad. But two weeks of Janet's instructions, directions, and advice about everything from her parents' life insurance settlement to her choice of cereal, soon became more than she could bear. She insisted on returning to Connecticut, telling her aunt she wanted to look at a college there and deal with her parents' stuff, that she'd come back to Kansas in a few weeks. Janet, of course, offered to help and it was only after much persuading that she reluctantly let her niece travel alone. Annabeth put a few bags in her mom's car, which Janet had driven cross-country with Chip, and headed east without telling Janet that her plan was to leave Kansas forever.

Chip, ever alert to her moods, was now gazing up at her with a worried look. Annabeth scratched behind his ear. "Oh, Chip," she said. "We did do the right thing, didn't we?"

Chip followed her as she left the kitchen and wandered around the other rooms, not bothering to clean a thing, instead reassuring herself that her decision to live in Connecticut had in fact been the right one. Freed of Janet's orders, in the early summer days of sunlight and warmth she'd begun to feel better. Long walks with Chip revealed that her extended hiatus from running had allowed her legs to heal. Two weeks ago, she'd tried a short run. For twenty-five minutes she'd been without pain, physical or emotional, and returned as some semblance of her former self. The enormous void in her center shrunk a tiny bit that day and when she sat down to a meal, she found she was hungry enough to eat it. She realized that for a little while, at least, she had been if not exactly happy, then not exactly sad. Those moments, though, were just intermissions from grief. Most of her days were, like today, lived in a gray half-light. When her parents' acquaintances called or stopped by to check on her, she always told them she didn't need a thing. As well-intentioned as they were, their visits were a strain. She didn't know these people well enough to be comforted by them and the effort to make small talk tired her. She'd only allowed her dad's friend David to come because his call had been short and business-like, closer to informing her when he was arriving than asking for her permission. She then forgot all about him until he was standing on the back porch. What a relief it had been when he didn't try to get her to talk about her parents or expect her to unload details about how she was doing. For the first time since she'd returned to Connecticut, she had felt comfortable in a kind stranger's presence.

"All right," she said to Chip. "We've got to accomplish something today."

She retrieved the cleaning supplies, went into the dining room, and got busy polishing the furniture. As she worked, she found a kind of Zen in the soundless, repetitive motion. The physical movement somehow connected her across time to her mother, whom Annabeth could recall polishing this same table in exactly the same way. A year ago, she wouldn't have even noticed that the old table was dusty, but today, restoring its luster became an act of tribute to her mom.

Chapter Three

"I NEED SOME big sister decorating advice," said Sarah on the phone to Ruth. "Could you stop by on your way home?"

"Sure—I'm all over it."

At six-fifteen, Ruth knocked on Sarah's front door and heard her call, "Come on in!"

Hannah flew through the living room ahead of Sarah and grabbed Ruth by the hand, "Will you play ponies with me?"

"Oh, Lovebug, I need to see Aunt Ruthie first. Why don't you play in the back for a few minutes," Sarah said. She picked up a shopping bag. "Okay, so two curtain choices for the living room. I have kinda wild and actually wild."

"How, um, wild," Ruth said. Sarah's entire house was beige. "Sounds like we are in for an adventure."

Sarah made a rueful face and laughed.

"Can you stay for a while? Do you want something to drink? We have wine, iced tea, water—"

"Thanks. Wine, if you are opening a bottle."

They went into the kitchen where Sarah opened a bottle of Pinot Grigio and poured Ruth a glass. She poured herself a glass of iced tea.

"You didn't need to open a bottle for me, but—I thought you liked this?" Ruth raised her glass.

"Yeah, I do, just not tonight. Cheers!" said Sarah, as she raised her glass in return. "Let's go out back and keep an eye on Hannah."

Once settled on the patio, Sarah turned to her.

"So hey, I have some news that is kind of a surprise."

"You're pregnant." Ruth knew before Sarah finished her sentence.

Sarah blinked. "Yeah, I am. I just found out."

She came out of her chair and embraced Sarah. "That's wonderful news! I'm so happy for you. A little brother or sister for Hannah. When are you due?"

"Probably around Christmas. I wasn't keeping track that closely—I'll know I guess when I see the doctor. We weren't really trying, also not really not trying, and we thought it might take a while, but it didn't and so . . . yeah, I'm pregnant. You're the first person I've told, besides Mark, of course. Too early to tell Hannah."

"This is just the best news. I'm thrilled for you guys."

"Thanks. We are, too." She paused for a moment. "Still, it doesn't seem quite fair . . . I'm sorry . . ."

"Oh no, don't be sorry. Be excited and know that I am absolutely fine. Better than fine. I'm over the moon." She hugged her sister again.

———

RUTH LEFT SARAH'S HOUSE BUZZED, not from wine, but from genuine excitement. What a relief to realize that she didn't have to fake it—she was delighted for her sister and pretty sure she would be even if she weren't secretly harboring hopes for similar good news for herself. It was too soon to say anything, but what a miracle if she and Sarah had babies at the same time!

"Settle down," she told herself. "You know better than that."

Over the past year she had become adept at keeping her expectations in check while her hopes ran wild. Now, on impulse, wildly hoping, expecting nothing, she drove to the chain pharmacy miles from home where she'd bought pregnancy tests in the past. It was essential to keep her suspicion secret until she had verifiable news to share. She had been embarrassed before by premature confidences, telling friends or David that maybe, fingers crossed, her fondest wish might be coming true. Her girlfriends understood because most of them had played this same waiting game—some, like Ruth, hoping for the stick to turn blue, others hoping just as fervently that it didn't. But there were only so many times she could drag them through her almost-symptoms before their eyes began to glaze over and their brows began to furrow. As for David, he would be overjoyed when it happened, but the hourly updates she'd plagued him with before had baffled, then silenced him. She would have gone crazy, though, if she hadn't talked to someone, and in desperation she began to bombard the great unknown with her worries and dreams. She discovered that she was able to take comfort in the benevolent silence that came back to her. "Please. Please," she said now, as she did a hundred times a day. Was this faith or delusion? She wasn't sure, but her words seemed somehow to go where she sensed they were heard.

Ruth scanned the aisles of the drugstore to confirm that none of the customers were people she knew. Just in case, she covered her tracks by picking up a tube of toothpaste, a box of tissues, and a book for Sarah's expected baby. It somehow seemed less ridiculous, and less of a jinx, to pretend she was there for more—as if God, or fate, or whoever was watching, wouldn't see right through the charade.

For most of her life, Ruth hadn't thought about God at all and could not have imagined choosing to be in church on Sunday morning. Last Christmas, though, a friend invited her to a service at the Congregational church, and Ruth had been charmed by the place and its three-hundred-year history. She liked sitting in the same pews and praying the same prayers that the pilgrims prayed. After a few visits, she started attending a weekly Bible study, too, although she never called it that, even to herself. Instead, she thought of it as her Sunday Morning Book Group. The Bible was a book, wasn't it? Ruth still had too many doubts and questions to identify herself as a believer, but since she'd begun attending church, it seemed that on occasion she did perceive the presence of something spiritual hovering nearby. In fact, she sensed it now, in aisle eight at Walgreens, of all places.

She knew her way to the test kits. She selected a familiar brand and joined the checkout line. Would it be wrong to ask God to predetermine a test result? She rejected the notion. No, that was inappropriate, like demanding a magic trick. By the time she reached the cashier, she'd changed her mind. Why not? They had tried everything else. She'd never foreseen that having a healthy body, a sound marriage, and a fierce determination still might not be enough to permit her to participate in the everyday miracle of reproduction. After years of tests, disappointment, charts, and disappointment again, asking God to load the dice in her favor wouldn't be wrong, would it? He was capable of all things, she'd been assured. Ruth paid and walked to her car, whispering words not dignified enough to be called a prayer.

Chapter Four

ANOTHER SPECTACULAR Saturday morning in June and somehow David had booked himself into an all-day indoor gig. Samantha Levine, the wife of one of Ruth's fellow attorneys and the woman whose garden gave David his start, was a freelance photographer who had recently published a coffee-table book, *Gardens that Break the Rules*. It was a work of art, full of gorgeous photographs meant to inspire landscape design creativity. Because Samantha was a local, as were some of the gardens, the neighborhood Barnes and Noble planned a book signing with her. The night before, though, she'd picked up a story on a flood outside Boston and recruited David to fill in for her.

"You'll be perfect," she said. "A lot of those pictures are of your gardens. You can talk to the customers about them. It will be great for your business, and you'll be doing me a big favor. I'd appreciate it, David. As payback, James and I will take you and Ruth out to dinner tomorrow night—you name the place."

"You know I'm happy to help, Sam, but I think they're going to be pretty disappointed when you aren't there—and what about the signing part? I don't think I can get away with being Samantha."

"No, I kind of doubt that, but I signed a few books yester-day in case anybody showed up early. You can use those and if you run out, have the B&N people get addresses and I'll drop notes to whoever didn't get a signed copy. It shouldn't be more than a few thousand fans, right?"

David was almost out the door when he remembered his promise to Annabeth. He quickly grabbed the phone and tried the number he had for Jack's house. No one answered and no voicemail kicked in. He intended to try again on the way to the book signing, but once in his truck, he realized he didn't have that number on his cell. Instead, he called Ruthie.

"Hey, I have to ask you for a favor. I forgot to call Annabeth to tell her I can't come today. Would you mind letting her know what's up and tell her that I could come by tomorrow or sometime next week if that is okay with her?"

"Sure. What's the number?"

He told her where to find it, and said, "I don't have a cell for her. The house machine is either off or she doesn't have one, so I couldn't leave a message. If you don't reach her by noon, let me know, and I will stop by there on my way home and explain or leave a note or whatever."

As David expected, there was not a big crowd waiting to greet him. As he feared, there was not a single soul. One woman did come looking for a different garden book and a little boy asked him where the story lady was, but otherwise,

David spent the morning chatting with the employees and trying to look as if he had something to do besides kill time. He didn't have much trouble convincing the store manager to let him leave after a couple of hours. David suspected it was as much a relief to the manager as it was to him.

He was surprised, coming out of the store, to see Annabeth walking toward the door. "Annabeth?" He hadn't noticed before how thin she was. She'd looked pale last week on her shady back porch, but here in the bright sunlight she looked wan, almost ill. She spoke in a quiet voice.

"Yeah, hi David. Your wife told me about the book signing. Is it over already?"

"That might be the right word. Not a big crowd today. But thanks for coming, so nice of you. I'm sorry I forgot to let you know I couldn't be there today. This thing came up last minute, a favor for a friend."

"That's okay. A book signing is a big deal!"

"Not this one," he laughed. "How are you?"

"I'm good." She looked around. "This is the first time I've been out and about in a while, I guess, but it feels mostly all right. It's pretty quiet at my parents' house. But I think it's good for me to . . . you know, mingle or whatever?" She shrugged, looking not quite convinced by her own words.

"Yeah, I think so. Again, I'm sorry to leave you hanging. I tried to call but couldn't get your voicemail."

"No, it's okay. Ruth came by. She's nice."

"She is, I agree."

Annabeth dug through her bag, looking for something, but came up empty-handed. "Anyway, the house voicemail was probably full. Sometimes people still call for my mom or dad. So . . . you know, I don't really like to answer that phone.

I'd text you my cell, but I can't find my phone." She thought for a moment. "I don't use that much either, but . . ."

She rummaged through her purse again, then grinned when she found her phone and showed it to David.

"I'm not much on cell phones myself, but I guess they are a necessary evil."

They exchanged phone numbers. Then, David said, "Hey, they didn't feed me in there and I'm starving. Have you had lunch yet?"

"Today? Yeah, I am pretty sure I did."

"Must have been quite the feast."

She laughed and David saw her shoulders relax. Despite her waifish appearance, the smile transformed her face. It revealed a hint of the sunniness that still existed beneath the darkness of her grief.

"Sure," she said. "I could eat."

They drove separately to the restaurant. She seemed calm when she got out of her car, but by the time they'd stood in the crowded line, dodging preschool soccer players and high school football fans, she was chewing her cuticles and shifting her weight from one foot to the other.

"Do you mind if we get this to go?" she asked David.

"Of course not."

The change in her demeanor was striking. When he noticed her hands shaking, he had to ask if she wanted him to drive.

"Yeah, maybe. I'm feeling kind of 'too many people' all of a sudden."

"Not a problem. You mind the pickup?"

"No." She shook her head and smiled a little. "I learned to drive in a pickup."

Once inside the cab, Annabeth clutched the bag holding her sandwich close to her body and gazed out the window.

"It's so weird," she said. "I wanted to get out today. For a while it was all right, pretty good really, but then . . . all that commotion—about nothing. When the yoga lady freaked because they didn't have fat-free cheese, I just . . . wow, gotta go *now*."

David nodded. "Me too, if that's any consolation. Want to take this to your house? We can get your car later."

They rode to Annabeth's without saying much. There, they sat outside on the porch while she nibbled on a corner of her sandwich. After a little while, she re-wrapped it and said it was time they got to work.

"Great!" he said. "That vine weed in the myrtle is really starting to bother me."

"Oh, yes," Annabeth said. "It is awful." She looked around. "What's myrtle?"

They both laughed. "I'll show you."

They worked in separate parts of the garden, David whistling over the sound of a distant lawnmower. From time to time, she'd ask if something was a weed or a *real plant*. He'd answer and return to his patch of ground. He stole glances at her occasionally, trying to gauge her mood. Although he couldn't describe it as jolly, he did notice her humming along with his whistling a couple of times. When she finished the bed she'd been weeding, she called him over to check her work. Her face lit up when he praised her, allowing him another glimpse of the sparkle her sorrow was hiding. By the end of the afternoon, he judged both the garden and the girl to be in a much-improved state. Helping Annabeth made him feel more than just useful. It made him feel needed, capable of making her happy, even if just for a little while. The spring in her step when he dropped her at her car he took as proof that his efforts mattered, that he could be key to her healing.

Chapter Five

RUTH AND DAVID didn't see each other until just before dinner. By the time Ruth finished working, stocked up on groceries, picked up the dry cleaning, and tackled the week's paperwork, she barely had time to hop in the shower before David returned home. As she put on her makeup, she filled him in on the plans for dinner with Samantha and James. She left the bathroom to avoid a fuzzy head of steamed hair from David's shower and waited for him in the living room. He raced downstairs just as Samantha and James arrived. The four of them spent a few minutes in the driveway so David could admire James's new Audi. Ruth and Samantha pretended to be interested, too, for a while. Then, Samantha said, "For God's sake, let's get in the thing. Isn't it supposed to move from point A to point B? I'm starving!"

"We could be driving a '72 Ford Pinto and Samantha wouldn't notice," James said.

"I'm happy that you love your new toy, dear James. I just think we should *oooh and aaah* in transit. That airline food I enjoyed today is not getting the job done." Samantha patted her tummy.

They piled in the car and drove to the restaurant. Along the way, James delivered a monologue about the car's many luxury features.

Once settled at the table, Samantha asked David how the book signing had gone. "Hmm. Pretty quiet, actually."

"How many books did you sell, would you guess?"

"If I had to guess, I'd say . . . none."

"Oh dear. David, I am so sorry. I wouldn't have asked you to miss a day's work for that. Why do you think no one came? The book had been moving well there."

"I'd say the first eighty-degree day of the season without a cloud in the sky pretty much took care of it. I bet all the gardeners were . . . gardening. And it was just too beautiful for anybody to be in a bookstore."

"That's the problem the production delay caused. What do you think? It's summer now. Should we rework the appearance timetable?" Samantha asked.

"I don't know," David said. "If the book is doing well. . . ?"

James had signalled the waiter and was now asking to order a particular wine from South Africa. When the waiter apologized for not stocking it, James explained in detail all the reasons why he should and initiated a long conversation about the qualities of the other wines on offer. The rest of them stopped listening.

"My agent thinks she can get us on television. You know,

those morning programs and local talk shows that are always desperate for guests?"

"You should definitely do that," David said. "I'd have to beg off, though. It's one of our busiest times and I need to be here with the guys."

"Great. That's settled." James rejoined them. "David gets to avoid crummy airline food by not going anywhere and Ruth gets to avoid crummy airline food by flying corporate."

"Excuse me?" Ruth said. "I am not aware of any corporate jets in my future."

"There may be," he said. "I've been wanting to tell you, but I had to wait until we got things more settled. We have a new client, Bishop Enterprises, based in California. Brian Bishop is a very successful real estate guy in several states—countries, actually—and he wants to get into the Connecticut market. He thinks the timing is perfect for him. All those unsold recession parcels that haven't bounced back yet, businesses moving to other states—I won't bore everyone with his long-term market strategy, at least not before I've had more wine, but he is planning to become a big presence here. He's hired us to be local counsel. It's a great opportunity for our real estate department after a long, rather dry spell, as you know."

"That's huge. But why would he want a small firm like ours? Our real estate department is three people."

"Our fees are lower, for one thing. And we don't have conflicts with the sellers that would be an issue with many of the bigger firms. And, that's just how he does it. Who am I to question the strategy of a guy who makes bazillions and wants to share some of it with me?"

"Great. Congratulations," Ruth said.

"Yeah, that's really great, James," said David, raising his glass. "Nice job."

"Thanks. It is great, but it means we have to make some adjustments to the department. We will probably need to hire a young associate and we're going to need to send someone to go between here and California. That's where your corporate jet comes in, Ruth."

He grinned at her. Ruth said nothing, waiting for James to explain.

"You are the perfect person to do it. You have the experience, and you will absolutely dazzle Bishop with the quality of your work. It's a wonderful gig for you and the firm. All the partners agreed that you were the right candidate for the job."

"Thanks, James. I'm pleased you guys think so much of me. But I'm not sure the timing is right. How much would I have to travel?"

Ruth tried to make eye contact with David who was too busy reading the menu to notice.

"Can't say exactly yet. It depends on how the deals work out, but my guess is two to three days a week, maybe more if things get going as quickly as Bishop hopes."

"That's a lot of time away. Private jets notwithstanding, David might forget to eat without me to remind him to stop working."

"I can manage two or three days a week without you, Hon," he said, missing his cue.

"Thanks."

"I said 'manage.'" He squeezed her shoulders. "I'd miss you a ton, but my days are so long this time of year, it's not as if you and I get that much time together during the week anyway. She'd be home on the weekends, right?" he asked James, taking Ruth's hand.

"I would think so, but to be perfectly honest, there might

be times she'd have to be away. It depends on how things work out. You know how that goes," he said to Ruth.

"Ruthie, you do what you think is best, but do not say no because of me," David said.

Ruth was flustered. She was annoyed with James for having this business discussion in a social setting and for bringing this up for the first time in front of David and Samantha. They were all friends, but it was inappropriate for him to put her on the spot like this. And she suspected James had asked her in front of the others because it would make it harder for her to say no. But how could she say yes? She might be pregnant. And if she weren't already, she was going to keep trying. She couldn't be crisscrossing the country. She couldn't tell them, though—too personal, too speculative. How could she say, "No, I won't do it," without giving a reason? On the other hand, how could she go and take a chance of missing all the right days?

"California, Ruthie, how great! My agent has been asking me to make a couple of trips out west for the next book. Maybe we could go together? Spend a weekend on a real beach. It would be so much fun," Samantha said.

"Yeah, Sam. That would be a blast. If I decide to do it."

James looked at her, frowning slightly. "Ruth?"

Ruth nodded yes to the waiter's offer of more wine, then said, "It is a lot of time away. If it involves Connecticut property, why couldn't I do the work here? All the law is here, the other lawyers will be here. I don't understand why I'd have to go to California so much."

"Bishop thinks one of the lawyers on the local team should work directly with his people as much as possible. He's always on the run and doesn't have time to hang out in Connecticut. But I'm sure once you get to know him you could talk to him about it. Maybe he'd be flexible about that. If anybody could charm him into it, it would be you."

Typical James, thought Ruth, rolling out the blatant flattery that worked with all his clients.

"How long do you think the whole thing would last? Weeks? Months?"

"I don't know," James said. "It's impossible to say right now."

David at last seemed to pick up on Ruth's hesitancy. "Ruth, if you don't want to do it, you don't have to. You do whatever you think is best and everyone will understand, right James?" He squeezed her hand again.

James considered. "Of course," he said. "But . . . I don't think I have to tell you there aren't a lot of Bishops out there in the world right now. New real estate *buyers* are not exactly knocking down our door. But yeah, obviously, you should do what you think best. If you don't do it, though, we'd need to bring in somebody else with your level of experience, not some young associate. That would be a more expensive and complicated process for the partners, I'm sure you realize. But of course, nobody is going to force you to go." His words were clipped.

Ruth looked down at the table. The others waited. "Let me think about it. I'll let you know on Monday."

"Fine," James concluded. He then sat up straighter and said with forced cheerfulness, "Okay, then. Now, dinner. Samantha, tell them who you saw today."

Samantha launched into one of her elaborate anecdotes, this one about running into a minor celebrity in an awkward situation. Ruth rallied as required. She laughed at Samantha's story and put the Bishop assignment out of her mind. She worked to ensure that everyone else had a good time, but her stomach was so unsettled she could barely look at the plates of fiery-red lobsters.

That night at home, Ruth tried to sort through it all. She got out of bed and wrapped herself in a throw, then wandered to her favorite spot in the house, a window seat in the living room where she often read. She turned on a small lamp and sat down with a legal pad and pen to make a list, pros on one side, cons on the other. She forced herself to be honest and was disappointed when, as she'd expected, the list turned out to be quite lopsided. There were many good, solid reasons for agreeing to this assignment. The items on the pro side ran down the length of the page, all of them concrete and unassailable. On the con side were only three entries: 1. Might be pregnant; 2. If not, need to *keep trying*; and 3. Will miss David/home. These were huge reasons that, to Ruth, outweighed all the others, but they were vague in comparison to the specific benefits of the pros.

"Okay, think about this logically," she told herself. "If I am pregnant, I will know in a few days. There aren't any health risks to flying early in pregnancy, so I could do it for a while and, by the time I can't fly anymore, I can convince this Bishop guy to let me work from Connecticut. After the baby is born, who knows . . . that was always going to be something to figure out. If I am not pregnant, we can still keep trying. I can come home on the right days, or David can come to California. A weekend near the Pacific Ocean wouldn't be the worst thing that ever happened to us."

It was clear from the beginning that her reasons for saying no wouldn't hold up to the reasons for saying yes, but she had to go through this exercise to provide herself with the illusion that she had been thorough in considering her options. She reached the inevitable decision with a feeling of resignation.

She would reevaluate in the morning, to see how it felt in the cold light of day, but coming to a decision at least settled her mind enough to make sleep a possibility. She climbed the stairs to the bedroom and quietly slipped next to David. Without waking him, she rested her head against his back. Tomorrow she would share her list with him, and they would talk this through, but for now, it was enough just to touch him.

She snuggled even closer and allowed a peacefulness to settle over her. Maybe it would be a good thing to have a new challenge, something else to think about besides baby, baby, baby. Before she drifted off to sleep, she prayed for clarity, for good judgment, for acceptance, and as she did every night, because she couldn't help herself, she prayed for a child.

Chapter Six

THE NEXT MORNING Ruth and David were both up early. David needed to be on-site at a large project that was taking longer than expected and had to be ready for a family wedding. He quickly grabbed some coffee, kissed Ruth goodbye, and jumped into his truck for what would be a long day of work.

Ruth dressed for church. She enjoyed it much more when she and David went together, but it wouldn't have crossed her mind not to go because he couldn't. Most Sundays she attended Bible study and then worship. It was food for her soul and balm for her nerves. In this community of high achievers, it was also intellectual stimulation. The class was full of people who asked hard questions and challenged assumptions. They were far from what would have come to her mind a few years ago if she had pictured a group of Bible students. No long-flowered skirts, no ringing condemnation of sinners, no political diatribes. Instead, these students were sophisticated world travelers, people who were at the top of the corporate ladder, graduates of name brand colleges who shared a common goal: to understand and live this book. This morning, they continued their study of the Ten Commandments. There were many differences of opinion about the meaning of "Thou shalt not kill." They questioned capital punishment, self-defense laws, killing words, war, abortion, drunk driving, and end-of-life medical decisions. No one point of view was deemed the winner, and no one insisted on the correctness of his or her opinion. The positions were vigorously presented and defended, though, and Ruth left class as revved up as if she'd been gulping Starbucks. After that, she welcomed the calm and quiet of the worship service, the opportunity to pray in silence and listen to the beautiful sacred music. The service offered her a chance to meditate, be grateful and still. Even the social hour afterward was a pleasure, a chance to chat with church friends before reemerging into the routine of daily life.

Driving home, Ruth felt tranquil, much more comfortable with her inclination to accept the new assignment than she had been last night. The fact that she was at peace told her it was the right thing to do. Maybe this new way of being busy was exactly what they needed. Hadn't she heard five thousand annoying stories of people who "gave up" and then got pregnant weeks later? The key to those success stories, Ruth always believed, was not to give up as a sort of fingers-crossed attempt to fool fate, but to get involved in something else that reduced the stress around the process of conception. Maybe a long-distance work assignment didn't qualify as an

all-around stress reducer, but it would provide a meaning-
ful distraction from the endless worrying about her fertility.
Whether it would be only that—a distraction—or the magic
key to success remained to be seen. Ruth knew she'd have to
jump into the project wholeheartedly for it to be successful
on either count. She'd have to force herself to give up, and not
even hope for anything more than an interesting professional
opportunity. Didn't that put it at least somewhat under her
control?

For the first time in a while, Ruth felt energized, back in
charge, ready to attack the problem in a new way.

THE WEIGHT that sat on Annabeth's chest was a little lighter
Sunday morning. Sadness, her almost-constant companion
since last February, was still right beside her, the first thing
she perceived when she awoke, but today it didn't also fill her
eyes with tears. Today, she acknowledged it, then got out of
bed and stretched in the warm sunlight shining through her
bedroom window. She pushed up the wooden frame and allowed the scented morning air to wash over her. That smell!
Freshly mown grass and all the flowers planted by genera-
tions of gardeners created a sweet and subtle perfume. She inhaled and smiled.

She and Chip made their way into the morning-bright
kitchen. She fed him, made coffee, then went with him into
the backyard. While he chased squirrels, birds, and anything
else he viewed as an intruder, Annabeth sipped her coffee.
Today it was not going to be enough to stay at home alone and
admire the summer weather. Today was a day that had to be
shared. I need a friend, she thought. But who? It only took
a few seconds for her to realize that except for her father's

friend David and his wife Ruth, she didn't know anyone here in Connecticut. Okay, then she could call Jessie or Emily from Kansas, or maybe both, and make plans for them to come here. It would be wonderful to see them again. They could go into the city, run in the park, come back, and make dinner together. It was still too early to call the Midwest, but she resolved to treat herself to a phone call today and a visit in the near future. Something to look forward to.

She went back inside and changed into shorts and a t-shirt. It was a perfect morning for a long run. No distance goal, no mile splits to worry about, just running until she felt like turning around and coming back.

"Sorry, Chip, too far for you today," she said as she ran out the door. She flew down the driveway, lightly skimming over the surface.

There was no car traffic on the road, but Annabeth encountered a couple of runners in the first half-mile. They acknowledged each other and went on their separate routes. The road soon became populated with more runners, cyclists, and fitness walkers. In Kansas she'd often had the early-morning streets all to herself, but she liked this better, the roads uncrowded but shared. She ran, full of energy, experiencing no pain, feeling as if she could go on forever.

After about an hour on winding, hilly roads, she decided to turn around and fix herself a feast of a breakfast. At first, she ran back along the route she'd taken with confidence, but after a while the scenery looked unfamiliar. She didn't remember that fallen tree, those new houses. But how could that be? She'd simply turned around! She ran on, hoping to recognize some landmarks. The roads held more cars now and fewer people on foot. After a few more minutes she realized she'd have to stop the next pedestrian and ask for directions home.

She crossed paths with an older guy and asked him, but he didn't know her street and couldn't help her. Annabeth kept going, now starting to worry as well as tire, and wondered if she was running away from her house instead of toward it. When the next person she encountered also had no idea about how to get home, she knew she'd have to stop at someone's house and embarrass herself. She chose a friendly-looking place with a front garden and an open garage door. She rang the bell and hoped whoever lived there would not think she was a crazy person. She was not expecting a guy about her own age to answer the door.

"Hey," he said, smiling as if he already knew her.

"I am sorry to bother you, but I think I'm lost." She gave an embarrassed laugh. "I've been running for about an hour and a half and I think I ran myself right out of my neighborhood."

"It's easy to do up here. The roads don't really make much sense. Where's home?"

"52 Winslow Road. Any ideas?"

"Not a clue! Let's get directions." He started to walk away. "Do you want some water?"

"Thank you. If it's not too much trouble, that would be great."

"Do you want to come in?"

Annabeth hesitated. "No, that's okay. I'll just wait here. Thanks, though." The guy didn't seem like an axe murderer, but you never knew.

A minute later he came back with a bottle of water and his phone. "Okay, let's see . . . oh whoa," he said, "this says you live twelve miles from here."

She tried not to look dismayed. "Okaaay," she said. "Can you tell me how to get back there from here?"

"I think I can . . . but . . . are you up for another twelve miles? Were you getting in a marathon today?"

She laughed. "Uh, no, that was not the plan. But I guess that's what I'm going to end up doing." She took another drink. "Thanks for the water. Now how do I get back?"

He looked at the ground a moment. "I know you don't know me, and you might not want to do this, but I'd be happy to give you a ride home. I'm not a lunatic. I promise. If my parents were here, I'd have one of them do it—or ride with us. But they are at church." He held out his arms, palms upraised. "See, I'm a guy from a nice Protestant family." He grinned at her.

Still, Annabeth hesitated, embarrassed to be so uncool and cautious. He did look safe. He had an open face and a mop of slightly disheveled hair. He was dressed in shorts and a Bates College t-shirt, wearing the same brand running shoes as all the guys on her old team.

He continued, "I'm a runner too, and I do know the difference between a twelve-mile and a twenty-four-mile run. I am a trustworthy guy, though if you'd rather, I could call a taxi or something. It might take a while to get one up here, but you're welcome to hang out until then."

Annabeth did trust this guy, although she knew she was taking a risk. He seemed genuine and his house, or rather his parents' house, looked normal enough.

"Thank you. If it really isn't too much trouble, I would like a ride."

"No problem. I'll grab my keys."

While she waited on the front steps, she wondered if she'd lost her mind. Her parents would have a fit if they knew she was doing this. Maybe they do, she thought. There weren't any alarm bells ringing in her head, though. Somehow, even now, she knew one of them would have a way of letting her know if this was a big mistake. She concentrated. No, no sick feeling in her stomach. It seemed okay.

The guy came outside and pointed to a black Jetta parked in front of the house. "That's my car," he said. "It's kind of a mess inside, sorry. I haven't cleaned it up since I got home from school."

"That's okay. I don't mind."

She decided she'd spoken too soon when she saw the pile of fast-food wrappers, discarded paper cups, and dirty running shoes in the passenger front seat.

"Oh, man," he said, "it's worse than I thought. Hold on." He quickly scooped up the pile and jammed it all in the already full trunk. "I guess I know what I'll be doing this afternoon." He laughed.

Annabeth laughed, too. "Hmmm, maybe so. I'm sorry to be a bother."

"No, really, it's no trouble. I need to get gas anyway. I can do that on the way back."

They got into the car. "Here," he said, handing her his phone. "Would you mind managing directions? The voice thing doesn't always work."

This brought Annabeth even more reassurance. If he were going to kill her, would he hand over access to 911?

"I guess I should introduce myself. I'm Theo Comstock."

"I'm Annabeth Brady. For both grandmas." Totally lame, she thought.

"Mine's for two grandfathers and my dad. We don't seem to have a lot of imagination when it comes to names."

"Theo is a nice name, maybe even a little unusual."

"Not so much in my family. But I was spared, actually—my full name is Ichabod Theodore Comstock."

"Oh!" Annabeth said, impressed and appalled.

"I got lucky. My dad is Ted. My grandpa is Theodore, but my great grandpa was called *Ich*, apparently."

"Wow," she said.

"Yeah, no kidding. Let's see—do I go right here, and then up the hill to Route 58?"

He pulled over at a stop sign and leaned close to her to peer at the tiny map on the phone. "Yes, that's what it says."

They drove the rest of the way to her house sharing stories of runs gone wrong, and soon arrived in Annabeth's driveway.

"Thanks so much for the ride," she said. "I am lucky to have knocked on your door. I appreciate it."

"No problem. At all. It was great to meet you."

"You, too."

She didn't turn around to wave goodbye but couldn't help wondering if maybe he was watching her in the rearview mirror as he drove away. Lame again, she thought.

Chapter Seven

THE PHONE WAS RINGING when Annabeth entered the
house. She picked up the old-fashioned kitchen phone without caller ID, and soon regretted it. It was Aunt Janet, calling
from Kansas to inform her that she was coming to visit. Aunt
Janet was nothing less than a force of nature. In her mid-six-
ties, she began every morning with a four-mile power walk,
the least energetic thing she did all day. She ran more com-
mittees and strangers' lives than anyone in eastern Kansas.
Now she was coming to Connecticut to "help" her "get things
sorted out."

Annabeth tried to sound accommodating instead of panicked when she said, "Oh, Aunt Janet. It is such a long trip for
you. You know I would love to see you, but things are sorting
themselves out here, and I'm doing much better."

"Nonsense!" replied her aunt. "I bet you haven't done anything about that overgrown pile of brush my brother called a garden . . ."

"Actually, I have. A gardener friend of Dad's has been coming by to tend to it. We have things sprouting all over the place."

"I am sure you do. Does this gardener friend know a rose from a radish?"

"Yes, as a matter of fact, he's written a book about gardening." Oh dear, big mistake.

"A book! That makes him quite the expert, I am sure. Have the plants read this book so they know what they're supposed to do?"

"I guess so because they look pretty good!" She tried a small laugh.

"What about those closets? Have you cleaned out all that old junk?"

"The closets are fine," she said, although she had no idea if that were true.

"Have you sorted through all the household files, met with the lawyer again? What about your father's office? I bet you haven't even thought of that."

Annabeth had seen to none of these things, but she wasn't about to let her aunt know. "It's all under control, Aunt Janet. There is no need for you to have to deal with a thing."

"I'm sure there are a million things you haven't thought of. I'll be there next Saturday. Don't worry about picking me up at the airport. I'll rent a car and drive up myself. Don't go into any trouble. I'll cook when I get in. We'll have a nice visit."

Annabeth tried one last time. "Aunt Janet, I appreciate your offer, but why don't you come later in the summer? I am going to be busy that week, and I won't be around much. Maybe another time would work better for both of us?"

"No, no, you run off to your weaving class or whatever. That will leave me free to make myself useful. See you next weekend."

"Bye then," said Annabeth, to the click of her aunt hanging up the phone.

The thought of Aunt Janet invading the house was almost unbearable, especially now that Annabeth had begun to feel better. She would have to hide somewhere for most of the days, pretending to be occupied elsewhere. And then when she came home—there Aunt Janet would be, organizing the spice drawer or pickling beets or something. Maybe she could pretend to get sick and call and tell her Aunt . . . No, that would never work. Janet would just come to bully her into recovery.

She sank down into a kitchen chair and petted Chip. "Chip, old boy, we are in for a time of it. You're going to be brushed within an inch of your life. And I am going nuts. We'll have to stick together and get each other through it."

She sighed and thought about the untouched closets, the unopened safety deposit box, the unsorted clutter in her dad's office, and her aunt's certain disapproval of all of it. How much could she get done in a week? Not enough. It was just too daunting. Outside, the sun was still shining, and the breeze was lightly rustling the leaves. Inside, Annabeth's heart was slowly sinking.

After almost succumbing to the gloom that threatened yet again to overtake her, she stood up and shook it off. "No! I will not let this day be ruined." She marched outside and threw the Sunday paper on the patio table. Then she went back into the kitchen and flung a pan on the stove. Determined to recapture the fragile optimism she'd felt earlier, she scrambled the eggs she'd been imagining on her run, microwaved some leftover coffee, made toast, and took the meal outside to enjoy while she read the paper. She would cope with next week when next week came. Until then, Aunt Janet did not exist.

Chapter Eight

MONDAY DAWNED PINK AND NOISY. The birds were screaming as they frantically flew from nest to shrub and back, collecting food for their hatchlings and fending off potential threats to their young families. Spring's chorus of a few morning bird calls had now become summer's cacophonous shriek. Somehow, Ruth could sleep through the din, but the noise served as an alarm for David. No matter how long before daylight the birds got going, they always seemed to be scolding, "Get up! Now!"

He got out of bed and tiptoed into the bathroom. Although the squawking would never register in Ruth's consciousness, his movements might, and he didn't want to disturb her. He closed the door and got dressed in khakis and a polo shirt, attire for a day in the office. He used to put off the paperwork until a rainy day, but there always came a day when there was just too much of it. This season, David set aside Monday for bookkeeping, ordering supplies, and client appointments. Every week he wondered how much longer he could handle this part of the business by himself, but he never seemed to find the time to look for an office assistant. Ruth sometimes came in on the weekends to help, an arrangement he realized wouldn't work once she started the California gig. Now he had to get around to writing an ad. He left before it was fully light, giving Ruth a quick kiss on the cheek as she was stirring awake. "Love you," he whispered, and she smiled back at him.

Once in the office, he started his ancient Mr. Coffee, turned on his computer, and began reading emails. His self-imposed rule of no business email on Sunday usually didn't create too much of a burden on Monday morning, but this morning he was dismayed to find a long rant from a dissatisfied customer, complaining about the deer-eaten plants in his new perennial garden. David sighed. He would have to call the guy and explain, once again, that without a deer fence, lilies and roses were risky propositions. He had advised against them, of course, but the client, some private equity guy, knew without a doubt that his yellow Labrador retriever would keep the deer at bay. David lost the battle of plant selection to his insistent client and now suspected he would have another losing battle on his hands—one about who would be purchasing replacement plants. Not an auspicious start to the day.

Relieved that it was too early to make the phone call, David spent the next hour taking care of other things. Around eight o'clock he forced himself to dial Sid Snyder's number, hoping for voicemail, but wasn't that lucky. The customer was only a little less upset this morning than he'd been yesterday when he fired off the email. He demanded that David come over that second to inspect the deer damage. "You cannot imagine the devastation!" he shouted. "It's Hiroshima!"

As a matter of fact, David could picture the scene well. He didn't need to see it to know it was bad, if something less than nuclear annihilation. He tried to sound calm and reassuring.

"I'll come by later to take a look. Then I'll make some recommendations about what to plant that the deer don't like quite so much," he said.

Sid, however, was having none of that and insisted that David drop everything to survey the scene and "take responsibility." David agreed to come before noon. "And elsewhere real wars are raging," he muttered to the empty office after hanging up the phone.

A dissatisfied customer was a relatively rare event for his business, and he always made a point of resolving whatever differences arose so the relationship with his customer survived intact. David knew he would have to muster a lot of patience to deal with Sid today. He also knew, even before leaving, that he would end up footing the bill for whatever came next. The morning's disruption did provide him with the final push he needed to write a help-wanted ad. He dashed off a few words: "Part-time office help needed for growing landscape business." Ha, he thought, we'll see who likes that. "Flexible hours and generous pay for someone with computer, basic bookkeeping, and good communication skills." He included all his contact information and emailed it to the local paper and a job search site before he headed out the door.

This trip across town was different than his pre-dawn drive. Now the roads were crowded with commuters and delivery trucks, everyone intent on being productive. The drivers were impatient, revved up on caffeine, most of them already at work, phones, and backup batteries charged for the day. David's own phone lay turned off on the seat next to him. He'd resolved when he began this business that he would not be a slave to electronics. If he needed to reach someone, he'd make the call. It sometimes drove Ruth crazy, but David figured there were very few garden emergencies that couldn't wait an hour or two. He usually called Ruth once or twice a day and checked his voicemail in the afternoon. It was a system that worked for him.

David pulled into the Snyder driveway, shut off the engine, and groaned. He could see from where he sat that the perennial garden had gaping holes where the lilies had been. The rose bed was barren. It still amazed him that deer would eat roses to the ground, even as the thorns cut bleeding gashes in their mouths. He walked to the border and began taking notes of the gaps. He intended to speak with Sid after he assessed the damage and had a new plan, but Sid spotted him and came storming out of the house.

"Thought you'd sneak in here and I wouldn't see you?" he yelled, bounding across the yard, face red, eyes bulging. "I won't stand for this! You are going to make this right or you will be hearing from my lawyer!"

Sid was short and round with stubby legs that rubbed against each other when he walked. Head forward, he charged toward David as fast as those legs could carry him. In the hours since David reassured him on the phone that all would be well, the man had managed to work himself into an even bigger rage.

"Hello, Sid." David extended his hand. "I was just taking a look to see what might work in here instead of those lilies. Looks like there are about fifteen areas that need new plants. I want to do a little more research about what will work best, but we'll get you fixed up in no time."

"Research? Aren't you the 'Expert Gardener'? The guy who knows it all? I paid you for a perennial garden and instead got a desert wasteland. I want all this damage repaired immediately! You should have gotten it right the first time."

David swallowed and looked at the ground as his stomach clenched in anger. He waited until any words he spoke would be under his control. Opposite him, Sid was a cartoon character of sputtering fury, an angry bull snorting his rage.

"Mr. Snyder, as you recall, you insisted on the roses and lilies. We discussed the possibility that the deer might find their way to your border because those particular plants are deer dessert. I—"

"Don't try to get cute with me, Crawford. You claim your plants have a one-year guarantee. So, stand behind it. Fix my garden today, or I will sue you before dinner."

"Mr. Snyder, as I said, I do intend to fix your garden, but I can't do it today and do it right. We want the finished product here to be something both of us agree is attractive and appropriate to the site. If I replanted today, it would have to be whatever the nursery happened to have on hand. I have no way of knowing what that might be. But you tell me—which is it? Gaps filled in with whatever is available or something that enhances this garden?"

Sid glared. "You are not getting it, Mr. Crawford. I am entertaining important businesspeople tonight. You may have heard, out there in the real world there is a recession going on?" He lowered his voice almost to a whisper. "The people coming here tonight want to leave me, take their money somewhere else. If they think there is the slightest chance I am in trouble. . ." he blanched, then finding a deeper register he almost growled, ". . . but they will not think that, because by tonight all this will be history." He gestured to the ravaged beds. "This place is going to be 'enhanced,' or I am going to sue you for more than you will ever have."

David had a powerful urge to grab the guy by the front of his shirt and throw him against something. His own heart was racing now, and he was breathing hard. He looked out over the still-lovely garden and imagined ripping it apart with his bare hands. Instead, he willed his pulse to slow, took several deep breaths, and spoke deliberately, without looking at Sid.

"I have never walked away from a project until the client was happy, Mr. Snyder, and I am going to do my best to keep that record. I will do what I can to restore your property today, but I will not ruin it to meet your arbitrary deadline. If at the end of the day you aren't happy, then I guess you will just have to sue me."

Now, he turned and looked at Snyder. "As a favor to you, my crew and I will be back this afternoon, but I insist that you allow us to work without threatening us or interfering in any way. If you do, I would be under a legal obligation to stop the job out of concern for their safety. Do you understand?"

Sid snorted. "I am not threatening you with anything but legal action, Mr. Crawford. I am perfectly within my rights to observe your work and that, I intend to do. As long as your crew does what they are supposed to be doing, they will have no problems from me."

David nodded. "I'll take you at your word."

He strode to his truck and drove away without looking back. He was still mad enough to spit, but he was not about to let anyone, especially Sid, see anything other than a measured and rational demeanor.

It was an odd feeling not to care about this garden. It was even stranger to want to see it in shambles. The process of designing a project and watching his vision come to life had always given David joy. It almost didn't seem like work. Even the hard labor was a pleasure, most days. This was the first time since he'd started the business that he didn't care what the thing looked like. He just wanted it finished with something deer wouldn't eat that would get Sid out of his hair.

He drove to the grower where he bought his materials. After looking at the existing inventory, he gave the manager a list of plants to load in the back of his truck. He didn't care whether they were perfect. Then he called his crew foreman, Rick, and told him to grab a couple of the guys and meet him at Sid's house.

Once there, David explained the situation and pointed in the general direction of where the plants were to go. Then he left, relieved he hadn't encountered Sid again, and drove to the job site where he'd pulled the crew. He fell to, digging holes and dragging trees, until one section of that job was finished. By the time he quit, filthy and tired, he was in better humor. The distraction of the hard work had been good for him, and he left for home, pleased with the day. By now Sid's guests should have been arriving and the fact that David's cell didn't show fifteen missed calls from him indicated that, at least for the moment, the guy was otherwise engaged.

Ruth was not home when he arrived. In the garage he stripped off his dirty clothes and threw them in the old washer kept there for that purpose. Then he went inside and grabbed a beer from the fridge on his way to the shower. He turned on the radio in the bathroom and listened to the good old boys while he cleaned up. By the time he came downstairs, Ruth was pulling into the driveway. He greeted her in the kitchen with an enveloping hug. Holding her tight, he told her, "You are a sight for sore eyes. I am one lucky guy."

Ruth laughed. "Rough day, honey?"

He laughed, too. "Not the best one I've ever had, but it's better now. Are you in the mood to cook?"

"If you're inviting me out to dinner, I accept. You want to talk about today?"

"Yeah, later. How about Portofino's—we could eat outside on the patio? It's gorgeous tonight."

"That sounds wonderful," Ruth said. "Give me five minutes to get ready."

Half an hour later they were seated at the restaurant, watching the day's last light fade from the sky. They sat side by side in silent appreciation of the approaching summer night. Not for the first time, David wondered at the change that being with Ruth brought over him. She was a cure for all his ills. Even if he never got around to telling her about a problem or a worry, he found her company a sufficient antidote to whatever was troubling him. Sometimes it was just too damned complicated to describe a difficult day that had already evaporated into manageable memory after a few moments spent in the warmth of her presence. As far as he was concerned, it didn't matter if Ruthie didn't know all the details or was aware of every thought in his head. As long as he could touch her, see her, smell her—all was right with his world. Tonight, there was no need to relive this frustrating day by describing it blow by blow. By the time they finished dinner, it was as if it had never happened.

Chapter Nine

ANNABETH looked at the piles of clothes she had stacked all over her parents' bedroom and sighed. Now that she'd made them, she wasn't quite sure why she'd done it. She knew why she'd started the project—The Coming of Aunt Janet—but after having spent almost the entire day sorting things into three separate piles of "keepers," "Goodwill," and "trash," what difference did it make? She should have just bagged and tossed them all without even looking at them. Other than making her weep and allowing her to save a very few special things of her mother's, the creation of these mounds seemed to make the whole project much more daunting than when they were clothes hanging in the closet. She sat back on her heels amidst the rumpled hills and thought about what to do now. Her first inclination was to close the door to her parents' room, make something to eat, and pretend the mess didn't exist. But even thinking about that plan made clear the impossibility of it. "C'mon, just get it together and finish." Still, she sat and surveyed the room. I probably do need to eat something, she thought. She couldn't remember if she'd stopped for lunch, which meant she hadn't. Her appetite was still almost nonexistent and often the only time she realized she needed to eat was when she got dizzy or confused. "After dinner. I'll feel better then."

She got up off the floor and willed herself not to close the door behind her. In the kitchen she ate a bowl of cereal while she rummaged through the freezer for something more like dinner. Realizing that there was nothing in there that hadn't been purchased by her parents made her aware of another job that needed to be done. She gave up, closed the freezer, and sat down to the second bowl of her whole grain dinner. Maybe the thing to do was just let Janet have at it. Leave those clothes, the papers—all of it. Sure, Janet would cluck and sigh, but she'd be delighted, especially if she could do it all the way she thought it should be done, without any interference from Annabeth. Ah yes, that was the answer to enduring Janet's visit—that and disappearing as much as possible. Only seven days of finding something to do away from the house, seven long dinners, seven nights of going to her room at nine o'clock, and then Aunt Janet would be gone. The closets would be organized, the household papers filed in labeled folders, the pantry sterilized and restocked. There would be no avoiding Janet's scolding, no matter how much she accomplished before Janet arrived. Better to be scolded for inactivity than incompetence; even more so if the inactivity was a conscious choice.

She spent the next hour or so scrolling social media and

googling former teammates. Seeing the various jobs they had for the summer made her think that she really should find one herself. She went to the local paper's site and began idly reading the Help Wanted section. There were lots of people looking for nannies and mothers' helpers, which did not appeal to her. She skipped over all the ads for telemarketers and pizza deliverers. She settled on a retail store looking for sales help and two businesses wanting office staff. She updated last summer's resume to include her year of college and emailed it to the places she'd selected. She didn't much care where she worked.

After more aimless browsing, Annabeth closed her computer and noticed that Chip was waiting patiently to go outside. She opened the door and they both went into the yard. It was almost dark, the very edge of the horizon hot pink and the sky overhead a blue-gray rimmed with glowing gold. The air was alive with the sounds of crickets and frogs and the last calls of the birds returning home for the night. Chip took off after some nocturnal creature as she walked around the yard. All kinds of plants had grown tall and thick since the last time she paid attention. Most of them were bursting with buds and some of them were already covered in blossoms. The perfumed air was dotted with a few early fireflies. Annabeth went from flower to flower, inhaling deeply, unaware that she was smiling as she went, unaware that some of the flowers had been planted by her father last fall. Even without that knowledge, the garden soothed her. Why didn't she spend more time out here? It was wonderful. She heard children playing in the street in front of her house. As she turned toward the sound, she caught sight of her mailbox and stopped. Mail. She hadn't checked the mail since—when? How had she forgotten about mail? She went to the box and opened it. There were two pieces of paper inside. One was a notice from the post office stating that all mail was being held because the box was overfull. The other was a handwritten scrap she could just make out in the last light of day. Standing next to the mailbox, she re-read the note, then read it again. She folded it with care, closed her palm around it, and turned to go inside. Without intending to, she began to run up the driveway. Within a few steps she was flying, outpacing the dark cloud of sadness that usually hovered just over her right shoulder. In its place she sensed the presence of something lighter that might have been a hint of happiness. It followed close behind her as she raced through the doorway. It was still there when she reached for the phone.

Chapter Ten

THE PREGNANCY TEST WAS NEGATIVE. Ruth tried to tell herself that she'd already known, and had no expectations. She made coffee without crying, collected the paper from the driveway without crying, ate breakfast and showered without crying. If David hadn't called, she might have made it through the entire day without crying. She attempted to report the bad news matter-of-factly, but in sharing it with him, her best friend in the world, the sorrow she'd been trying to ignore overwhelmed her. She broke down before she finished the sentence. Unable to speak, she sat alone in a kitchen chair, cradling the phone and herself as best she could, weeping almost without sound.

At the other end of the phone, David also sat in silence. After a few minutes he spoke. "I'm coming home."

Ruth was tempted to agree. "Yes, come here now. Hold me and cry with me and make it all better." But she knew he couldn't make it all better. He could comfort her and share the disappointment with her, as he had before, but how many times could they replay this painful scene? As much as she was heartbroken, she was also tired of their recurring roles.

"No, no," she said. "If you come home, I don't know when I'll stop crying. So—I'm going to get moving. Just needed to grieve a little. I'll be fine."

It took a bit more of convincing before he was willing to hang up, but Ruth meant what she'd said. She needed to get moving. Going to work, though, would mean telling James yes, the only answer she could give him now. She wasn't ready to rush headlong into the planning for the new role she knew James would be chomping at the bit to do. It wasn't a lie to say she didn't feel well, so she gave herself a few hours and let her assistant know she wouldn't be in until later.

Something else had to occupy her mind. She couldn't mope at home all morning. Samantha was out of town, but maybe Sarah was free. Sarah would think of something fun for them to do and she wouldn't pester Ruth to talk, not now that Sarah herself was pregnant. She called her sister and left a voicemail, hoping it was a preschool morning for Hannah, and that Sarah, too, would have a few hours free. Around nine-thirty Sarah called back.

"Hey, I am so glad you called. Hannah has Lunch Bunch today and there's nothing I absolutely have to do. I'd love to hang out with you. What do you want to do? Go for a walk? Have lunch? Give your Amex a workout? I'm up for any and all of the above."

"Oh good, let me think. How about some shopping? I haven't bought anything new since I don't know when and

I actually need clothes for my new work assignment, which I haven't even told you about. We can have lunch, too. What time do you pick up Hannah?"

"She stays until three o'clock today. Do you want me to come get you?"

"Where are you?" Ruth asked.

"I am still in the preschool parking lot. I am wearing sweats, though, so maybe I should run home and change?"

"I'm not dressed either. Let's meet behind the library in forty-five minutes."

Ruth got dressed and did what little she could for her red, swollen eyes. For now, she'd cried enough. A year ago, she couldn't have imagined how efficient she'd become at bundling the hurt and setting it aside. In the early days, before she'd been through the disappointment so many times, each month was a fresh loss that caught her off guard. Now, even as each not-unexpected recurrence was another blow, it became even more necessary to avoid feeling the force of it. Somewhere in her unconscious being, she sensed that she and God had made a pact. In return for the ability he gave her to put the pain aside, she wouldn't blame him for causing it.

By the time Ruth met Sarah she was able to concentrate on the trivial decisions immediately before her—which shoes to try, what to order for lunch. She was able to chat and laugh, and when Ruth told Sarah her disappointing news, she tossed it off in such a casual way that even her sister believed her when Ruth shrugged and said, "Not this time. I had zero expectations."

Sarah waited a few seconds before saying, "Oh, I am sorry, Ruthie. But I guess at least it's good, you know, that you weren't counting on it."

"No. I wasn't. I mean, it would have been great timing with your news, but not the best for work." She sat up straighter and smiled brightly. "Because—I haven't had a chance to tell you, I have a big-deal new client."

"Tell me," Sarah said.

"I am going to be the lead lawyer working with a major real estate investor from California who's eyeing some Connecticut properties for development. It's huge for me and for the firm. James specifically asked me to take it and I just couldn't say anything but yes."

"No kidding. Congratulations! That sounds very exciting. Wait—you're not moving there, though, are you?"

"No, I'll be back and forth. I guess I'll find out the details when I talk to James about it. I am pretty curious to get to California and meet this guy."

"When's that?" Sarah asked.

"Don't know yet, but I'll probably find out tomorrow."

"Where in California?"

"I don't know that yet either. Bishop, the guy, lives in San Francisco, but his company has an office in Los Angeles, too. I'm assuming I'll be working both places. I've never been to either one, so I guess I'll finally get the chance. But," said Ruth, leaning forward, "this is the important question—what am I going to wear? San Francisco seems like a pretty sophisticated city. Los Angeles—totally different. I wonder what the lawyers there wear?"

"Spray tans and Botox?" Sarah guessed.

"Probably!" Ruth laughed. "I am afraid my wardrobe right now says, 'Here's Ruth, our thirty-six-year-old Connecticut preppie.' I need help."

"Yay! This will be fun. Please tell me you don't have a budget because I'm dying to go to Francine's and I don't think we should even go near the place unless you are seriously ready to go crazy."

"Let's go crazy."

They walked down Main Street toward Francine's, a tiny exclusive shop that carried expensive designer clothing. Ruth had been inside a few times but had always limited her purchases to the semi-annual sales rack. She wasn't a regular and one didn't just wander into the store to browse. It was in a narrow, tree-shaded courtyard, almost hidden from the main street. The courtyard was underplanted with impatiens, ivy, and flowering herbs in antique iron pots. Francine herself lived in an apartment above the shop. It was all very old world and charming. Inside, even during these hard economic times, each article of clothing was displayed as a work of art. No racks of identical dresses squeezed onto crowded rods in this shrine. Instead, one-of-a-kind items were down-lit and displayed in solitary splendor. It was like being inside a museum, if not a cathedral. The space demanded whispers and respectful nods in the direction of the clothing. It was almost impossible to imagine touching any of these sacred objects, let alone trying them on.

Ruth had forgotten how intimidating the place was. She took Sarah by the elbow and had turned to leave when a young saleswoman, not Francine, came from the back to greet them. "Good afternoon, ladies," she said with a friendly smile. "Would you like to look a bit, or could I help you find something in particular?"

Sarah, an innocent in this foreign land, responded, "I am just here to help my sister find something for work."

Ruth knew that the script called for her to request a very

specific item that would put the saleswoman to task. Before she could say her lines, though, the unassuming young woman answered Sarah casually. "Great. That's our specialty." Then to Ruth, "Do you prefer dresses or pants?"

She showed them the clothing, allowing them to touch all the silk and cashmere fabrics. The saleswoman soon filled a dressing room with outfits that each cost as much as a monthly mortgage payment. Ruth allowed herself to be convinced by the woman and Sarah that these "investment" purchases were just what she needed to feel confident in her new job. She tried on a few things, then had to stop because everything was beautiful and she could have bought them all. In the end she chose several pieces that went together and were versatile enough to be appropriate for a corporate office or more casual occasions. Ruth had to admit that buying them and hearing the compliments they elicited from Sarah and the saleswoman did make her feel better, to her chagrin. In fact, it wasn't an exaggeration to say that in these new clothes she felt like a different person. And maybe that's just fine, she thought.

Chapter Eleven

DAVID HUNG UP the phone after talking with Ruth and sat for a few minutes. When they first started on their baby journey, he'd get his hopes up too, and cry with Ruth every time they were disappointed. Over time, though, he noticed that his crying only compounded her hurt and the responsibility she took for their failure. Like Ruth, his tests had come back without pinpointing any reason for their inability to conceive. It should have happened. But it didn't. He'd run out of words of consolation and, by means of some unspoken pact, they carried on pretending not to be as devastated as they were. Now, he wracked his brain trying to think of something new to say that would be healing for them both. He came up with nothing, as seemed invariably to be the case. Maybe when they were together words worth saying would come out of his mouth. He sat a little longer, then got up, made more coffee, and returned to his email. Whatever else, running the business would provide a distraction.

The inbox contained three responses to his ad. He scanned each of them looking for previous experience that would be relevant. None of the three had ideal resumes, so he went back and read each one more carefully. It wasn't until he clicked on the third email address that he realized it was Annabeth's. Her message had been impersonal, with no mention of the fact that she knew him. After considering for a minute, he decided to acknowledge their acquaintance and sent her an informal reply, asking if she was sure she wanted to hang out in a glorified potting shed. By noon, he'd heard back from the two people he didn't know and set up appointments for the following day. He worked all afternoon, too busy to check email again until it was almost time to leave. Still no reply from Annabeth. As David was closing shop, the office phone rang. It was her, explaining that she'd applied for the job without realizing it was his business.

"I hope you don't think you have to hire me. That was so dumb. I just thought the work seemed like something I could do, and I need to do something, so I sent my resume. I wasn't trying to take advantage or anything."

"I didn't know you were looking for a job, or I would have offered it to you in the first place. Saved myself the cost of the ad. Do you want the job?"

"Sure, I do," Annabeth said. "I have to tell you something, though." She sounded very serious. "I am not too proud of my math skills. I will try to be careful, but I don't feel confident about that part of the job."

"What I need isn't advanced math. Ruth or I will show you. It's mainly just adding and subtracting, and we have a calculator," David joked.

"Hmmm. Yes, well, I have a calculator, too, but that may not be enough. I promise I will try hard, though. I know I can do the other things—the phone and filing and stuff."

"I know you can. Why don't you start next Monday? I can explain most of what you'll be doing. I may ask Ruth to show you how to do the Saturday deposit. It's not complicated. She often does that, but she's going to be away a lot and won't have time anymore. Would working an occasional weekend be okay?"

"Yes, sure. The only thing I have to do all summer is be run over by my aunt, but that is another story. Maybe I'll tell you when I come in."

"Yes, that sounds . . . interesting."

"See you next Monday!"

David hoped Annabeth would be up for the job. Her resume only listed a couple of stints as a camp counselor and one summer as her father's research assistant, not skills that would come in handy dealing with the Sids of the world. But thank goodness, there weren't many Sids in the world. She needed to occupy her time and he needed a little office help. It ought to work for them both. He did sometimes get a little bored in the trailer with no one to talk to—and if he could figure out how to get that smile of hers to appear on a regular basis, he'd be doing much more for her than just helping her kill time.

"THAT WAS SMART. I applied for a job without even knowing where it was. David must think I am just an idiot. But . . . I got it." Now that she had it, she wasn't sure how pleased she was. It was one thing to get out of the house during Aunt Janet's visit, another to be committed to a job all summer. At least she already knew David and wouldn't have to pretend to be some efficient office wiz. But all that was next Monday. Tonight, she was seeing Theo. On the phone, he'd told her he was going to be job hunting himself all day and wouldn't be free until evening. Annabeth preferred running in the morning, but she'd had no trouble agreeing to this particular nighttime run. They'd made plans to meet at a park in the middle of town for what Theo said was one of his favorite routes, five miles through a mix of streets and trails that he thought she would like, too.

Only one more hour to kill, she thought, as she checked the time. She toasted a freezer-burned bagel, then tossed it in the trash after one bite. She went to her room to change. All day she'd been back and forth about what to wear—faded shorts and a t-shirt or something newer and nicer. She tried several outfits before she ran out of time and left wearing an old top but new shorts, hoping she looked decent, but not like she was trying too hard.

She arrived before Theo. She watched him park, check himself out in the rearview mirror, and then climb out of his car and look around. She redid her ponytail, took a deep breath, and got out to meet him.

"Hey, Annabeth."

"Hey, Theo. This is a pretty spot." She looked around, taking in the view of the quiet river.

"You've never been here?" Theo asked.

"No, not really. I've driven by, but I haven't stopped. I never lived here. I guess I am more of a tourist."

"I think you'll like this run. Not *too* many hills."

"Oh great! When someone from Connecticut says not too many hills that means it's going to be brutal!"

He laughed. "No, it isn't! I haven't been running too much this summer, and I wouldn't do anything terrible to either one of us. But if it gets bad, tell me. We can change it up or turn around. No problem."

"If I slow you down, just go ahead. I'll do an out-and-back and we'll meet here."

Theo gave her a skeptical look. "Like the out-and-back you did that day you needed a ride?"

"Oh!" She widened her eyes at his grin, then she laughed. "No, maybe not exactly like that one."

"I'm sure you'll be fine. A run you don't know in a town you don't know—what could go wrong?" he teased.

"When you're stuck at a ten-minute pace the last two miles, you'll regret those words."

For a second Theo's face fell.

"I'm kidding!"

They set out together, running side by side through the winding residential streets. At first, they talked and laughed so much that their pace was slow and irregular. Theo played the tour guide and Annabeth the impressed visitor. After a while, though, they picked it up. Still together, they finished the run in a respectable time, moderately tired and not, as Annabeth had worried, drenched in sweat.

"We should do this again—maybe later this week," said Theo, as they walked toward the river's edge.

"Definitely. But—I forgot to tell you—I got a job."

"Congratulations. My parents are not too thrilled that I don't have one. I think they hoped for an internship at JP Morgan or someplace like that, but I'm too late for this summer. Where are you working?"

"At a landscaping business. I'll be an office assistant for a friend of my dad's. He's a nice guy and seems flexible about hours and stuff like that."

Theo nodded. "Does he need a finance intern?"

"I don't know. I can ask?" She had no idea what a finance intern might do.

"I think my parents have something a little more train-to-New York in mind."

"Sorry. I can't help you there."

He leaned against the railing that ran along the river, facing her. She moved to stand next to him and peered over the edge, watching the swans and geese swimming below them. Families were gathering on the riverbank, some of them unpacking picnics, others just closing out the day. They watched as a young child learning to ride a bike wobbled down the sidewalk, his father running behind him. When the boy made it to the end of the path, he half-fell off the bike and yelled, "I did it! I did it! Now can we get ice cream?" The father high-fived his son. "Yes! We can definitely get ice cream."

"Hey," Theo said. "That sounds good. Do you like ice cream? There is a place right near here."

"How I feel about ice cream is way beyond liking it," Annabeth said solemnly.

"I knew you were my kinda girl."

She chose to ignore the leap in her chest.

They made their way to the store and waited in line behind the excited new bike rider and his dad. A week ago, the scene might have brought sad tears to her eyes. Tonight, it struck her differently, evoking happy memories of similar moments with her own parents. She wished she could tell the little boy, "File this away. Someday the memory of this night will make you happy all over again." She smiled, watching them, and felt Theo at her side, doing the same thing. It was so very nice not to be alone.

Chapter Twelve

JANET'S IMPENDING SATURDAY ARRIVAL had put Annabeth in a state of near panic. The thought of even a single dinner alone with her aunt made her heart sink. But a whole week? She needed a backup, other friends around to parry with Janet, or at least to divert her attention away from Annabeth for a while. Theo had volunteered to "help" with Aunt Janet, but he didn't know her—or the scope of the task he was offering to take on. And Theo was too nice. Aunt Janet would roll right over him. What she needed was a crowd to run interference, but there was no crowd at hand. The only other people she knew in the entire town were David and Ruth. They were nice too, but older, maybe less cowed by someone else's bossy aunt. Would they think it was totally weird if she asked them to dinner? Maybe to thank them for giving her the job?

She dialed the office number and was a little surprised when Ruth answered. She explained that she was trying to get everything caught up before Annabeth took over.

"Thank you," Annabeth said. "I appreciate having the job. I just hope I don't screw it up."

"You won't!" Ruth reassured her. "It's a win/win for all of us."

"Actually, I was wondering if you and David might be free for dinner tomorrow night when my Aunt Janet gets in town? I am not such a great cook, but my friend Theo said he'd grill something and, um, my aunt is kind of a big personality, so I thought this might be a the-more-the-merrier kind of situation . . ."

"Annabeth, we'd love to help you, but we have plans tomorrow," Ruth said.

"Oh," Annabeth half-squeaked, half-groaned. Her evident disappointment prompted Ruth to reconsider. David had told her the girl was all alone.

"Although, now that I think about it, we see those friends all the time and we were just going to do dinner and a movie. I'm sure they wouldn't mind if we rescheduled."

"Really? I don't want to cause you a hassle."

"We'd love to. What can I bring?"

THE NEXT MORNING Annabeth made the rounds, gathering the food she needed for her first dinner party. She stuffed everything into the refrigerator and thought about what other prep she should do—ah yes, set the big table in the dining room. Somewhere in her mother's cabinets she knew she'd find everything she needed, so she began opening doors. She quickly glanced into a couple of them, not quite sure what she was looking for when, without warning, the contents of the dining room buffet sent her reeling. Inside was her mother's wedding china, an old-fashioned floral pattern her mother had chosen when she'd been a newly engaged girl of only twenty years old. She had used these dishes for every special dinner since. The entire set was stored as if for display behind the closed cabinet door, with hand-cut felt circles between each plate, the cups arranged so that all their handles faced the same direction, serving dishes on one shelf, place settings on another.

Annabeth froze. Her mother's hands had last touched these dishes, so perfectly placed, their arrangement made a still life. To disturb them would be to cancel the evidence of the day her mother stood here, alive, creating this hidden work of art. She could picture her mother unpacking the china boxes herself, tending to this task when no one else was around, quietly content in what her mom called "playing house." The sight of those dishes made the reality of her mother's existence, and the reality of her absence, so immediate that it took her breath away. She reached out a hand and hesitated near the edge of one bowl, her fingers stopping just short of the delicate gold rim, as her eyes filled with tears. "Oh, Mommy," she whispered. "Please, don't be gone."

Annabeth sank to her knees in front of the cabinet and began to cry. For some long minutes, she lost herself in sorrow. When her throat and eyes began to hurt so much she had to stop, when her vast supply of tears was temporarily depleted, she sat up, breathed a ragged breath, and wiped her eyes with her hand. Chip, who'd wrapped himself around her like a blanket, began licking away her tears.

"Okay, buddy. That's enough." She petted him and moved

out of his reach. She looked back at the shelves, her mom's china still perfect, expectant, and eager to be put to use.

"Go on," she imagined her mother saying. "Use them. It would make me happy."

With trembling hands and a pounding heart, Annabeth touched the dinner plates and moved her fingers to count the number she needed. She took the stack and hugged it close to her. A poor substitute for the warmth of her mother's body, it nevertheless brought her some comfort. Young Lydia, Annabeth's age, had chosen this china for herself and her future family. Though the dishes had been used for some portion of their purpose, the task Lydia had imagined for them remained incomplete. Annabeth knew that her mother had envisioned this china in her daughter's hands, too. She felt in some inexplicable way that her mom was there again, loving her, pleased that one small part of the future together they'd been denied was nevertheless coming to pass. She closed her eyes, cradling the plates, then placed them with care on the table.

Chapter Thirteen

RUTH AND DAVID were the first to arrive. They came bearing wine, flowers, bread, and dessert.

"Thank you. That pie looks yum. And those flowers are so pretty. What are they?"

"Anemones. I know you're not supposed to bring the hostess flowers she has to deal with in the middle of her preparations, but I couldn't resist. I'll put them in water, and you can keep doing what you were doing."

Annabeth shrugged. "I was just waiting for you guys."

David came into the kitchen after a detour to check out the grill. "Hi, Annabeth," he said. "The grill looks good and there's charcoal in the garage. I'll get the fire going later, if you want. Sometimes it takes a while."

"Actually, my friend Theo said he would do the grilling. He should be here any minute."

"Great," David said. "I would never interfere with another man's grill. I'll leave him to it."

Ruth turned with her hand on her hip. "With another *man's* grill?"

"Oh . . . I just meant . . ."

"I don't care!" Annabeth said. "I hate that messy charcoal and I'm afraid I'd blow something up with the lighter fluid."

"Sometimes David thinks the damsel is in distress when she's actually got everything under control. He can't help riding in on a white horse. But he's very sweet about it." Ruth put her arm around him.

"I don't care about the grill. But David did already rescue me."

"You mean the job?" Ruth asked.

"Yes," Annabeth turned to him. "If you need me to work late, come in early . . . that would be fine with me."

David laughed. "I'm guessing that applies to this week in particular?"

"This week for sure. But next week, too, or whenever you need me."

Theo arrived, toting a large bag of charcoal. After introductions and some getting-to-know-you chat, he said to Annabeth, "I should probably check out the grill."

She agreed and together they went out the back door.

"I'm so glad you're here," she said when they were alone on the porch.

"Me, too. I'm glad I met your friends."

"They aren't so much my friends. They're more like my parents' friends, and now—whoa—one of them is my boss.

But David and Ruth have been looking out for me. I'm so glad you came."

Theo smiled at her. "How could I pass up the opportunity to meet Aunt Gladys?"

"Aunt Janet."

"Oh, yeah. Janet. Can't wait to meet her. Where is she?"

Annabeth looked at her watch. "I thought she would be here by now. Don't worry, you won't miss her."

At that moment, a car appeared at the end of the driveway.

"She's here," she said, her eyes wide, feeling dizzy.

He put his hand on her elbow. "C'mon. Let's face the dragon together."

They walked around the side of the house to greet Aunt Janet, who was hauling a suitcase from the trunk of her rental car.

"Here," Theo said, "let me help you with that."

Janet ignored him and hoisted the bag out of the trunk and plopped it on the driveway. Then she removed a large zipper tote and a well-taped cardboard box and set them on the ground next to her bag.

"Tomatoes," she said without turning around. "Jack told me there wasn't a decent tomato to be had in the entire state of Connecticut, and I'll be damned if I'm eating mush when I have a garden full of Better Boys that would melt in your mouth."

"Hi, Aunt Janet," Annabeth said. "How was your trip?"

"The usual hell that happens when you get the inmates running the asylum. Boarding the plane from the front, no food, seats designed by a CIA interrogation squad. I told the flight attendant to just keep the darned Coke if she was too cheap to leave the can."

"Oh. My. Well, Aunt Janet—this is my friend, Theo Comstock."

Janet turned and stuck out her hand. "Glad to meet you. You from around here?"

"Yes, I live one town over. Are you sure I can't help you with your things?"

"Here. Take that suitcase and I'll get the tomatoes. Don't want you dropping them after I held them on my lap the whole way here. Except for takeoff and landing, of course, when that flight attendant made me stuff them under the seat. As if it made any difference at all! Rules for no reason, that's just what that's all about."

Janet put the tote over her shoulder, picked up the box, and started toward the house. Now Theo looked at Annabeth with his eyes open wide. She shook her head, then giggled. They trailed behind Janet until she arrived at the back door and shouted, "Any chance somebody could open this door?"

Annabeth ran to grab the handle, but David was already pushing it open from the other side. Janet stepped into the kitchen, saying, "Thank you. It's nice to know there are still gentlemen in the world."

Annabeth quickly glanced back at Theo, who returned the look in bemused puzzlement as he stepped through the kitchen door pulling Janet's suitcase. Janet placed the box of tomatoes next to the kitchen sink, sighed grandly, and surveyed the room. "Are we having a party?" she asked.

"Just having some friends for dinner," Annabeth said. She made introductions as they all maneuvered to shake hands with Aunt Janet, who pointed at Theo, still holding the suitcase handle. "Just put that anywhere," she said. "I don't want to deal with it now."

"I'll take it up the guest room," he offered.

David spoke to Janet. "Can I get you a glass of wine?"

"No, thank you. I'll have a scotch on ice."

"All right," he responded. "Where is the scotch, Annabeth?"

"The liquor is in the cabinet above the fridge. I don't know what's up there. Probably some scotch, I think."

"While you try to organize a search party, I'll just go wash up, if you don't mind. Where's my room, Annie?"

Annabeth hated it when her aunt called her that. "I'll show you," she replied and led her aunt out of the kitchen.

When she returned, she discovered that the rest of the crew had recovered from Storm Janet and were discussing some local news story she'd missed.

"Was there scotch?" Annabeth asked.

"Yes, good stuff, too. You're all set," David said.

"Whew." She tried to relax her shoulders.

Theo winked at her. "Thinking about trying some yourself?"

"No, I hate scotch."

"I'll check back with you about that in a few days," Theo whispered as Janet reentered the kitchen.

"I'll take some of that," said Janet, nodding in the direction of the bottle. "With ice, please."

"Sure thing." David sprang into action and filled a glass with ice, then scotch, and handed it to Janet with a tiny bow. "Welcome to Connecticut," he said, raising his glass. They all followed suit and sipped their drinks.

"Ah . . .," Janet sighed, slightly smacking her lips. "I guess my egg-headed little brother knew one sensible thing after all—how to buy booze."

David flinched and Ruth looked toward Annabeth who stared at her aunt in horror.

"Theo, why don't you make yourself useful and open that box of tomatoes so we can have them with dinner?" Janet ordered.

"Okay, um, sure." He gently touched Annabeth's arm before he picked up a knife and started working on the box. She put her hand on his back in grateful response.

The silence in the room continued as they all watched Theo. Only Janet was unperturbed. "Careful with that knife. Don't cut in too far or you'll ruin them."

Theo kept his back turned but politely responded that he would. Annabeth slipped out of the kitchen, wandering into the living room and away from the others. She'd not expected Aunt Janet to continue her my-brother's-so-smart-he's-a-fool routine after he was dead. The clash of images—the one Annabeth held of her father as brilliant, and the one Aunt Janet promulgated of Jack Brady as preposterous—had knocked the wind out of her. She never liked the cruelty in her aunt's jibes when her father had been standing there to jibe back, but now it was utterly unbearable. She couldn't imagine eating at the same table with this woman, let alone hosting her for an entire week.

She opened the front door and absentmindedly walked even farther away from the house. Of their own will her feet moved down the drive. In the chaos of her careening thoughts, she almost walked in front of the car slowly coming up the drive. A couple she didn't know waved at her, smiling. The woman lowered her window and said, "Are you Annabeth? I'm Ruth's sister, Sarah."

Confused for a second, Annabeth made her way back to coherence. "Oh, hi, Ruth told me you were coming. Glad to meet you."

"This is my husband, Mark."

"Hi," he said. "Thanks for adding us to the party."

"I'm glad you could come. Park in front of the garage and I'll walk in with you."

David and Ruth approached from the kitchen door. Ruth reached her first and put her arm around her shoulders. "You okay?" she asked.

"Yeah. I just wasn't quite expecting that."

"Who would be?" Ruth looked her in the eye. "I think you are going to have to put on a suit of armor this week. Can you do that?"

"I guess I have to." Annabeth swallowed, then firmly nodded her head. "I can."

Ruth reintroduced Sarah and Mark to Annabeth. "I hope you don't mind that I brought an appetizer. The first tomatoes from our garden! I made that tomato, mozzarella, and basil thing."

David, Ruth, and Annabeth burst out laughing. Ruth said to her sister, "You won't believe this . . ." and began telling Sarah the story of Janet's tomatoes. As they walked toward the house, David fell in next to Annabeth.

"You know, you can come into the office as much as you want this week. If we run out of regular stuff to do, we'll find something. Might not be exactly riveting, but this could be a challenging week for you."

"Ha! What makes you say that?"

"I just want you to know that we've got your back and whatever we can do to help, we'll do it. If you want to just hang out and read, no one will bother you."

"Thank you. I think I will be spending a lot of time at work. And running. And shopping. And driving around town memorizing street signs. If I were here all alone . . ." She shuddered.

He put his arm around her. "Well, you're not."

She was grateful for his words, which she knew were sincere, and for his simple physical presence. She felt lucky that all her new Connecticut friends had her best interests at heart.

As they reached the back door, he paused. "If I thought your aunt would be a sleepy drunk, I might start pouring the scotch big time. But somehow, I have a feeling we might not want to encounter a tipsy Aunt Janet."

Annabeth agreed. "No, I think we'd better not run that risk. A sober Janet is scary enough."

They entered the kitchen to the sound of Sarah's stammered apology for showing up with "red rocks on a plate," and to the sight of Janet wielding a butcher knife with a whole speared tomato on the tip as an example of what the fruit should be.

DINNER PROGRESSED, after a fashion. Brave volunteers served as Janet's minder, then retreated as others took up the task. Theo did his best to keep the conversation on neutral topics and his eye on silent Annabeth, who seemed to absent herself from the table.

During dessert Aunt Janet fired a question her way. "All right, then, Annie. Where do we start? I'll bet Jack's office is a sight not to be believed. He never threw a thing away. Have you made any headway in there?"

"Headway?"

"Clearing out that clutter. You can't let those papers just sit there. It's probably a fire hazard!"

"I haven't been in my dad's office. The lawyer went through things to find some legal papers . . ."

"And you thought you didn't need me?" Janet sighed. "You cannot just let those things sit."

"I can't? Why not?"

"Because it's unhealthy. My father kept my mother's clothes in the closet till the day he died. Ridiculous! Clean out, move forward, get on with your life, Annabeth."

At this point Ruth spoke up. "I wonder if the cleaning out isn't something Annabeth should do when she feels the time is right. There's no need to force anything. She's not sell-ing the house—?" She looked to Annabeth for confirmation. Annabeth indicated yes and shrugged at the same time. "So, there's no rush."

At this comment, Janet dropped her arms to the table. She looked over the rim of her glasses and let loose her powerful voice.

"Why in the world would she not want to get rid of that stuff?"

"Maybe she wants to take her time sorting through it all," Ruth said.

"Yes, there is a lot—" Annabeth said.

"Then best to get to it!" Janet said. "No time like the pres-ent. We are not doing that girl any favors by treating her like some little Orphan Annie. Life moves on. I'm here to help and I will *not* be sentimental about that junk, I can tell you that right now. A bunch of moldy old papers about nothing. I never did understand how a grown man made a living at all that nonsense. We'll just take the whole lot up to the college and say, 'Here you are, good luck,' and be done with it. I don't suppose you've sorted through Lydia's closet, have you?"

Annabeth shook her head no. At this point Mark had to speak up. "Janet! Take it easy. You want to clean out some-thing? Our basement is a nightmare. Right, Sarah? Come over tomorrow and have at it. You'll be doing us a favor."

Sarah looked stricken.

Janet ignored him. She stood and began clearing the table.

David also stood and told her to stop, they would do it. Once again Janet would not be deterred. She built a towering stack of china and carried it into the kitchen where she began to rinse and load the plates into the dishwasher. David looked Annabeth's way and shook his head in apparent sympathy and exasperation before he followed Janet into the kitchen. Annabeth picked up her own setting and walked a step or two before she wobbled and stopped short of the kitchen door. Theo took the dishes from her and whispered, "I'll do it. Just wait a sec."

Ruth met him at the kitchen door and took the plates from him.

"Pretty crowded in there," she said.

Theo backed away and returned to Annabeth, immobilized next to the table, and grabbed her arm. "C'mon," he said, "let's take a walk."

Chip recognized the word and came to join them. They went out the front door and circled the garden a few times to calm down and fool Chip into thinking he'd been somewhere. They stopped after several laps and Theo pulled Annabeth close to him.

"Hey," he said. "I'm here for you. Just call me or text me and I'll be right over. No dragon aunt is gonna keep me away."

Annabeth looked up at him and sighed. "Thank you." She tried to smile. "I'm afraid I'm going to take you up on that."

"I hope so," he said, pulling her closer. He took her face in his hands and kissed her for the first time. Although she wasn't expecting it, she was thrilled. It was right, perfect, exactly what she'd been wanting him to do.

PART TWO

July / August 2009

Chapter Fourteen

RUTH WAS AWAKENED, as she had been most mornings for the last three weeks, by a subconsciously perceived sense of fog creeping over the world. Through the narrow gap in the hotel room curtains she could sense the misty dawn of a new day in San Francisco. It was strange that something silent could penetrate her sleep, but the damp clouds somehow managed to do that. She looked at the clock and saw it wasn't yet six o'clock. Sleeping any longer was out of the question now that she was awake, so Ruth got out of bed and walked to the window. Beyond the glass she saw—nothing. Just dense swirls of opaque gray. In this old hotel the windows were still operable, so she pushed one up and listened to the muffled sound of light traffic beginning to stir. The whoosh of a passing truck or car through the fog sounded mysterious and otherworldly, the noise of ghostly vehicles traversing some alien planet. Later the sun would shine weakly over the city, and she would look out the window of the skyscraper where she worked these days and see the gorgeous blue San Francisco Bay, the boats of Marin County, and the Golden Gate Bridge in the distance. She would be dazzled anew by the splendor of this place and wonder at the miraculous mid-morning transformation that would occur, changing the city from a Gothic crime scene to a three-dimensional vacation brochure.

She hadn't had time to get to know the city or its inhabitants, but Ruth wondered if the dual personality of the city affected its residents. Did the same sunny afternoon Californians stalk the streets in the early morning hours with dark mayhem on their minds? Not Brian Bishop, of course. If he'd been up and out before dawn, it would only have been to exercise for hours or snap up some vast swath of property for sale in a faraway land. *Dark* was not a word that would ever have applied to Brian. Ruth could almost imagine him being the solitary force of energy that dispersed the San Francisco fog every morning as he made his way around town, the wake-up call the city needed to clear its head and get on with the business of being its picture-postcard self.

No matter how early Ruth arrived at the office, Brian was already there, on the phone with someone in Europe or banging away on his computer. Simone, his very busy assistant, would begin each day with an inbox full of emails from Bishop referring to the stack of papers sitting on her desk. She didn't seem to mind. Bishop loved his work, reveled in it, in fact, and his enthusiasm was contagious. Everyone in the office seemed to be dying to get to the next deal, finish the next project, and toast the success of another completed acquisition or sale. Initially, Ruth was skeptical of all this unbridled enthusiasm. She couldn't believe it was genuine and kept waiting for these people to roll their eyes or sigh. But after three weeks she'd come to believe they were sincere. They all loved coming to work and adored Bishop. It seemed any one of them would have cheerfully thrown themselves under a bus for him, which made it puzzling to find out that Bishop was divorced. How had anyone had the desire, let alone the will, to leave this guy? Maybe today Ruth would get a hint because his ex-wife, Maeve, and their two daughters were coming to the office for Brian's forty-fifth birthday lunch celebration, a catered affair Simone had been planning for weeks.

Ruth threw on some exercise clothes and made her way to the hotel gym. She was relieved to find herself the first one there and thus able to control the single television in the small space. She climbed on an elliptical machine, picking up the pace as time passed. After forty minutes she slowed the machine and hopped off. She switched the television from the science documentary she'd been watching back to the usual sports channel and returned to her room.

It was only seven-fifteen when she left the hotel, but she had plenty to do at the office and could never bear to stay in her room with her post-breakfast dishes. Even though it was early, and still very foggy, the streets around the hotel were beginning to fill with others on their way to work. Most of them hurried along, deep in thought, their minds already on the tasks of the coming day, skillfully stepping around the homeless who still caught Ruth's involuntary attention.

She dialed David's work number, then his cell, but got no answer either place. Annabeth must not be in yet, she thought. And, of course, David would never have his cell turned on. She'd have to try again later. Although Ruth had gone home once already, it felt like she and David had been separated for much longer than three weeks. It was also now clear that the back-and-forth she had been promised was just a sales pitch. She had so much to do and so many meetings here in California that going home was almost impossible, at least so far. She missed him terribly. They tried to talk as often as they could, but those conversations did not compensate for all the solitary dinners and breakfasts alone. For the first time in her married life, Ruth was lonely. The people she worked with at Bishop had been kind and welcoming to her, but every night they went home, or out, at any rate, back to their own lives, which left Ruth with a lot of evening hours to fill. Although she was pretty good at keeping busy at home, and during the day here, there were only so many hours she could spend reading or walking or television watching before she began to long for company. She missed her girlfriends and Sarah, but most of all she missed her best friend. How her priorities had changed. Not so long ago she would have been worried about whether the timing of his next visit would be "wrong" for baby-making. Now she only cared about seeing him, whenever it was.

As usual, Brian was already at it when Ruth arrived. His office door was open and she could hear him speaking what— Mandarin?— to someone on the other end of the phone. The guy was amazing, she had to admit. It was hard to get to know what was inside the whirlwind of Brian Bishop, but there was an impressive person on the outside, to be sure.

Ruth got a cup of coffee, then headed toward her windowed office next to the company's general counsel, Mallory Mitchell. Mallory was away setting up a satellite office in London, which made it a little tougher for Ruth to learn how things were done in this legal department. The two other law-yers on staff were helpful but overburdened. They'd given her a ten-minute orientation and made themselves available for questions as much as their time would allow, but for the most part, Ruth was on her own. She had read reams of paper rang-ing from past contracts, current mission statements, and pol-icies about the use of the corporate plane—as if. When it came to the Connecticut deals, however, it was more or less up to her to sort through state and local requirements and elimi-nate any legal hurdles. There was no question of ever, ever telling Bishop that something couldn't be done. It had only taken Ruth a day to understand that her role was to find a way to allow him to do whatever it was he wanted, no matter how difficult or time-consuming. If he had decided that a project should go forward, that was all there was to it. That made the pace and nature of this place completely different from the cautious firm at home, and Ruth was still a little off-balance by the constant demands on her intellectual resources. She was beginning to like the challenge, though, of maneuvering through the rules to ensure that she won, Bishop won, they all won, whatever prize it was they'd set in their sights.

"Morning, Bernard," she said to the young man sitting out-side her office, the assistant she'd been assigned. He was as caffeinated as the rest of them, efficient and, for some reason, a bit miffed that he'd been assigned to Ruth. He didn't much enjoy slowing down to explain anything about office pro-cedure to her, but he did approve of her willingness to trust his competence across a wide range of other subjects. His oc-casional impatience with her lack of knowledge was a small price to pay for all the missteps he'd saved her already.

"Morning, my dear," he replied. Although he was at least ten years younger than Ruth, he considered himself to be the superior in the relationship. "Whatever you've bought for Brian's birthday gift, you can just leave it in the box and regift it next Christmas. We've all gone in together to make a donation in his name to Kids in Crisis. You can pay Simone one hundred dollars anytime today."

"Okay, thanks," Ruth said. She hadn't even considered getting Bishop a gift. At the office back home, someone brought a cake and that was about it. For big birthdays, like a fortieth, there might be a few joke cards, but no one would have ever dreamed of birthday gifts.

"I'll go take care of that right now." She hastened to leave.

"Not now! He's in his office and Simone is sitting right in front of him. He notices everything. This is a surprise, remember? Here, give it to me. I'll put it in an envelope and send it to her in the interoffice mail."

She could tell it was all Bernard could do to keep from shaking his head at her stupidity. Then he smiled at her. "What *would* you do without me?"

"Blunder about in error-filled oblivion, obviously." Ruth smiled back. There was something about Bernard's imperiousness that was endearing. In fact, he was looking out for her.

"Obviously," he replied.

She went into her office and turned on her computer. As usual, the inbox contained several messages from Brian. Dispatches about overnight developments in Asia, questions about the details of some of the Connecticut deals, and other spur-of-the-moment musings. It frustrated the in-house lawyers to no end that he continued to record so many of his random thoughts in emails.

"Brian," they'd suggest, "it would be better if you communicated orally. Just pick up the phone. Hackers are real, you know, and all those emails are a permanent record that would be discoverable if anybody ever sued us. To you they're just 'how about this?' but to somebody else's attorney they might be turned into litigation gold."

"Lawyers ruin everything," Brian would respond, not entirely in jest. And he continued to keep the emails coming. "I need to get it down right away, or I'll forget. Besides, aren't you guys the best in the business? I'm not worried. You'll keep us out of trouble."

It was hopeless to get him to see that keeping him out of trouble was just what they were trying to do. Still the lawyers would from time to time make another futile attempt to convince him to change his ways while keeping a wary eye on all he wrote.

This morning's emails didn't contain anything that raised red flags for Ruth, so she answered his questions and added his items to her own to-do list. Then she tackled the long list with a vengeance. Her morning flew by in a rush of research, phone calls, memos to Bishop, and constant communication with Bernard. When he announced it was time for the birthday lunch, Ruth couldn't believe it. She was in the zone, and hated to break away, but had no choice.

"Um, Bernard, how long do you think the party will last?" she asked as they walked down the hall to the large conference room.

"Long enough to honor the occasion," he replied firmly as he shot her a look of warning. Ruth had no idea how long honoring the occasion might take, but got the message that she would not be leaving early to get back to work.

The conference room had been transformed. Simone was running around in a frenzy, rearranging already beautiful platters of catered food, keeping everyone out of sight, and fretting aloud about whether Brian was going to be surprised. Ruth didn't think so. Nothing got past him to begin with, and all this loud whispering and nervous energy was something even a blockhead would perceive. She wondered how good an actor he'd be in a situation like this. An excellent one, it turned out. He entered the room and appeared to be stunned. He sputtered and gasped and laughed and pretended to be angry in a convincing way. Maybe his surprise was authentic, maybe he was practiced at the art of deception, or maybe he was a nice guy who wanted to make the people who had gone to all this trouble feel good. Ruth couldn't yet tell, but she was impressed by his reaction and how happy it made Simone, who kept saying, "We did it! He *was* surprised!"

As the initial hubbub was beginning to die down, she announced, "I have another surprise!"

She disappeared into the hallway for a minute and then reappeared with a woman and two little girls, who could only be Bishop's family. Ruth wondered how he would react to the "surprise" of his ex-wife showing up at the office birthday bash. She watched him closely and saw his face break open into a smile of delight.

"This is the best!" He grabbed his kids and then Maeve, hugging them and laughing out loud. "I thought you guys had to be at your mom's?" he asked Maeve.

"You mean we actually fooled you? No, we just wanted to surprise you. And I see we did."

The girls were jumping up and down, excited to see their father so pleased. The whole scene was one of TV-movie cheerfulness and the party unfolded in much the same way, Bishop's contagious happiness turning a luncheon in a conference room into a real celebration. Simone was beside herself with pleasure, beaming in maternal satisfaction.

When people began settling in to eat, Maeve approached Ruth.

"Hi," she said. "I'm Maeve O'Connor. You must be the new lawyer?"

Ruth shook her hand. "Yes, Ruth Crawford. Nice to see you."

"You, too. So, how are things going? Are you working yourself to a frazzle?" Maeve, naturally pretty without make-up, seemed open and relaxed.

"Not quite to a frazzle." Ruth laughed. "I am plenty busy, but I enjoy the work. It's something different for me. Everyone in the office is helpful."

"When they aren't busy working themselves to a frazzle," Maeve said. She grinned and raised an eyebrow at Ruth. "But I'm glad it's going well for you. Remind me how long you've been here?"

"About three weeks. Somehow it seems like I've been a part of this crew for years. It is beautiful here."

"Here in the office?" Maeve asked, deadpan.

"No! Yes, the office." Ruth laughed. "But I meant the city."

"You've seen the sights, driven Lombard Street, all that, I imagine?"

"Actually, not *all* that. I've walked around the neighborhood near my hotel, memorized the view from my office window, all *that*."

"Um-hmm," Maeve said. "I see Brian hasn't changed his spots. He often forgets that not everyone in the world lives to read real estate contracts. Although if you do—" she added, "you've come to the right place."

Ruth laughed again. "They are all right."

Maeve said, "Must be a little tougher with Mallory away. She and I are good friends—we went to grade school together if you can believe it—and she's worried you might be feeling stranded. She's sorry she can't do much from London, but if you want someone to show you the sights, help you get your bearings, I can show you around."

Ruth looked at her in surprise. "That's so kind of you. Thank you."

"Would you like to see the city? I can give tours in my sleep. Not that I'm bored by them," she added. "Just that it would be very easy for me to show you around sometime. Have you been to Marin County?"

"No," Ruth replied, "but I know that's what I'm seeing from the window. It looks like a fairyland."

"Oh, it is. But we muddle through somehow."

Ruth liked this woman's irreverence. It was a welcome counterpoint to all the urgent, deadline approaching, seriousness of the office.

"Anyway," Maeve continued, "I'd be happy to give you the grand, or not-so-grand, tour anytime, if you're interested."

"I would love that. I am just not sure when . . ."

"You'll have a second to call your own?" Maeve finished.

"Yeah, things have a way of popping up, and I just keep running around after them . . ."

"Far be it from me to suggest you play hooky, but you might just have to disappear for a few hours if you want to see anything besides the inside of this lovely office and your undoubtedly charming hotel room."

"My disappearance would give Bernard a heart attack."

"Bernard? Not being in the know would give him a heart attack. If you asked him to help orchestrate a disappearance, he'd put the CIA to shame."

Ruth knew Maeve was right and decided on the spot to make a plan for an afternoon off.

"He would love it, trust me." Maeve nodded her head in satisfaction. "In fact, I am free as a bird tomorrow. Brian is going to be at an all-day soccer tournament with the girls, which means he will be relying on wireless communication devices. And you know how sometimes they can let you down . . ."

"Oh, yes, I do! Okay, then. I'll talk to Bernard and make it happen. What time is good for you?"

"I could pick you up around two o'clock, maybe? We could do the city first, and if you want, you could come to my house for dinner. Brian will have the girls overnight and I didn't make any other plans."

"Sounds lovely."

"Glad I could talk you into it."

Chapter Fifteen

BERNARD was more than eager to help cover Ruth's truancy. He devised a code for text messaging and complicated plans A, B, and C that Ruth was quite certain were not needed, especially with Brian otherwise engaged, but all that planning did give her the confidence to take the risk.

"Thank you so much, Bernard," she told him. "Let me know if I can ever do the same for you."

He snorted. "Thank you, dear Ruth. I'll keep that in mind."

"Why do we have to go through all this anyway? Is it a crime to leave work a few hours a month?"

"Only here in Bishoplandia."

"Thanks again. I will treasure every moment and think of you with gratitude while I do."

Bernard half-bowed. "My pleasure. Now get out of here. Be gone. Buy shoes or eat chocolate or do whatever it is you've been dying to do. It's already almost noon."

Ruth fled the building and raced back to her hotel to change clothes. As long as she was taking a risk, she might as well have a little time on her own first. She hurried through a couple of errands, then bought a book and a sandwich and headed for a pocket park near her hotel. There she found a sunny spot on a quiet bench where she could alternate between people-watching and reading until time to meet Maeve.

In the park Ruth saw a side of the city she hadn't experienced before. There were families playing together, friends meeting for coffee. She'd been in the city for weeks and only now saw that it was at least partially inhabited by real people, not just financial wizards and the homeless. She loved seeing this aspect of San Francisco and wished that David were here to share it with her. She pulled out her cell to call him and saw a text from Bernard she'd overlooked. Her stomach leaped in panic, then settled down as she read his code for "all quiet." She responded "thx" and then dialed her Connecticut home number. No answer, so she called David's cell.

"Hey there. You finished early today?" he asked.

"I did. I am about to have an entire afternoon away from the office, if you can believe it."

"I'm not sure I do. We got done a little early today, too. It stinks we are still three time zones apart. I miss you so much, Ruthie-belle."

"I wish you were here. I keep seeing all these great restaurants and picture us having dinner at every one of them. You have to get out here!"

"That would be so great." He paused for a moment, then said, "I've worked like a madman for weeks, but we are slowing down a little with the heat. I could get away for a couple of days, let Rick and Annabeth handle things."

"Yes! So, she's doing well enough to leave the office stuff for her?"

"Actually, she's terrific. She plans to get our whole system on the computer—invoices, orders. It's incredible."

"Wait—I have been trying to get you to do that for two years. What's she got that I don't?" Ruth pretended to be put out.

"Time. She would have changed the oil in the mowers if it kept her away from Aunt Janet. It's going to work out for both of us."

"And for me. Now go make a plane reservation. I need to see you!"

"Oh man, me too, you, Ruthie-belle. Love you."

"Love you."

Ruth was happier than she'd been her entire time in California. An afternoon off and soon a visit from David? Who cares who got credit for bringing David's business into the twenty-first century. She changed again, picked up a bottle of wine from the hotel gift shop, and reached the main lobby just as Maeve pulled up. "I see you haven't had to don the in-visibility cloak," Maeve noted as Ruth got in the car.

She laughed. "No, I haven't had a phone call or email or one word from Brian all afternoon. Just a couple of 'all clears' from Bernard. It's almost too good to be true."

"Brian adores his girls. And his soccer. Put those two things together and he might not notice if the entire continent of Asia went on the market. At least for a few hours."

Ruth lifted her eyebrows.

"Okay, well, that's a lie. But I know he will be distracted all day. And exhausted by tonight. He'll spend the day running from one match to the next, taking notes on how each of them played, checking the girls' hydration status, handing out energy snacks. And here is my prediction for their evening: overtired girls barely staying awake long enough to eat Brian's nutritious dinner, eyelids drooping while Dad recaps key plays and shares practice tips. By the time Brian gets around to his work email, he'll be too worn out himself to bother you. I think you're safe until tomorrow."

"Hope so."

"Let's make the most of the moment, then."

Maeve began her official off-and-on-the-beaten-path tour of the city. She was a fun and funny expert on all things San Francisco and the two of them covered more ground in the waning Saturday afternoon traffic than Ruth would have thought possible. Ruth was knocked out by the beauty of the city, and equally delighted in Maeve's company. It was a pleasure to be with someone who knew Brian well and didn't stand in awe of him. The two of them clicked right away and the hours flew by.

As dusk was falling, they made their way to Maeve's house in Marin County. Once again, Ruth entered a world she hadn't known existed. Its stunning vista made it impossible for her to imagine everyday life in such a place.

"This is a movie set," she told Maeve as she looked through the living room window to the boat-dotted bay below her, the purple outline of the city in the background, seemingly a million miles away. They both took it in.

Maeve said, "Yes, it is gorgeous. When I first moved here, I wondered if I would ever take this view for granted. You know, get up in the morning, glance out the window without even noticing what was there. But I have to say, that hasn't happened, and I've lived here for almost five years now. I do make a conscious effort to really see it, yet even now there are times I have to pinch myself."

They walked outside and breathed in the fir-scented air. Ruth sighed and continued to gaze as the dusk deepened into evening. Lights began to appear in the bowl below her as the last of the sailboats made their way to shore. The air grew cooler. After a few minutes, Maeve said, "Let's eat inside. It's getting cold."

Maeve had purchased dinner ahead of time. They fixed their plates and moved to the dining room, which also overlooked the bay. How easy it is to sit and talk and share a meal this way, Ruth thought. One dinner like this and she was convinced she had wasted too much time on complicated entertaining. When she and David hosted, they'd work for days creating a perfect homemade meal, but who cares that they shopped at the farmer's market at six a.m. and spent hours making every single dish from scratch? All anyone needed for a lovely evening was something decent to eat and someone enjoyable with whom to share it.

"Maeve, how did you and Brian meet?"

The two women had cleared the table and now sat in the living room with their wine.

"In college. We were in the same dorm our freshman year. He was funny and good-looking and very—magnetic, I'll say. We weren't in the same classes. Brian double majored in business and philosophy, and I studied English. If the computer hadn't assigned us to the same dorm that first year, we'd never have met."

"Fate," Ruth said.

"Random," Maeve said. "But he was, and is, as you know, a force of nature. He did favors for me, bought me snacks, gave me off-campus rides, because, of course, somehow he had a car as a freshman," she laughed. "I was courted. And, Dear Reader, I married him."

Ruth smiled. "I can imagine." She was curious about how the happily-ever-after ending had evaded them but would never have asked that question. Instead, they sat in companionable silence for a moment, each keeping her thoughts to herself.

Maeve asked Ruth. "How about you? How did you and your husband meet?"

Ruth took a sip of wine and recalled the first time she saw David, incongruous in his flannel shirt and work boots, carrying a briefcase stuffed with books. He'd caught her studying him and gave her a smile so intimate, so familiar, that it was more like recognizing someone from the past than meeting someone new. To Maeve she simply said, "In line at the post office. He needed a pen. I had one. He asked me for coffee, and I was intrigued, so I said yes. It turned out he was fun and smart, so I said yes to another date. David wasn't like the other guys I knew and nothing like the lawyers I worked with. That date was mostly him helping some stranger change a flat tire." She finished her glass of wine and waited for Maeve's response.

"Irresistible!" Maeve said.

"It was. He was teaching high school in those days, but he spent a lot of time as a kid on his grandfather's farm where, apparently, they grew their own—everything—and he liked 'playing in the dirt,' as he put it. He taught himself landscape design and now that's what he does. He's still pretty cute and fun, I'm happy to say."

"Lucky you." Maeve poured Ruth another glass of wine and topped off her own. "Sounds like you two have what it takes."

Ruth didn't know quite what to say. She thought so, she hoped so, but it would be tactless to declare that to Maeve, whose own marriage seemed to have lacked what it took. She lifted her glass and said, "From your lips . . ."

Maeve lifted her own glass. "Yes."

Then, "I still can't pinpoint exactly why Brian and I didn't make it. Isn't that awful? We got divorced and put our two girls through all that because—why? Brian was never home, and I had imagined a different life for all of us, and my friends kept telling me what a fool I was to put up with his never being here, and then one day he was moving out and we all were crying, and the lawyers took over and . . . now, here we are. A big cliché. Ugh. And too much information. Sorry."

"Not at all." Ruth hesitated, but then, because Maeve was so open, risked saying, "I don't know either one of you well, but—is it too late? Maybe you could call the divorce the mistake and give it another go? I can tell he still cares for you a lot. How his face lit up yesterday when he saw you."

"Maybe once upon a time that would have worked." She looked out the window. "I think I was either *air* or *Paris* to Brian."

Ruth waited. "I'm not sure I understand?"

"He loves me the way we all love air. It keeps us alive. It's essential, ubiquitous, but does anyone ever consciously think, 'Man, how much do I love oxygen?' No. It's everything in a way, but we take it totally for granted."

Maeve must have spent a lot of time regretting what went wrong with her marriage, despite the breezy way she analyzes its demise, thought Ruth. It had to hurt to come last in Brian's priorities. She's moved on now, or so it seems, but this particular failure and the logistics of shared custody had to be front and center of her every day now, at least as long as the girls are at home, probably for the rest of her life. All the pretty views in the world wouldn't compensate for that.

"Interesting to think of it like that. Paris?"

"Paris is just the opposite. The most wonderful city in the world, but you have to think about it a *lot* to experience it. Plan the time away, book the flights, the hotel, the restaurants, remember your passport. It's a big deal and while you are planning for it, and even more while you are there, Paris is everything. The most special, wonderful, present thing there is. But, once you come back home, Paris is out there, somewhere else." She waved her arm toward a faraway distance. "And after a while you hardly think about Paris as a real thing at all. It's a memory, maybe a future destination, but it's not real, it's not a part of your conscious being."

Ruth murmured in agreement.

"So, I was Brian's air and Brian's Paris. I was never just his regular Wednesday morning." Maeve sighed, then covered her mouth with her hand. "Can you tell I've had maybe half a glass of wine too much?"

Ruth gave her back a semi-sad smile. "I do think I understand."

As she vowed on the day she got married, Ruth recommitted herself to never getting divorced, come what may. Some people, like Maeve and Brian, did seem to find a post-divorce way of being that appeared mature and satisfying. But there had to be pain beneath that veneer of civility.

Maeve looked at her. "Good grief, I really just put it all out there, didn't I?"

"I guess so. But that doesn't seem weird to me. Maybe that's weird!"

They both laughed. Maeve tucked her legs under her and spoke again, "After a lot of work—and a lot of talk therapy, as I am sure you can tell—I have come to enjoy my freedom. Brian's very generous financially and, ironically, devotes more time to the girls now on a set schedule than he did when he was living with us. And besides, I'm sorta-kinda-almost seeing someone else now." She held her hand up, palm outward. "That's all I'll say about that. I'm superstitious. Ha! What we let happen was a mistake in many ways, but I can't see any way in which undoing it would erase the mistake or even make things better. We make things better from where we are going forward, don't you think, instead of trying to go back to where we've been?"

Ruth thought this over. "I guess so. As long as we learn from our past mistakes."

"Oh, yes, agree. We have tried to do that."

Mauve lifted the wine bottle and looked toward Ruth, who shook her head no. Then she said, "Anyway, Brian gave me my beautiful babies. The best gift ever. And onward we go, Jeffrey, onward we go."

"Yes, they are beautiful." She tilted her head. "Who's Jeffrey?"

"Ha! I have no idea. My mom used to say that. So now the whole family does."

"It sounds . . . inspiring."

"I'm sure it was for Jeffrey."

As the evening wound down, they agreed to try to get together again soon. "There's almost always a soccer tournament somewhere," said Maeve, as they bid each other goodnight.

Ruth took a premium car service back to the city, courtesy of Brian, and Maeve insisting. She settled in the back seat. Maeve's complete candor was unexpected, and in someone else it might have scared Ruth off. Instead, her openness seemed to invite a friendship where they could both just be themselves.

Chapter Sixteen

ANNABETH arrived for her first day of work wearing her best— a minidress she and her mom had bought for her college interviews. She'd blown her tangle of curls into a smooth style that fell halfway down her back. When she saw his "office," a stand-alone metal building situated in an open field, she felt ridiculous. But Aunt Janet stood between her and her closet, so she got out of the car and knocked on the trailer door.

David called out, "It's open."

She ignored the butterflies in her stomach as she stepped into the tiny, tidy space. Overdressed and under-prepared, she stood in the doorway and hoped David wouldn't perceive how uneasy she was about this whole enterprise.

"Wow!" he said, taking in her appearance. "You look . . . just . . . amazing."

She blushed and glanced down at what she was wearing.

"Thought I should dress up for the first day. It was pretty much this or running shorts."

"I am not complaining."

She felt heat rising to her face again, confused to be pleased by his comment.

"Um, I see you're already busy," she said.

"Yes, ma'am. Help yourself to some coffee. There's a small fridge in the back with some milk if you want some."

"Just black, I'm good. Thank you."

"Oh that's right. I need to get this materials order faxed. Do you mind if I finish and then show you around?"

He hadn't intended the comment as a joke, but Annabeth could see every square inch of the office and the small back room from where she stood. It consisted of a desk and chair, a small table, a computer, a fax/printer/scanner device, a couple of filing cabinets, and an ancient Mr. Coffee machine. On the desk was a multi-level letter tray and nothing else. She also noticed a tiny restroom, as well as a wall lined with open shelving that contained general supplies.

A minute later the fax machine signaled that all was well. Annabeth started to bend down to retrieve the documents, then hesitated when she realized that her dress was probably too short for the maneuver. She straightened and turned to see David watching her. After a moment, he rose to squeeze past her and get the papers himself. Now it was his turn to blush. He cleared his throat and looked down at the papers in his hand.

"Okay. So, um, I realized this morning that there is only one desk chair. But that's fine for today because I have to be on-site pretty soon. If I show you where the files are and the papers that need filing, will you think I'm the world's worst boss for leaving you alone on your first day?"

"No, not at all. I can do that." Annabeth stood with her back against the wall, sipped her coffee and looked around. "Will any of your customers come in?"

She dreaded the thought of having to admit to anyone that she knew absolutely nothing.

"No, not likely. They call or email me. There is no reason for anybody to come here. We don't stock any plants. I design the gardens, and then order the materials from the growers. We usually pick them up ourselves. The heavy equipment is stored by that old barn across the road. The guys are already out today, and they won't be back until later. That's it—your orientation for the entire business."

She didn't feel much more knowledgeable, but she nodded. "Sounds very organized."

"In theory." David glanced at his watch. "I've got to go. Okay, these are the hard copies of the shipments and here is the file cabinet for them. They are filed by last name of the job site. Then chronological order within the folder. Soon all these files will be electronic—thank you for that—but for now, this is how it works. You sure you're okay? I hate to just bark orders and run."

"I have an Aunt Janet in my house, remember? I'm getting used to barked orders. No, it's fine—happy to do what *you* want me to do. That's why I'm here, isn't it?"

"I won't go all Aunt Janet on you, I promise. If you have any questions, you have my cell, right? I don't often answer it . . ." he said and laughed as she looked at him a bit puzzled, "but today I will check to see who's calling."

"I guess you can be like me and skip the phone altogether?"

"Are you the only person your age on Planet Earth who does not use a cell phone?"

"I have one, but I keep losing it. And without my mom and dad to worry about me . . . I don't much miss it."

Annabeth realized her statement revealed the sad fact that she had few friends to text or call. She looked down at the floor and David changed the subject.

"Okay, the landline here sometimes gets calls because—"

"You don't answer your cell?" Annabeth finished for him.

"Hmm. Could be. If you don't mind answering it, just take a message. Or if you are busy, there is also voicemail. I should be back early afternoon."

"Okay. I'll see you later."

David grabbed his worn backpack and again negotiated the narrow space to brush past Annabeth. Just outside the door he seemed to remember something.

"Oh—I should tell you one of our clients has been giving me no end of grief."

Her concern must have shown on her face because he hastened to reassure her.

"Don't worry—that's not our usual drill. He's just kind of intense. I heard this morning that he's been charged with fraud by the SEC, so I think he'll be too busy to bother with us for a while, but if the name Sid Snyder shows up on the caller ID, don't answer it. I'll deal with him later. Or maybe never. I plan to ignore him for as long as possible."

She was relieved she wasn't going to have to deal with this guy and whatever the SEC was.

"Okay," she said. "I won't answer."

With that, David was gone. She let out a breath she didn't realize she'd been holding. The space felt much larger without him standing next to her. She took another deep breath and felt her shoulders relax.

"All right, all good," she said aloud. She picked up the stack of papers and opened the file drawer. Within a few minutes she was concentrating on the work. It wasn't challenging, but she did have to pay attention, a blessing that pushed aside all thoughts of David, Janet, even her mom and dad. For several hours she felt productive, focused, and free.

When she got in her car to drive home, though, the reality of Aunt Janet came rushing back to her. Annabeth slumped against the steering wheel for a moment and groaned. She glanced at her watch and saw it was only three o'clock. Plenty of time to be eviscerated by Janet's criticism between now and bedtime, even if she followed through with her plan to crash by nine. She started her car and opened the windows. David waved good-bye from across the street where he and the crew were unloading the trucks. She waved and put the car in drive.

Grocery store, she thought all of a sudden. That could take a while. She headed for the market farthest from her house and strolled the aisles. She examined every item in the produce department with care and perused every shelf in the store. At last she filled her cart, paid for the groceries, and began a slow drive home.

Aunt Janet was nowhere to be seen when Annabeth arrived. Bracing herself, she grabbed a couple of bags and headed toward the back door. To her relief, the kitchen was empty except for Chip, who greeted her with much enthusiasm. "Hey, buddy! How are you? Did you miss me today?" She set the bags on the kitchen counter, then stooped to pet him. His delirious tail-wagging made her smile. Having no problem resisting the urge to call out for Janet, she left the kitchen and went back down the drive with Chip to collect the rest of the groceries. As she passed by the garage, she noticed at least six large trash bags, stuffed full and tied closed, stacked against one wall. "Uh-oh, Chip. What's all this?" She stopped and opened one bag, relieved to see that it contained plant stalks. Doubtful that they all held garden debris, she tried another bag and found it full of grass clippings. She looked around the yard now and saw that it did indeed look tidy. The flowers were front and center instead of mere hints among the weeds. Okay, give Janet her due: she did know what she was doing.

When she went back to the kitchen, Janet was there putting away the groceries Annabeth had already brought inside. "Hi, Aunt Janet," Annabeth called out as she came through the door. "Thanks for putting that stuff away. And thanks for the gardening. The place looks great!"

"Tomorrow, I'll tackle that pantry," Janet responded. "Who on earth would put canned goods on the same shelf as batteries?" She sighed. "The whole thing needs to be stripped and repainted."

"Oh my. That seems like so much work. I can't let you do all that." I can't let you stay that long, Annabeth thought.

"If you won't let me deal with closets and the office, I am going to find other ways to make myself useful," Janet said.

"I would say you already have. I saw all those bags by the garage. That must have taken you all day. I don't think I could have done it in a week."

"I should say not. Seems to me you haven't been able to do it in several weeks."

She refused to show even a flicker of anger. "No, you're right. I haven't done much work in the garden."

"I might think that fancy pants *landscape designer* friend of yours would have helped out a little, but I guess hoeing and raking are beneath him."

"He did help. The weeds just—grew—I guess." Annabeth would not allow Janet to criticize David unfairly. "He did a lot for me, but it's his busiest season now. That's why he needs me to work in the office. He would help again if I asked him. But now," she gestured to the yard outside, "he won't need to."

Janet said nothing as she continued to put away the food. "I don't suppose you know how to cook any of this?"

She counted to ten, as her mom had taught her, then responded. "Some of it. But since it's so hot, and we both worked all day, I got some prepared stuff for tonight. Chicken and salad. Is that okay with you?"

Janet seemed to be just tired enough not to offer to butcher a cow for steaks on the grill, because she said, "It is hot. That's fine."

They took their cold supper out to the porch. By now, the sun was setting and the sounds of the day beginning to fade. In their place frogs croaked, crickets chirped, and the birds squawked their final calls as they retreated to wherever it was they spent their evening hours. Dusk settled over the lovely garden, which Annabeth had to admit looked better than she'd ever seen it. The two of them sat in the quiet, enjoying the view. After a while they gathered the dishes and went inside. By nine-fifteen it was Janet herself who declared she was ready for bed.

"Goodnight, Aunt Janet. Thank you again for your help today."

"You got your money's worth, that's for sure. Tomorrow, I'll tackle that pantry." She harrumphed and went to bed.

———

THE NEXT MORNING Annabeth was up early, tiptoeing around the kitchen, hoping to escape before her aunt awakened. She whispered to Chip to come with her and slipped out the back door onto the porch. While Chip investigated the scent of the night creatures who had dared to trespass his domain, Annabeth sat on the steps and ate breakfast, laughing at the old dog's burst of morning energy. She couldn't linger, though, because she and Theo had plans for a run this morning. Leaving Chip to it, Annabeth sneaked along the lawn beside the gravel drive and threw a bag with her work clothes into the trunk of the car. Then she made her escape. She thought as she drove away, maybe I should have left a note, but she excused herself with the knowledge that Janet would figure it out and assume she'd already gone to work. Annabeth wasn't interested in Janet's plans for her own day. Actually, she was interested, but didn't want to hear all the criticism that would accompany their description. Why say, "I'm going to tidy the pantry," when she could say instead, "It's a miracle we all don't have botulism, given the state of this kitchen."

Freedom! And Theo! The two of them had been texting almost nonstop since the night of that gruesome dinner. For the first time in a long time she was keeping her phone at hand. She poured over every message for deeper meaning and waited the amount of time to respond the girls on the team had told her was required. At first, he mostly asked how she was holding up, then threw in a few tomato jokes, and as of this morning was texting "can't wait to c u" followed by the grinning emoji. She held back from texting him a face with a heart—he had to go first. She did seem to be on his mind a lot, though, and he was topmost on hers. "U 2." She had responded just before she left the house.

The fresh air and her successful getaway lightened her mood as she drove to the river. Although it would be hot later, for now the cool morning promised a comfortable run. When she pulled into the commuter parking lot, she recognized Theo even with his back turned. He had an unusual build for a runner, one Annabeth preferred over most of the scrawny boys on her high school team. He was as fit as any distance runner, but also had some muscle on his frame, despite the fact that she never heard him mention working out with weights. Maybe, like David, he was strong from doing physical labor. But he never mentioned that either. Maybe he just came this way.

He glanced up at the sound of her car, smiled and waved, then put his phone in his pocket and came toward her. He kissed her hello without hesitation.

"Just getting ready to text you."

"Good morning in person, then."

"It's a great morning. Do you feel like running a little longer today?"

"Yeah, sure. How long?"

"There is a loop from here that's about eight miles. It's pretty flat and shady and it follows the river most of the way, so it's kind of scenic. You up for it?"

"Yep, all set."

They made their way toward the path next to the river. Initially, running took a back seat to their animated replay of Saturday night's dinner, the two of them laughing and exclaiming about almost every moment. After covering the topic in extensive detail over several miles, they fell into silence for the last half of the run. By that point, the only sound accompanying their breathing was their synchronized footfall. Annabeth was mesmerized by it. This had happened before, and she loved the serendipity of it—separate bodies with otherwise separate rhythms somehow falling into sync for a sustained period of time.

In the past, it had always happened with other girl runners. She couldn't remember having ever matched pace with a long-legged guy before. Could it be accidental or was he slowing his pace to match hers? She had an unreasonable belief in the cosmic significance of running synchronicity, but only if it occurred spontaneously. Did it count if one of the runners contrived to make it happen? Or . . . maybe . . . did making it happen signify something more?

When they slowed to a walk, she paced the parking lot, hands on her hips, away from Theo. He headed toward his car, brought out a large jar of water, and began chugging it. Annabeth watched him for a moment, then returned to his side.

"Want some?" he asked her, proffering the container.

"Yeah, actually. I sneaked out before I remembered to grab water. Thanks."

She gulped down a generous amount and returned the jar. "That was a good run. I haven't done eight miles in a while. Except accidentally."

He laughed. "I remember. Day One of The Annabeth Experience."

"Oh my, is that a good or a bad experience?"

Theo took another drink as he stood staring into the river.

"It was the best day of the summer."

Chapter Seventeen

RUTH SAT IN the hotel lobby trying to read as she waited for David's taxi. He'd texted the "landed" emoji about forty minutes ago and now she was expecting him to come through the revolving front doors any second. She was as excited as a kid waiting for her birthday party. Finally, his cab arrived. Ruth saw him climb out of the taxi and retrieve his bag from the trunk. She popped out of her chair and hurried to meet him on the sidewalk. She smiled and extended her arms to give him a hug.

"Hey,"—he smiled back at her—"just a sec." David put down his bag and said to the taxi driver. "We all set?"

"All set. Enjoy your stay, sir."

As the cab drove away, she stepped toward him and nestled her head in the spot just below his collarbone, wrapping her arms around him. She leaned in and held him tight, until the suitcase she was straddling caused her to lose her balance and she had to step away.

"You look amazing," he exclaimed as he held her at arm's length to look at her face. "My Ruthie-belle." He kicked the bag aside and pulled her close again.

She smiled up at him as he gently broke the embrace and picked up his bag. "Are you tired from the flight?" she asked.

"I was. But I'm better now." He put his arm around her waist. "I am so glad to be here."

They walked arm-in-arm toward the elevators where an open car was waiting. They were joined in the compartment by a couple of kids, so they rode without speaking until they reached her floor. Ruth knew what would happen when they got to the room: David would drop his bag, take her in his arms, and squeeze her hard enough to hurt. Then he'd steer her toward the bed, and they'd make up for all the days apart.

At last, they reached the door to her room. She entered before he did, took a few steps toward the window, then turned to receive his embrace. He gave her a quick squeeze and announced, "I have got to have a shower right this second. The guy next to me spilled his third drink all over our seats— and me."

"That's what I'm smelling. Not exactly your usual scent. Take off those clothes."

He raised an eyebrow at her. "Mrs. Crawford!"

"I'll put them in the laundry bag while you shower." Ruth playfully pushed him toward the bathroom.

"Give me five minutes." While David showered, Ruth stuffed the clothes in a plastic bag and filled out the laundry tag. Then she sat on the bed and waited.

He reemerged wearing the hotel robe, his hair still dripping down his back. "Whoa, that is so much better." He started rummaging through his bag for clean clothes. "Shall we hit this town of yours?"

Ruth made an I-can't-believe-you face and said with a laugh, "Yeah, sure, but this town of mine isn't going anywhere any time soon. You don't want to stay here awhile?"

"You know I do. I just thought you might be disappointed if I ran out of gas before we got to do any sightseeing."

She got off the bed and stepped in front of him. "*You* are the sight I want to see. I've missed you so much."

He wrapped his arms around her. "Oh wow, this feels so good. You feel so good. I've missed you, too. I wish you'd never left."

She relaxed in his embrace. "Let's just be together, then. Okay with you?" She tried to raise her head to smile at him, but he locked her close to his chest, and said, "Oh, Ruth."

They moved toward the bed, navigating around the open suitcase and stumbling over two pairs of shoes, which made for a very uncinematic encounter, but they both pretended not to notice. At first, they were a little shy with each other. Then, a combination of instinct and long-standing affection carried them past the worst of the awkwardness that time and distance had created. If it wasn't the most amazing sex they'd ever had, if they were a little out of sync, Ruth told herself, it was only a momentary hiccup. They still had tonight to get it right. She realized suddenly that she hadn't been counting the days—and that she was not going to. "Let us just be us," she offered a short prayer. It's been so long since we loved each other without a calendar in our heads.

David had fallen hard asleep. Ruth retrieved her clothes and tiptoed into the bathroom to freshen up. When she returned to the bedroom, David was still sleeping, but no longer seemed dead to the world. She crossed the room and climbed into an armchair to wait for him to awaken on his own. As she watched him, loving him, re-memorizing him, she was a bit saddened to realize that "her town's" famous fog had made an unusual midday reappearance. David was not going to be able to see the incredible view from the hotel window. Nothing to be done, of course, but still, it was not the scene she'd imagined. After twenty minutes or so, she woke him up. Together they made plans for the day, fog be damned, Ruth happy at last to be able to show David the world where she now lived.

They left the hotel and began walking through the busy streets. The fog had lifted enough so David could get some sense of the physical beauty of the city's terrain, horticulture, and architecture. In this tourist area the shops were mostly national franchises. The streets were crowded with shoppers, gawkers, and many homeless people. She noticed David's noticing them and took his arm. "It's strange, isn't it? This gorgeous place and all this money and sad people just lost in the middle of it? I know there are lots of ideas about how to make things better for them, but so far nothing seems to make much difference."

"Yeah, pretty surprising. It's not what I expected."

"Me either. I might be putting my head in the sand, but I figure I'm just visiting here, there isn't much I can do. I pray for them and feel for them. Doesn't seem like enough, though. Sometimes, I just get mad about it."

As they walked a little farther, David kept his arm around Ruth, steering her through the crowd and around the mess on the sidewalks.

"Forgive me if this is wrong, but I don't want to spend our time worrying about anything. I just want to be together. Is that awful?"

David squeezed her tighter. "I don't think so. We can't solve San Francisco's problems in thirty-six hours."

"You're right. Do you want to grab a cab and go see the gardens?"

"Sure. Let's go."

They hailed a taxi and spent the next few hours strolling hand in hand and catching up on each other's separate lives. Ruth laughed, moaned, and marveled over the further antics of Aunt Janet and was cheered to hear all the ways Annabeth was doing better. She tried to convey to him the frantic life inside Brian Bishop's kingdom. Ruth didn't even attempt to describe Brian the person. He was so much more complicated than a king of everything in overdrive, but it was impossible to get the full picture of him across to someone who'd never even met him without sounding like she'd invented some paragon of male perfection. They talked of many other things but, as much as they shared, time was short and they couldn't cover it all. Topics of conversation that seemed important yesterday—her budding friendship with Maeve, Bernard's funny imperiousness, the challenges of the work—slipped into insignificance today. Practical decisions, like when and where to eat, turned out to be impossible to make. Who cared, really, but then again, they had just the single special dinner, so maybe it did matter at least a little. Ruth wanted to keep the reservation she'd made, and David wanted to buy something from a food truck and eat in a park overlooking the water. They ended up in Chinatown, sharing a compromise meal that neither of them much wanted. At least they ate together. It was fine, good enough, beside the point. Over the course of their short visit, they caught up incompletely, in bits and pieces, their hearts full of affection and the very best of intentions.

David had to fly back to Connecticut on Monday evening. Ruth told him good-bye with reluctance, wishing they'd had more time, or had used the time they'd had better, or somehow managed to pull all the dangling threads back into the usual pattern. But they couldn't quite manage that, so they'd have to try harder to do long distance better, to be together more often, for longer periods of time. She would insist on breaks to go home, per the original agreement with Brian, and he would just have to deal with it. But for now, and the immediate future, there were contracts to write and gardens to plant. So, they each got to it.

Chapter Eighteen

Before she'd realized quite how long she'd be staying in San Francisco, Ruth treated Sunday as if she were on vacation—order room service, read the paper, then head out later for a long walk. But after several weeks here she felt the need to reconnect with the core part of Sunday she'd left at home. She'd resolved to make her way to church. The city churches were different from her little white clapboard in New England. They tended to be stone, or stucco, grand or at least large, and populated with people she'd never see in small-town Connecticut. She hadn't attended the same church twice and viewed these excursions as anthropological forays into unfamiliar lands.

This Sunday she set out for a cathedral within walking

distance of her hotel. She dressed in nondescript clothing so she wouldn't look either too Protestant Sunday Best or Tourist Slob and grabbed a cup of coffee from the hotel lobby to drink along the way. Her destination was an old and beautiful building. She settled into a pew midway on the right side and felt a familiar peace descend. The formality of this place appealed to her. The size of the congregation guaranteed anonymity, which also pleased her and allowed her to relax. No one here was going to ask her to deliver meals, go on a mission trip, or increase her pledge. Although she missed her Sunday morning "book group," she was eager to experience worship as simply that, an hour to listen, pray, and reflect instead of the analysis, socializing, and task-undertaking that worship was at home. While she realized it wasn't quite fair to take without giving anything in return, she justified her passivity with the excuse that she was only here temporarily and much too busy to sign up for anything. Although there was a soupçon of guilt in her self-indulgence, it did not cancel the restorative pleasure of an hour spent being all Mary and no Martha.

When the service ended, she walked without making eye contact toward the door where the priest was shaking hands. She greeted him and accepted his blessing, then descended the stairs and looked around for a place to grab another coffee. She was startled when someone behind her touched her elbow and asked, "Ruth?"

She could not have been more shocked to see that it was Brian. "Brian? You're here?"

He signaled good-bye to a couple walking down the steps with him but seemed to be alone. At her remark, he burst out laughing.

"I see by the look of utter astonishment on your face that you are surprised to see me."

"Not because you're here. At church, I mean, but because you're—anywhere." She stammered as she tried to cover up her faux pas implying he must be some kind of heathen. "I mean not at work."

Again, he laughed out loud. "Yes, I guess that would be rather shocking."

"No, wait. I thought you worked every minute of every day. I didn't mean to imply that I couldn't imagine you at church."

"You did imagine me at church?"

"No, I never imagine you anywhere but work!"

"Now you know. I've never seen you here before though?"

"No, my first time. But sometimes I do go—"

"Somewhere?"

This conversation was a mess, but he was getting a kick out of it, Ruth could tell. He had an amused half-smirk on his face and seemed ready to be entertained by where she would blunder next.

"Yes, why, yes I do. On Sunday mornings I church-hop. Before I get to my work, of course."

"But of course. Do you usually tear out the door and race to the factory floor, or do you ever stop for a bite of food along the way?"

"Always straight to the factory floor, sir. I try not to let anything interfere with my work." She mimed a half salute. Ruth had never seen this Brian. Relaxed? Kidding around? Maybe he had a personality disorder?

"I try not to go to the office on Sunday. You might have noticed?" he asked.

"I just thought my Sunday hours didn't match yours."

"No, I think it's important to take a day away from those phones and desks and computers." He seemed to have a straight face as he made this statement.

"You *never* work on Sunday?" Ruth was wondering why he allowed himself the day of rest he denied everyone else. But thinking back, it was true, she'd never seen Brian at work on the Sunday afternoons when she'd been in the office.

They'd started walking together down the sidewalk.

"As much as possible. I usually go to church, sometimes with the girls, and then try to spend time with them. Maeve even invites me to Sunday dinner often, if I promise to leave my laptop, iPhone, and iPad in my car. I often manage to keep myself from twitching until eight or nine o'clock Sunday evening."

"Aha," Ruth said. "Now I get it." But she couldn't imagine it.

"By the time I get home I *am* twitching, so I fire up the devices and work until midnight. A light day, I agree, but by then it's already Monday in Asia, as you know."

"When do you sleep?"

"Whenever I get tired."

"That's an . . . interesting schedule, but I don't think it would work for me. I need some time between last email and bedtime or I can't stop thinking about work. And I can't relax when I'm thinking about work."

"I know." Brian grinned at her. "That's why you're here."

"So, I'm guessing you're not about to urge *me* to take the afternoon off, then?"

"Actually, I was going to ask you if you had time to grab a bite? I know a great place, but it's breakfast, not brunch, if that's okay with you?"

"Okay, sure."

After a couple of blocks, they reached a tiny cafe on a side street. There were only six tables, all occupied, but the chef/owner greeted Brian like a long-lost brother and produced a table for them from thin air. Brian introduced Ruth to Ernest, who took their orders. A friendly, young waitress brought delicious strong coffee and a complimentary basket of croissants.

"Oh my gosh!" Ruth said. "These are delicious. This place is right by my hotel, and I've never even seen it before. I may become a regular myself."

"Yeah, it's terrific. They are only open for breakfast and lunch, but I try to get here as often as I can. Wait till you taste the eggs Benedict. Incredible."

"Do you live in this neighborhood?"

"I used to. It still feels like home—my church, my breakfast place. Maeve and I used to live here together before we moved to Marin, but when we got divorced, I got a place in a different neighborhood, not too far from here. I miss it though. Maybe I should have bought our original apartment back."

"Umm. It's never the same, though. I would guess you did the right thing by moving on. Do you think you'll stay where you are now?"

"Maybe. For a real estate guy, I'm an odd duck in that I don't care much for personal relocations. Once I'm settled in, I like to stay where I am. How about you?"

"No, I don't like to move either. I lived in the same house my entire childhood and since law school I've only lived in three places—a tiny apartment in New York, my starter condo, and the house my husband and I have now. It's home and I can't imagine moving for any reason. I do like to redecorate, but I'm partial to a foundation that stays solid beneath me. David, my husband, is pretty much the same. Even if we won some mega millions jackpot, we'd probably just do a little spiffing and call it a day."

They chatted, waiting for their food to arrive. They ordered more coffee and watched the sun begin to peek through the clouds.

"Ah, the sun," Brian said.

"Yes. I do sometimes miss the sun," Ruth agreed.

"I love the beauty of this place, and the climate isn't bad, but the gray mornings sometimes get old."

"Why did you choose San Francisco? You could run your business from anywhere."

"Now I could, but when I started, I was dealing in properties in northern California, and I didn't have fourteen electronic devices to carry around. I needed to be here. Maeve and her family were here, and now the kids are here." He shrugged. "I'm here."

Ruth nodded.

"How about you? How did you end up in Connecticut?"

"I was born there, raised there, went to college and law school there. Except for a brief stint at a big firm in the city, I'm there."

"So did you like the service this morning?"

It took Ruth a second to understand that Brian was referring to the church service. "Yes, I did. It's not very Congregational, but I like a change from time to time. And I don't have the self-discipline to do worship on my own."

By now their food had arrived. It could have been photographed for the pages of a magazine and tasted even better than it looked. Ruth pointed at her plate and widened her eyes in appreciation. He smiled back, accepting her unspoken thanks.

"No, not too many people have that kind of discipline, I wouldn't think," Brian picked up on her comment. "And it's supposed to be a group thing, at least part of the time, isn't it? Lots of instructions about that in the New Testament. I can get a lot of meaning out of climbing a mountain trail alone, but that by itself wouldn't do it."

"Yes, I agree. I belong to a Sunday Morning Book Group—a Bible study—and I miss it. We are lucky enough to have a brilliant leader. It's so far from what I thought a Bible study would be, and it brings me to places I'd never reach all by myself. I think it is part of the two-or-three-gathered thing."

"Yes, undoubtedly. I haven't been in a Bible study for years, but I used to do that. In college."

Ruth managed not to fall off her chair at this announcement. Who was this guy?

He continued, "I got a lot out of it. I guess I back-burnered it for work—other stuff— some time ago." He paused. "I should now say 'I need to get back to it' and I know I do, but I also know I won't find the time in the near future. It's my loss."

"You don't seem to have a lot of down time," Ruth agreed.

Brian laughed. "And because of me, nor do you."

"Not too much, no, but it's okay for me because it's temporary. At some point I'll go back to Connecticut and the work I was doing there. But what about you—do you see yourself working like this for the rest of your life?"

"I guess I do. I love it. Every deal is different, so they are all interesting. I'm good at it, if I can say that without sounding like a total jerk. I've made money for a lot of people, even since the recession, and I'm happy about that. At some point I may want to slow down . . . you never know."

He signaled for the check and finished the last of his coffee. She glanced at her watch. Somehow, they'd been together for more than an hour.

"Well, on that note, I suppose I'd better make my way to the office. I have some work I need to do before my boss gets in tomorrow morning."

"Is he completely horrible?"

"Yes."

He looked dismayed. She laughed. "No! I'm busier than I have ever been, but I like the work and I don't have much of a non-office life here, so it's fine."

"If you want to take a break and go back to Connecticut for a weekend, or whatever, please, you should do that. I'm sorry if I kind of did a bait-and-switch on you. It's not *all* urgent, in spite of how I treat it, and you know the difference, so you should go, anytime."

"I am going take you up on that. It's true that it's not all urgent, but the deal we're doing with the people in China is getting down to the last details, so I don't think I can get away right this minute." She paused and looked at him sideways. "I'm sure you remember it— that Asian work mysteriously 'connected' to the Connecticut projects?"

"Why, yes, I do." He beamed at her. "I guess you figured out that's my way of saying I like your work?"

"Feel free to say it another way, if you're ever so inclined."

Brian nodded. "Point taken."

"Once we get this China deal wrapped up, I will be taking that break."

They left the restaurant and separated after a few blocks. Brian was headed to Marin for this week's soccer games, with "some interesting information about the ratio of goals scored to field position of closest defender" for his daughters, and Ruth turned in the direction of the office. There was a lot of work waiting for her, but the combination of the worship service, her first regular conversation with Brian, and the possibility of a trip home was worth the late hour she'd see before she left for the day. For the rest of the afternoon, she marveled off and on at the Brian she met today and wondered whether she'd ever see that guy again. She should plan a trip back to Connecticut, China deal or not. Maybe Brian would even remember he suggested it?

RUTH STAYED UNTIL NINE THAT NIGHT. She left the office tired, but satisfied with her work. Bernard, on the other hand, would not be pleased by the many new documents that would greet him Monday morning. He made no secret of the fact that cleaning up Ruth's drafts and emailing copies to all the other lawyers were tasks beneath his talents. In fact, they were, but nevertheless had to be done. Ruth had learned to ignore his huffs and sighs of disdain. But she'd also learned to leave a misspelling or a question about some fine point of grammar for him. It thrilled him to be able to correct or elucidate her, oh so patiently, on an arcane rule of English composition. It pleased her to see that he was paying that much attention. He was in fact knowledgeable and exacting, and often Ruth learned from him through her questions and unintentional mistakes.

"Thank you so much, Bernard. I guess I'm a lawyer, not a writer," she would say, and Bernard would reply, "Remove all doubt from these pronouncements, my dear."

Leaving the office so late meant Ruth probably would not

be able to talk to David. He had called earlier and texted her a "call me, miss you" message, but she'd been in a meeting and encased in a steel building and had not seen it until she walked out the door. Ugh. They were already back to the old drill, it seemed. It was too late to call him now. With their schedules so different, their time zones so incompatible, it required real effort for them to speak live and in-person. Not that they each didn't try, but it didn't happen often enough. They'd always talk on Saturday evening after they each finished work, but too many other nights there were missed calls back and forth that resulted in a final voicemail, "Love you, Ruthie. I'm dead on my feet and headed for bed. Call me tomorrow?" Often when she tried to reach him in the morning, he didn't pick up, the summer planting season putting him in the middle of jobs that started at first light, even on Sundays. And then the work claimed each of them and another day was lost, an endless cycle that was pulling them further and further apart. She had to listen to Brian and get out of here. Suddenly she missed David so much she had to fight back tears. She texted him "Hey! Brian says I can spring an escape. Can't wait to see you in person. Love you so much."

Chapter Nineteen

DAVID'S TEXT in response was the first thing she saw the next day. "Yes! ASAP. Miss you." She grabbed her laptop to search for flights before she even got out of bed. First, check email . . . her smile faded. The inbox was full of messages from people from the office—Brian, her co-workers, even Bernard—all marked URGENT! What in the world could have happened in the last seven hours?

She scanned the most recent messages as she scrambled out of bed and headed toward the bathroom. In escalating states of panic, the emails described a negotiating process that had run off the rails. Terms long-ago agreed upon were now unacceptable. The closing was in jeopardy, and it was all hands on deck (this from Bernard). Her phone, silenced overnight,

began vibrating and she saw seven missed calls. Ruth decided to ignore the overwhelming amount of information
being blasted her way and just head for the office. She turned
on the shower and ignored the hotel phone, which now was
also ringing. Before she'd consumed a drop of coffee, she was
shaking with adrenaline. She told herself to calm down. Five
minutes in the shower wouldn't make a bit of a difference
to the crisis, but would make a big difference to how she approached the day. It would take something way worse than a
shaky closing to send Ruth Crawford out the door without
a shower.

She forced herself to stay calm, but didn't waste a second
getting ready. This morning, she took a cab instead of walking to work and started listening to voicemails in the back
seat. Bernard's message was the most recent. He was practical, as always. "I'd advise you to bring your passport and a
packed overnight bag. They are discussing who should go to
Asia and, at the moment, perhaps because you are still not
here, you are the most frequently nominated candidate. Do
not stop for breakfast, they're bringing everything in. Don't
worry. I ordered yogurt for you. I'm sure I will see you in a
very few minutes."

She sighed and decided to go on to the office instead of
turning around for a bag. Bernard most likely was right.
He often was, but maybe by the time the decision was made
about who should travel, someone else would be assigned the
task. The building lobby and elevator were as serene as ever,
but the fourteenth floor was so hyperkinetic that Ruth could
hear the buzz of voices the second the elevator doors opened.
She stepped out into a room that vibrated with tension. She
could see Brian on the phone in his office. He'd abandoned
his jacket and rolled up his shirt sleeves. She couldn't yet

hear what he was saying, but he was saying it with force as he jabbed at pieces of paper on his desk. She walked toward his door, but was intercepted by Bernard.

"Did you get my messages?"

"I got a hundred messages and a million emails. Can you give me the edited, up-to-the-minute news, Bernard?" Her head was already aching from the atmospheric adrenalin filling the hallways where they stood. She needed to get to the crux of the problem so she could start dealing with it.

"Yes. The Beijing deal you and the Asia team have been working on is, uh, going up in flames."

"I gathered that. What happened?"

"It is China, you know. The buyers want to renegotiate about half the terms of the deal."

"No way. That contract was locked in. We can't reconsider a single one of those terms without dismantling the whole thing. I don't think there is much to talk about."

"That seems to be the general consensus here, but it appears that the buyers have other ideas. You'd better sneak into the conference room and listen for a minute or two. You'll get the drift. Although why *you*, the big shot lawyer, should be able to ignore your phone and I, the lowly assistant may not, is a question that we might discuss further once this little problem is solved."

"We might. Thank you, Bernard."

"Where's your bag?"

"I was already in the taxi when I heard your voicemail. If I need to go, I'll have to go back to the hotel first anyway."

Bernard frowned and turned on his heels, then stopped and spun around. "Please tell me you have your passport with you and that it is not in some pilgrim's trunk back in Connecticut?"

"You know I do. It was on the must-have checklist you sent me before I left home."

He allowed himself a tiny smile of self-congratulation. "And aren't you glad?"

"No, not really, because if I didn't have a passport I couldn't go to Asia on a moment's notice, could I?"

At this he laughed out loud. "I love the simplicity of your thinking, my dear Ruth. Of course you could go at a moment's notice. But now I won't have to spend my entire morning in the emergency passport line."

He waited for an acknowledgment that he'd been right as usual. Ruth said nothing.

"You'd better get in there. I think it's too late to save yourself, but maybe you could try."

Ruth joined the semi-hysterical crowd in the conference room and learned the details of the calamity that had befallen them. Despite not speaking Mandarin or any other Asian language, they'd all decided Ruth was the perfect person to go, meet up with the firm's translator, connect with local counsel in Beijing, and sit down with opposing parties to try to work things out.

"It should be Brian. He knows the players, speaks the language, has the lay of the land. He's done this a million times. It should be Brian and you all know it. Why isn't Brian going?" Ruth was incredulous that they were still arguing for her to be the one to try to cobble the agreement back together.

"Brian's going to London tomorrow. He and Mallory are officially opening that office. He suggested you. He thinks you can do it better than anyone else *because* they don't know you."

"That's ridiculous. They will try to play me like a fiddle. I won't know how to credit anything they propose."

"Our local counsel is fantastic. She's been there for years, speaks the language, has a well-respected team. She'll fill you in and can do the face-to-face talking," said Brian, coming into the room.

"Brian, I am not trying to be modest, or lazy, or coy—but I am not the right person for this assignment. I don't know all the previous deals like you do."

"And I don't know this one like you do."

She stood staring at him. "But of course you do."

"No, I don't. I trust your work, Ruth, and I know what a quick study you are. I also know they will fall in love with you, and I think that you dazzling them could be exactly the advantage we need."

"I'm not sure what you just said is even legal, Brian. I don't think you can give me an assignment because I am a woman any more than you can deny me one because I am a woman."

"It has nothing to do with your being a woman. It has to do with your particular set of skills and knowledge."

They faced off for a moment without speaking. "If you insist, I will go represent you, but as your lawyer, I have to say that I don't think this move is in your best business interests."

"I respect your opinion as my lawyer, but in this particular instance, I choose not to take your advice."

They stood another moment. The others in the room looked elsewhere. Then Ruth briefly nodded her head. So she, as was inevitable, gave way to the force of this manipulation by flattery and guilt. She was too constitutionally accommodating to stand a chance against it.

"All right, Brian. I'll go." She refused to meet his eyes.

In a quiet voice Brian said, "Thank you, Ruth. I truly do appreciate it."

———

RUTH LEFT THE OFFICE and packed for a flight that evening. She tried to reach David, but as ever, got his voicemail. She opted against leaving a message and instead just texted, "call me." It was anyone's guess whether he would bother to look at his phone before she had to leave. If he hadn't called by the time she got to the airport, she would try again on all fronts—home, cell, office, email—and hope one of the methods of communication used by most modern humans would raise him.

She was more than a little peeved at Brian, although once she'd said yes, he had made every effort to make her trip as comfortable as possible. Simone made arrangements for first-class passage every step of the way, from car service to the airport to flights to hotels. They'd promised her a translator/guide to meet her flight in Beijing and local counsel to accompany her to all the business meetings. If she weren't still irritated, she might have allowed herself to get a little excited. Instead, she got even angrier as she stood before the contents of her small hotel closet and tried to decide what to pack. She chose to go with the ubiquitous uniform of professional women everywhere—black pants, a black dress, a black skirt and several tops that would work with all of them. Francine's elegant clothing did not let her down. She managed to squeeze out an abbreviated stint on the elliptical machine and another shower before her scheduled pickup. For the trip she dressed in a gray pantsuit and stashed her red wrap in her carry-on bag, remembering that red was a lucky color in China. She tried to reach David again every half hour or so, and in the end left a voicemail that said, "Hey! I'm going to China! Can you believe it? Not sure when I will be back, so call me before my flight tonight at eight. Pacific. I'll go nuts if I have to miss seeing you *and* talking to you. I love you! Answer your phone once in a while!"

With plenty of time to kill after clearing international security, Ruth chose to walk to the airport instead of hanging out in the first-class lounge. She checked her phone every few minutes, each time with an ever more sinking heart. It was almost nine back home. Surely David wasn't still out working?

The time came when she had to board the plane. For a brief moment or two, the plush accommodations took her mind off her failure to connect with David, but she intended to keep her phone turned on until the last second. She was staring sadly out the window when someone asked her if she had anything else that needed to go in the overhead. She turned to respond to the man, who turned out to be Brian himself.

"What? I thought you couldn't go?"

"I couldn't. But then I could. I realized I wasn't being fair to you. Mmm, no that's not quite right. I realized I was being a jerk. I'm sorry. I do think you can handle this, but I couldn't stop thinking of how mad you were."

Her mind was reeling. If it was this easy for him to go at the last minute, why all the hubbub about sending her? He did look chagrined, she had to admit, wearing an expression she'd never seen on his face before.

"But Brian, I didn't show any anger at all."

"Nope. You didn't. But I could tell you were mad, and then I started thinking about it from your point of view, and it seemed pretty unfair. Maeve used to claim that I could never admit when I was wrong. So, I'm admitting I was wrong. I'm sorry, Ruth. I do need your help on this, but it isn't right to send you off on a moment's notice to handle it alone."

Ruth looked at him skeptically.

"I'm sorry and I think we should tackle this thing together."

Still, she said nothing. She held his gaze and considered the sincerity of his apology. He did seem to mean what he was saying. And he sure was right—he had been a jerk, but she needed to show him she wasn't a pushover.

"Okaaay, then. Do you think you can forgive me long enough to do the work together?"

"Of course, Brian. I was always going to do the work."

"I know, I know that. Will you accept my apology?"

She paused and then gave an honest answer. "Yes, I accept your apology."

Brian smiled, and said, "Thank you." Then after a pause, "Maybe we can do some brainstorming before we arrive. I asked Bernard to download all the docs on thumb drives for us."

"Sounds like an efficient way to pass time over the Pacific."

She turned away as the flight attendant passed through the cabin one final time, reminding all to power down for takeoff. She picked up her phone and saw that she'd missed a call from David. "Oh, no," she groaned. "I missed a call from my husband, and I had my phone in my hand the whole time. How does that even happen?"

"I don't know," Brian said. "It is weird—the wireless limbo where calls land sometimes. I hate it."

"Ugh." She risked the flight attendant's wrath and hit redial, but the connection dropped before David picked up and she was more sternly reprimanded for using her phone. In frustration, she tossed her phone into her purse and found her eyes welling with tears. Don't cry, she warned herself.

"I'm sorry, Ruth."

"It's okay. Just not how I wanted this day to end."

Saying the words made her remember a fragment of scripture, she forgot it exactly—something about thanking God for his grace, more than enough for this day. Ruth leaned back into the seat, closed her eyes, and prayed her ad-libbed version. She made herself practice what she'd been told she should do and gave thanks for her many blessings, including a chance to see China, with an old hand like Brian, going first class all the way on someone else's dime. She thanked God for having a husband she loved enough to miss and asked him to bless her trip and her loved ones. Then she sat in silence for a few minutes and felt a tiny hint of peace. The plane moved down the tarmac and lifted into the sky. How many times does one have to experience flight before all sense of wonder disappears? More often than she did, it would seem. As the plane rose above the buildings and twinkling lights below, out over the water and into the evening sky, Ruth felt the same sense of awe she'd felt on every flight. Awe for the miracle of this enormous piece of machinery breaking the bonds of Earth, and awe for the stunning beauty of the Earth it left behind. A moon was rising over the water, reflected in every wave, so deceptively gentle from the perspective of this magnificent height. All was silent and hushed. She kept her back to Brian and gazed until her neck hurt.

"It's still a marvel, isn't it?" asked Brian, peeking over her shoulder into the darkness.

"Yes. It is."

Chapter Twenty

IN A TIME ZONE where it was the middle of the night, David sat wearily on the edge of the bed. Unable to change the events of the day no matter how many times he replayed them, unable to accept the reality of the waking nightmare he'd just been through, he decided that making a list of all the broken things he needed to fix might be a way to stop his brain from flashing like a strobe light through the disconnected and surreal images of the past few hours. He trudged down the stairs and into the kitchen. He switched on the light, picked up a pad of paper and a pen, and sat down at the counter with the hope of creating a plan. Despite his worthy intentions, though, all he could do was play back the events of the day, yet again.

The morning had begun like any other. He rose early, got ready for work, and headed to the office to make the schedule and check messages before anyone else arrived. He penciled in the crew's responsibilities and flew through email, deleting most of the messages as junk. He forwarded a couple of invoices to Annabeth and answered the messages that required a response. So far, so normal. After about twenty minutes he'd cleared his inbox. He stood, stretched, and tossed out the now-cold cup of coffee he'd picked up along the way, then made a fresh cup from the single-shot coffeemaker Ruth had bought before she left for San Francisco. It was much better than the Mr. Coffee, circa 1987, he had to admit, but he found it to be a little bit fancy for a landscape guy in a trailer. Well, now he was a landscape guy with an assistant in a trailer, so maybe getting all Keurig was justified. David now recalled the peace of that moment as he savored the last of the morning's quiet. Within a few minutes the guys arrived, calling out to each other and joking around before their day of labor began in earnest. A few minutes after their arrival, Annabeth pulled up in front of the trailer with a huge smile on her face.

"Aunt Janet has left the building," she sang when she got out of her car.

He gave her a thumbs-up in celebration of her first Janet-free day of the summer, then walked across the road to talk with Rick. As he was going over the day's plans with the guys, he heard behind him the sound of a car roaring down the gravel road at insane speed. He stopped talking and spun around to see what kind of fool was driving like that. To his amazement, the car careened into the grass in front of the trailer, barely stopping in time to avoid a head-on collision with a large tree. All the guys on the crew stared open-mouthed, as did David, who called out, "Hey! You almost got yourself killed there. Take it easy."

The driver threw open his door and hurled himself out of

the car, shouting, "Take it easy? Take it easy! Just see how easy I take it."

As the man charged across the field toward the trailer, David recognized him: Sid, his disgruntled client, was in a rage.

David dropped his coffee cup and ran across the road toward Sid. "What exactly do you think you are doing, Mr. Snyder?" he called.

Sid whirled. For a moment he stood, red-faced, breathing fire, glaring at David. Then, he wheeled again and stomped toward the trailer, shouting, "See how you like it, Mr. Crawford. Let's see how you like your life destroyed. You will not get away with ignoring me." He jerked the door open so hard the top hinge separated from the jamb. Then he barged inside.

By now David had reached the trailer and, angling through the lopsided door, plunged after Sid. "What are you doing? Get a grip."

The guys in the crew had also run across the street and were gathered around the door behind David. Sid lunged for the printer, picked it up, and hurled it at David. David ducked and avoided getting hit, but the printer careened off the wall and broke into several pieces when it hit the floor.

Annabeth, who had been standing in shocked silence, shrieked and dived beneath David's desk. Sid was hardly placated by the physical exertion of tossing a small printer and went even more ballistic. He grabbed a broom leaning against the wall and began using the handle to smash everything in sight—the light fixture, the coffee machine, the computer, Annabeth's table. He was a purple fury of violent animal noises. David watched in horror as he demolished the inside of the trailer. When he approached David's desk where Annabeth was crouching, instinct kicked in and David jumped him.

They went at each other, each trying to throw punches and anything else they could get their hands on. David was taller and stronger, but Sid was fed by stoked anger and at first got the better of things. After a few minutes, though, he was sucking air, his fists missing their target. The guys on the crew, who wouldn't all fit inside the tiny, trashed door opening, were nevertheless trying to push their way inside when David heard Rick call 911. Sid looked ready to collapse from exhaustion as he leaned, gasping against the back wall. He glared down at Annabeth.

"Snyder," said David, panting himself. "This is insane. The police are on their way. For God's sake, just stop!"

"You refused to fix what you broke and left my property a wreck for the most important night of my life. People were laughing at me. 'Maybe next year you'll have a house *and* a garden, Sid.' 'Were they having a big sale on anorexic shrubs, Sid?' How dare you? I lost everything because you made me look like a fool!" With a burst of energy, he jerked himself upright, reached into his jacket pocket, and pulled out a gun.

Annabeth gasped and the room became silent.

"What in God's name are you doing, Sid? Put that down so we can talk."

"Oh, now you will talk to me?" He snorted a laugh. "That's funny." His laughter turned hysterical. "I pictured this. I knew this is what it would take for you to respect me. Ah, yes, funny how a little piece of metal focuses the mind, isn't it, Mr. Crawford?"

"I'm focused, but we're not going to accomplish anything with a gun between us. Put that down and we'll go outside to talk."

"No, we won't be going outside, Mr. Crawford. It's *all* shit and it's all your fault." His wild eyes roved around the trailer, unfocused and terrifying. Suddenly he pointed the gun at Annabeth under the desk.

"It's all shit," Sid repeated.

Annabeth whimpered through tears, "No, no."

In an instant, David flew over the desk toward him. At that same moment, the trailer started shaking wildly from side to side. Sid lost his balance but got off a shot that went through the roof of the trailer. All three of them inside were tossed around so much that it was as hard for David to grab Sid as it was for Sid to aim the gun.

Annabeth left the semi-shelter of the desk and began crawling toward the bathroom door. Amid the chaos, David heard the trailer separate from its foundation and felt it begin to tilt. Sid was roaring like an animal again. None of them could control their limbs or movements. Sid tried to take aim at David, stumbled, then pointed again at Annabeth and fired another shot that missed both targets. David could hear his guys outside, shouting to each other to keep rocking the trailer. All at once it crashed to one side. Everything went sliding. Sid lost his balance and was hit by the moving desk. David, also knocked down by the impact, was able to recover more quickly. He grabbed Annabeth's arm and pushed her out the now-sideways partial door opening, then scrambled out after her. They sprawled on the ground and stumbled away from the door as two police cars pulled up and the officers leaped out.

The crew shouted to them in Spanish and English, "He has a gun! Inside the trailer!" The two officers drew their guns and approached the trailer with a steady caution that hardly matched the frenzy of the scene. They were a commanding, confident presence and within seconds took control. From inside, Sid was moaning in apparent agony. Now injured as well as spent, he crawled through the door and collapsed on the ground. The rage that fueled his savage attack depleted, it was a silent and docile man who allowed himself to be hand-cuffed on the ground and half-carried to a police car. He didn't raise his head or say a word as the police put him in the back seat and drove away.

MANY HOURS LATER, after giving interviews and sign-ing statements, David and Annabeth left the police station, a venue the officer had suggested would be more comfort-able than the trashed work site. David drove them back to the trailer in silence. Even though the police had said it would be off-limits for a while, he was shocked to see yellow crime scene tape all over the site. They got out of the truck and stared at the disaster in front of them. David was dismayed to contem-plate how much work it would take to clean up, regroup, and get the business running again. No longer frightened, he was exhausted, and angry.

Annabeth's reaction was different. He watched her turn pale and then crumple to the ground. Although she seemed to get through the police procedures well enough and had been praised for being strong, now she was shaking so hard her teeth clacked together. David dropped down next to her. She was so small. He wrapped his arms around her shoul-ders and held her tight, rocking her back and forth, telling her, "It's okay, you're safe, it's all right now." Still she cried and trembled. He pulled her closer, enclosing her fully in his arms. He could feel her heartbeat, the wetness of her tears on his shirt. He held on, rocking her as she sobbed, repeating,

"You're okay; it's okay; I'm here; I've got you," until at last she wound down and slumped against his chest. He didn't let go. He would hold her forever. It felt so good to be close to her, making things better for them both. After a while she lifted her head and pushed herself away from him. She got to her feet, wiping her eyes with both hands.

"Annabeth, what can I do?"

"I don't know. I just want to go home."

"I'll take you home."

She looked over at her car.

"Or I'll follow you to make sure you get there safely."

"Okay," she said. "Let's just go."

Through the truck's open windows, the scents and sounds of an ordinary summer night were incongruous to David at the end of this anything-but-ordinary day. He followed her into her driveway where she jumped out of her car and cried, "Chip! Oh my gosh, he's been in the house for hours. Poor thing. He hasn't even had dinner." She ran up the driveway, calling over her shoulder, "I have to take care of him." She then stopped and exclaimed, "Don't worry! I'll be fine. Chip will forgive me. He'll be on guard."

"Annabeth—I'm . . . I . . . Do you need me to go in with you? Stay here tonight?" He held his breath.

"No, no. We'll be okay."

"If you change your mind, call me. I'll come any time. And lock your doors for once."

"I will."

She ran into the house. He hoped that she would do both— lock her doors now and call him later. He sat in the truck and watched as lights came on in the downstairs windows. A little while later, he heard Chip bark from the backyard and then the sound of the screen door slam. After he saw light shining through the windows on the second floor, he thought, good, she must be okay. And yet he stayed.

When all the lights were dark and he realized he was inventing excuses to gaze at her bedroom window, he made his embarrassed way home.

SITTING AT THE KITCHEN COUNTER, David rested his forehead on the palm of his hand. He hadn't made any progress on his list, but it was so late, and the day had been so long that he was growing tired enough to think he might fall asleep. As he climbed the stairs to the bedroom, he looked again at his phone and the stream of messages from Ruth, responding to his earlier call. Was that this same day? He wasn't quite sure. He'd missed talking with her before she left for China, for God's sake. Could things possibly get any more screwed up?

He sank into the bed, hoping sleep might come. Before he turned out the lamp he texted Ruth a quick message: "China! Wow! Been an interesting day here too—fill you in tomorrow. Love you." Then he placed the phone on the charger on his bedside table in case Ruthie or Annabeth reached out to him in the night. He hovered for several hours on the edge of an almost-sleep. His phone didn't ring. His mind couldn't rest. Before the first light, he dragged himself out of bed, ready or not, for the next day to begin.

Chapter Twenty-One

HALFWAY ACROSS THE WORLD, Ruth was virtually in-communicado with everyone beyond the range of her sight. She'd hesitated, incredulous, when Brian told them all to turn off their phones for the duration of the trip, no exceptions. "Assume someone is listening to everything we say, except when we are in the local counsel's office, and maybe even there. Do not leave a single piece of paper behind."

When she kidded him about being paranoid, he'd said, "What's that old joke? Just because you're paranoid doesn't mean they aren't out to get you." Then, more seriously, "They are very good at information gathering. We have to try to make it at least a little bit harder for them." She'd obliged, de-spite her skepticism, and did as she'd been instructed.

She, Brian, and the local counsel's team kept a grueling schedule of meetings and meals that left Ruth, stupefied with jet lag, almost incapable of cogent thought. Brian, on the other hand, appeared unfazed. He could strategize with Ruth, meet for hours with the team or the Chinese contingent, suggest new provisions, arrange dinner, even banter in Cantonese or Mandarin, the two languages indistinguishable to Ruth, while she struggled to remember the most rudimentary changes to the contracts that were written in her native tongue. She felt compelled to apologize to Brian for being such an idiot, but he didn't seem to be bothered. She, along with Bernard, had kept meticulous and invaluable records of all the back-and-forth emails and revisions that both sides had agreed to before the whole thing fell apart. Ruth's hardwired organizational skills somehow functioned even when other parts of her brain shut down, and in this minimal way she contributed to the effort. She wondered whether Brian regretted even having her along—and was certain he must be relieved he hadn't sent her alone. Horrendous disaster averted.

By the third day, she was able to sleep most of the night and could form two consecutive sentences during daylight hours. At the end of that day, she was able to offer a new modification to a key issue—and to everyone's delight the buyers accepted it. One issue down, twenty-seven thousand to go, she thought. Everyone on both sides needed a break by then and they agreed not to meet on day four. Ruth assumed that meant that her group would be holed up in a hotel conference room hammering out new language for the next big hurdle, but Brian decided they all should get out and about. He arranged for a private guide and treated them to an inside look at the major sights of Beijing.

Until then, Ruth had assumed she would be answering the question "How was China?" with the only honest answer she could give: "Far away." Their enormous Western-style hotel and the huge office building where they met were like hotels and office buildings everywhere. The subtle differences—tea instead of coffee, the color red instead of beige—didn't much enlighten her about the culture. She hoped the bland, gloppy food they'd been served at the working dinners had been Americanized for their supposed taste. She longed for something crunchy that didn't also come with eyes. But, of course, Brian had been to Beijing many times and not only knew how to get personal tours of the Forbidden City, an original *hutong*, and an uncrowded section of the Great Wall, but also where to find real local food. After a full day of information and sensory overload he took them to a tiny restaurant in a part of the city that hadn't yet been modernized or made international. He asked them to allow him to order for the table, a suggestion to which they agreed with relief. The group settled into a large comfortable booth. After placing a long, detailed order in another language, Brian faced Ruth sitting next to him.

"How are you doing, my jet-lagged friend?"

"Awake. At 7:05 p.m., Beijing time. How's that for adapting?"

Brian laughed. "The day didn't exhaust you?"

"No! It exhilarated me. I am trying to tuck it all away to retrieve it later when I can read more about this amazing place. I have never studied Asian culture. I'm embarrassed to say that until now, I haven't been all that interested. This enormous, ancient place has been here all the time and I barely thought about it."

"I'm glad you enjoyed it. It's a complicated place. I won't even get into the current politics. Although it isn't possible to do five minutes of business here without thinking about the current politics. But understanding takes years. And just when I think I've got all the players and rules more or less sorted out, it changes. Someone is out and someone else is in and the contacts I've made are suddenly third rail. For a while. Then it all changes again."

"And you were going to send me here alone?"

"Not alone. You would have had all our local people . . ."

"Who might have been suddenly 'out' while I was here relying on them?"

"Highly unlikely. It usually doesn't happen in a week."

"Usually?"

"Okay. I admit I was wrong. I thought I had too much going on to make the trip and was happy to convince myself that Ruth, my superstar, was ready to go solo in China. Sorry."

Ruth was floored by the superstar designation. She had no idea he thought she was anything but efficient and competent. "Hardly," she responded. "And definitely not ready to fly solo on this one."

"With our people here, you would have been fine." He paused. "As long as you'd arrived early and slept for a month."

"That, or some serious pharmaceuticals. How do you do it? You never seem the least bit affected."

"I used to travel constantly, and I think that set my inner clock on permanent spin. I just switch to wherever I am. I can sleep on planes, as you noticed. Hope I didn't snore! I don't have to do anything; I seem to just work that way. The one perk of nomadic life."

"Not the only one. You speak—what—four languages?"

Brian just shook his head.

"Oh, more than that? Clearly being able to speak the native tongue when you land is another perk. I bet you know great little restaurants like this everywhere. You have friends all over the world. I'd say your travel comes with a number of perks."

"Yeah, the restaurants and a few basic words in other languages are good things, I agree. But I hardly have friends all over the world. I know a lot of people. I've hired a lot of people. I've negotiated with a lot of people. Circumstances haven't allowed me to become friends with a lot of people." He took a drink of wine and shrugged. "With the plusses come the minuses . . ."

The restaurant was starting to fill now. All the diners seemed to be local people. Unlike their previous meals, there were no other groups of business types burning through their expense accounts. Most of the guests here were dressed in typical Chinese clothing, not western office attire that predominated in their hotel lobby. Leave it to Brian to know about a place like this.

Ruth said, "It must have been hard to leave your family. Or did you bring them with you?"

"I brought them when the girls were little, but once they started school, that didn't work anymore. Maeve sometimes came on a short trip, but, you know, she wasn't going to leave the kids for two or three weeks. They needed one of us at home with them. She is a fantastic mother, as you can tell."

Ruth agreed. "She's fantastic altogether. I like her a lot."

"Me too. And she doesn't hate me, as much as she's disappointed in how things turned out. I guess you could say she's forgiven me."

"She's great."

All the food Brian ordered arrived. He described each dish as it approached, after first reminding them that most of the fish and seafood would come with heads and tails attached.

There were enormous spicy prawns, well worth the battle with their appendages. Another dish, with a name that gave Ruth pause—mutton hot pot—turned out to be similar to fondue. The diners dipped thin pieces of raw mutton and fresh vegetables into a simmering pot of hot broth and then dipped the cooked food in sesame paste. It was delicious and very filling.

Everyone relaxed as the wine flowed and the dishes kept coming. Personalities began to emerge, and they started to get to know each other as individuals in addition to their work designations: "the girl with the files," "the translator," or "Mighty Math Man." Over the course of the meal, they went from being a group of people working side by side to a cohesive team. In spite of the trite frequency with which that phrase is thrown about and misapplied, now Ruth observed the transformation as it happened, brilliantly orchestrated by Brian, of course, who no doubt had done this many times. She sat back and watched him charm, tease, flatter, regale, and empathize his way toward making each one of these people feel known and appreciated. She could tell already that the next day would begin the period of their best work and could imagine that soon they would be racing together in a whole new gear toward the now-achievable goal of a contract on their terms, the Chinese group's stubbornness notwithstanding. Of Brian's many gifts, this was perhaps the most impressive—his ability to identify what made a person tick and provide the means by which he or she could be motivated. And, even as Ruth observed and admired it, she knew he was doing it to her as well.

But if she allowed herself to be seduced, it wasn't quite seduction, was it? And in this context, was seduction even the right word? Something closer to inspiration. Or manipulation. Ruth laughed to herself and thought, I don't care. She was here to get this thing done and get back home. If Brian thought calling her a superstar would impel her to work even harder and better, that was fine. Why am I not furious with him anymore? Because I am on to you, Brian Bishop. I'll be deciding from now on when you get to me and when you don't.

She leaned forward and helped herself to more of the exotic food and accepted a wine refill. It had taken a while, but the perennial optimist in her had resurfaced and allowed her to see this entire experience as something precious, worth appreciating. It wasn't something she chose to do, but now that she was doing it, she could choose to be grateful and thrive in it. She sipped from her glass, laughed with the others, and offered a silent prayer of thanks for this incredible gift she'd been refusing to accept.

Chapter Twenty-Two

BY THE MIRACLE of camaraderie and conversation, Ruth was able to stay awake until midnight Beijing time and realized that, thousands of miles away, David would be awake too, working or maybe having lunch and perhaps even in the vicinity of his cell. She hesitated before turning on her phone, then chanced it. She would not say one word about the work; she'd never put the deal at risk. But after so many days she had to hear David's voice. She started dialing his number the second she reached her room. The phone rang several times and then, blessedly, David picked up.

"Ruth! Oh, man, Ruthie."

"David! My gosh, are we actually speaking? It is so good to hear your voice. I've missed you so much."

"Can't tell you how much I've missed you. How are you over there on the other side of the world?"

"I'm good, adjusting. I wish you were here though. This is an incredible place. Until today we were cooped up working all the time, but we finally got out and saw so many sights I never thought I'd see in person. Just amazing. The number of people, the scale of the buildings, the bicycles. Almost everybody wears surgical masks. There's some virus going around, I guess. I took lots of pictures—some of gardens for you—so different from home. Oh, I wish you were here. I can't begin to describe it in a way that does it justice."

By now she had shed her jacket and taken off the heels she'd been wearing for hours. She curled up on the bed and snuggled into the pillows, eager for the intimate conversation with David she'd been missing for so long.

"That does sound incredible. I'm glad you are having such a great time."

"I wasn't. I've been dog-tired and practically in lockdown, working every waking minute, but it's better now. How about you? How have you been? So frustrating I couldn't call you. Brian thinks all our phones are tapped. Crazy! I had to call you, though. Tell me about what's going on."

She heard him take a deep breath, then begin. "Umm. Actually, there was an incident. With an irate client. It got a little out of hand and, uh, the guy went nuts. I mean, I knew he was kinda nuts, but this was beyond. The trailer is trashed. The cops came, the guy was arrested. It was pretty bad."

"What? That's terrible. Who was it? What happened? Are you okay?"

She sat straight up and tried to picture what he described happening in a real place to a real person, this person, the one she cared most about in the world.

"I don't know if you know him. Sid? The one who has been a pisser all summer? He must have gone off his meds or whatever because he just went wild at the office. Yelling, throwing stuff. It was surreal, and now the place is a total wreck. I'm okay, though. Kind of shocked, or in shock, I guess." Ruth heard him take a breath, then groan.

"Sid? That little guy? Who would ever imagine he would do something like that? He seemed like, you know, just a big-mouthed bully, not someone about to snap. Are you really okay?" She sensed there was more to the story that he wasn't telling her.

"No, yeah. I'm all right. Just trying to figure out what's next. I'm not sure when we can get back in the trailer. The guys were great—saved the day actually—and they said they'd all be there to help get us up and running again, but the police still won't let us back in, so now we're just kind of waiting around, not sure what to do. I am about to let them go home, I guess."

Her mind continued to reel as she imagined the scene and its aftermath. Thank God he wasn't alone when it happened.

"Was Annabeth there?"

"Um, yeah, she was there and was pretty shaken, I have to say. I haven't seen her since it happened."

"That poor girl. She's been through the wringer. Does she have anyone nearby she's close to? I guess Janet's gone home, although I don't know if that's good or bad."

"Janet finally left. She has Theo, I guess."

"Yes, he seems like a good guy."

"Yeah. A kid though, so . . ."

"David, honey, you don't sound all that great yourself."

"No, not great, but I'm okay. Mainly it's been—shocking—and now a giant pain."

"If you need me to come home, I will be on the next plane out," she said, and meant it.

"No, no," he said, as she knew he would. "I am okay. It just happened a couple of days ago and I am still trying to sort things out. I've never enraged a client to the point of mayhem before. I guess it has thrown me off a little."

"I would think. Did you call James?"

"James. Why?"

"You probably have a civil suit for damages, lost income, and such in addition to the criminal charges I am sure are going to be filed. You'll need to file a complaint, most likely. You should talk it over with James. I mean, I would advise you, but I may be a little too close to the client." She laughed a bit but heard nothing from David's end of the line. "Anyway, it wouldn't hurt, and he might be helpful."

"Yeah, okay, I will call him if anything comes up."

"Uh, David, something has come up. I think talking to him might help you figure out what to do next."

At this, he did laugh. "Yeah, right. Okay, sure. I will call James. Got a lot of phone calls to make. I'll add him to the list."

She winced at the note of irritation she heard in his voice. They were both silent long enough for Ruth to realize that she was too tired to think, no matter David's state of well-being.

"I hate to hang up, but it is so late here and I'm not going to be lucid much longer. Can I call you tomorrow, or later today here?"

"Of course, Ruth, go ahead and get some sleep. Nothing you can do from China. Sorry to drop all this on you."

"What? You didn't drop anything on me. Good grief. I love you, David. I wish I were with you right this minute holding you, I wish I could—rewind, undo it."

"If I could hold you right now. . . ," David sighed. "Love you so much. Goodnight, sweet Ruthie."

"Goodnight, David."

Ruth expected another brutal night of insomnia after that, but she'd had too many of them in a row and reached that inevitable point when her weary body's need for rest trumped all else. She fell asleep within moments and slept deeply for hours. When she awoke, she had to rush to get to the conference room on time but felt like she had at least regained her physical stamina, even though she was distracted with worry about David. But there was nothing she could do from here. Just get this thing done and get home.

It turned out to be a breakthrough workday. Their pooled insights about the people on the other side and the free flow of ideas made possible by a supportive environment led them in an entirely new direction on a number of sticking points. By the time they stopped after their working dinner, they had come up with improved and, in some cases, inspired new proposals on all the major items of disagreement. They couldn't wait to meet with the other side in the morning. Ruth was tempted to call home again when she reached her room, but Brian had issued another one of his no-phone reminders (did he know she'd broken the rule?). By an act of tremendous willpower, she limited herself to a brief "love you" text and, missing David terribly, went to bed.

Chapter Twenty-Three

DESPITE THE SUMMER HEAT, Annabeth had felt freezing cold since Sid's attack. No afternoon sun or thick sweatshirt could warm her enough to stop her from shivering. Now she sat on the back porch wrapped in an enormous quilt her mother had made and watched Chip try to catch the rabbit who'd been feasting in her father's garden. Her mind was blank. The victims' counselor who met with Annabeth had been very kind. She'd listened to Annabeth's description of the attack, then asked her a series of questions about it. She must have answered all the questions correctly because the counselor said, "You seem to be processing this very well. But if you find over the next few days or weeks that you need to talk to someone, please call me. It wouldn't be unusual for you to have times when this bothers you, even after you seem to have moved on. Please don't suffer in silence. I am here to help." Annabeth appreciated the woman's gentle concern and took her proffered business card. Every ten minutes or so she thought, maybe I should go in and call her but was too cold to move from her refuge. It was in this blank state that she heard a car crunching over the driveway gravel. Her first reaction was to run and hide, but she lacked the energy, so she remained in place and waited for the sound of the car leaving again. Instead, she heard Theo calling her name as he came around to the back.

"Hey, Annabeth." He squatted down next to her. "Are you okay?"

Better now, she thought, looking at him, his concern written on his face.

"A few bruises and my knee kind of hurts."

Theo held open his arms to hug her. She welcomed his embrace and rested, quilt and all, against his chest. "It must have been awful. That guy . . ."

"It was awful. I was so scared. He had a gun. He shot at me." Her eyes filled with tears that threatened to overtake her yet again. Chip, ever her protector, sensed the potential deluge and squeezed next to Theo to comfort her, too. She tried to push him away, but Chip refused to give up. He started licking her face, butting Theo out of the way.

"It's okay, Chip. I'm okay," she soothed him as she tried to avoid his slobbery sympathy.

When he still didn't stop, Annabeth sat up. "Okay, that's enough!"

The dog backed off a foot or two, then sat at the edge of the quilt, on full alert in case she needed his further ministrations. Annabeth went into the bathroom and splashed cold water on her face, thinking she might brush her hair and try to look presentable. A glance in the mirror revealed that her appearance was beyond redemption with a mere hairbrush.

When she returned to the backyard, Theo had folded the quilt and was sitting on the steps, tossing a tennis ball for Chip, who seemed to have forgotten all about his nursemaid responsibilities. He ignored her return.

"I see Chip's recovered," she said. "I'm sorry I was such a wreck when you came up."

He stood and hugged her. "You don't have to apologize. Do you want to talk about what happened?"

Not really, she thought, but she managed to sum it up without reliving it.

Theo was dumbstruck by her description. "Oh my God. What happened to the guy?"

"They arrested him. I think he's in jail now."

"I just can't . . ."

"I know. It was nothing like in the movies. There was no time to process that it was happening and no time to think about what to do. I think we are only okay because the crew was there, and the guy was not a great shot."

Theo pulled her toward him and held her. He said, "I don't know what to do to help. Have you had breakfast? Are you hungry? I know how to cook omelets and grilled cheese"—he pulled back to look at her—"my family believes strongly in eating through all crises."

"That sounds good, actually. No, I haven't had breakfast. Not sure what there is to cook, but either one of those sounds good."

With the four eggs on hand, Theo made a cheese omelet to share.

"It's good," she said.

"Thank you. Next time, I'll make a sausage one. That's my specialty."

She smiled weakly. "Sounds great."

"Hey, listen," he began. "I wonder if you mind if I change the subject for a minute?"

"Good, yes, please do."

"Sunday is my dad's birthday, and we are having brunch for him. I'm not cooking." He grinned. "But I wondered if maybe you might want to come? If you are up to it?"

"Oh." She thought for a minute. "Well, maybe I would like to come."

"It will just be my parents and my little sister. Not a big production or anything."

Annabeth smiled. "I'd like to meet them."

"I want them to meet you. You'll like my sister. My dad will tell a lot of corny jokes. My mom will make too much food and try to get you to have seconds, but she's a good cook, so maybe you will want them."

"A mom-cooked meal sounds fantastic. We could run first."

"Not this Sunday. On my dad's birthday we're all supposed to go to church together. I'd invite you to come with us, if you want to hear forty-seven times how much I've grown, how much you've grown . . . you know—all the news."

"I know pretty much what I'll be missing. Thanks, but I'll pass."

She got up to clear the dishes and Theo rose to join her.

No, you don't have to help," she said. "You cooked, I clean up."

"Okay. That works." He sat back down. "You feeling any better—do you want to run later? No problem if you don't."

"Yeah, I do. Where should I meet you?"

Theo thought for a minute, and then said, "I'll pick you up. We need to drive to get to this place, but it will be worth it."

Annabeth walked Theo to his car where they lingered over good-bye. They kissed so long that Chip, who'd been expecting to play ball again, gave up and lay down at their feet. After Theo drove away, she rewarded Chip for his patience with a session of fetch. His joy knew no bounds, but his old body did. He soon tired and lay down again, panting and smiling at her. Feeling much less gloomy, Annabeth was able to replay the events of That Day. Big chunks of it were lost to her. Other moments flashed before her, forever imprinted on her psyche, but she couldn't quite form them into a coherent order. Somehow, even though she knew they occurred, they didn't add up. Someone tried to shoot her? Was she in a building that turned over? Did David save her life? Who was the person who experienced all those strange things? For the first time since all this had transpired, she was able to remember them without being overcome, because something equally strange in a different way had happened to her just now, while she was with Theo. It was coming to the surface of her conscious mind and affecting her even more than all the drama of the awful day. Before Theo arrived, she had been crying for the umpteenth time, sitting like a lump in a well of self-pity. Poor you, poor thing, she thought in a kind of chorus, the familiar background music of her life. But after a time, the words began to have a different effect on her. Instead of comforting her, or even describing her, the words started to repel her. While with one part of her mind she engaged with Theo, on another level she was coming to a new insight. Some wisdom deep within her unconsciousness was telling her: "Enough of this. Aren't you sick and tired of being sad?"

Now, alone again, she became aware of a buried longing to conquer her woeful state of mind, a state that was threatening to become permanent, and be done with it once and for all. She perceived that without intending to, she'd built a safe house designed for a wounded bird and had settled in for a long stay. But the structure wasn't safe at all. It was a house for her fear and anxiety, and staying inside it was making her more and more fragile. The death of her parents, her loneliness, and now Sid's monstrous attack all contributed to the structure. But she didn't want to inhabit it anymore. Finally, after all these months, Annabeth had reached the bottom of the large stock of self-pity she'd been hoarding. Weary of cowering inside her wounded self, she made a conscious decision to claim a life beyond her grief and weakness. The relief of coming to that decision elicited a few quiet tears once again, but these were healing tears. At the moment of reaching that decision, she was transformed.

When Annabeth blew her nose and wiped her swollen eyes this time, she did so as a different person. Where had it come from, that insight, that strength of will? What made it available to her now, within hours of an experience that could have sent her tumbling back inside her despair? The wonder of the change remained with her throughout the day. Anyone observing her closely would have discerned the subtle difference. Her shoulders were less rounded, her neck less bent. Her steps were lighter, the fearful look on her face was gone. After a quiet afternoon alone, an evening spent with Theo, and a night spent in peaceful sleep, she awoke before dawn, renewed and hopeful.

Chapter Twenty-Four

Sunrise found David drinking his umpteenth cup of coffee and pacing the house. He'd been up for hours after another night of wakeful tossing in a hostile, uncomfortable bed. Funny how exhaustion can become a stimulant. Funny how thoughts can deteriorate into spasms of incoherent brain bursts. Not funny how ill-equipped David was to cope with this altered state. All his capable competence had never been so severely challenged. His grace under pressure turned out to be fleeting and circumstantial, a quality he possessed by virtue of never having much need of it, and it was not available in endless supply as he had always presumed. "So now what?" he kept asking himself. He would begin a mental checklist: call the insurance guy, find out when the police will let him clean up, call Rick about the crew, call

James—ugh—call Annabeth . . . and the process would come to a halt. Okay, no. Maybe just go over to the trailer, see what things look like today. No, call Rick first and have him meet me there. Wait—the police first? And definitely need to check on Annabeth in person. So her house first, right?

He got in the truck without a particular destination in mind. Of its own ingrained habit, it took him to the trailer site. The crime scene tape was down, although no one had told him they were doing that, and his stuff was left strewn about the grass, bits of this and that fluttering in the breeze. He got out of the truck and walked toward the mess. Out of this chaos he was supposed to reconstruct a business? Rage toward Sid surged again. How dare he. A violent fit by a mentally deranged egomaniac resulted in this destruction, unjustified and out of scale to the slight that triggered it. The unfairness of it clenched his gut. David had never before borne the brunt of such deliberate cruelty. A storm or an accident? He would have already been picking up the pieces and making plans for an even better next go-round. But the malice in this calamity shook him. While Sid had been busy fuming and plotting, David had carried on unaware, unable to do anything at all to avert catastrophe. And it could happen again. Even now some evil plot could be hatching in the mind of some dysfunctional someone and there was nothing he could do about it. It was like 9/11 on a personal level. For a man who'd always found the world to be a generally good and predictable place, coming to terms with the reality of unforeseeable evil was disorienting.

He moved in the direction of the main mess. Papers were blowing in the slight breeze. He peeked inside the trailer and saw the old printer shattered, beyond saving. The contents of one file cabinet were most likely what he saw outside blowing in the wind. Annabeth hadn't started scanning the files yet, so those papers were all he had. He spotted the old desktop computer—also smashed and broken—and the vintage Mr. Coffee, more or less intact. How was that possible? He looked around for the new one Ruth had given him but couldn't locate it.

He called the number on the card the police officer had given him to ask if it was okay to begin the cleanup. He reached the officer's voicemail and left a message. Then he called Rick and asked him to notify the guys to be on standby. Within a few minutes, Rick himself appeared, impatient for the work to begin. Soon the crew joined them, each one re-telling the events of that day from his individual perspective. David learned details he hadn't been aware of and filled them in on what had happened inside the trailer. In this way, the specifics of the story came together.

While they were talking, the police officer called David and gave the okay for them to start putting things in order. As happy as that made David, it thrilled Rick, who took charge of the crew. With considerable effort, they were able to right the trailer. It looked like it had been through a tornado, but at least upright they didn't have to crawl through the debris on their hands and knees as David had just done. The crew spent the morning sorting the various items into piles by category until they could determine what was salvageable. David left at midday with a shopping list of essentials, while Rick and the guys continued to work and wait for the metalsmith and lock-smith to arrive.

Progress and purpose had put David in a better frame of mind as he filled the truck bed with the items from his shop-ping list. He'd been so intent on getting the task completed that he hadn't noticed he was hungry. In the old days, a whole week ago, he would have left the stuff in the truck and not given it another thought. But now, in a new awareness of his vulnerability, he decided to have lunch at home, where the contents would be safe. After a moment's driving, he realized that going home meant that a slight detour would take him past Annabeth's house. The truck would be safe there, too, and he wanted to check on her in any case. He would find something to eat there, even if it were just some of her endless supply of protein bars.

When he reached her house, Chip popped up behind the window, barking at first, then wagging his tail in delight when he realized it was David.

"Hey, Chip, how you doing, buddy?" Chip continued to smack his tail against a chair leg while David waited for Annabeth to answer. He knocked again. Chip barked again, but Annabeth did not appear. He was disappointed and a little surprised that she wasn't home. Where was she? He'd kind of thought she would be lying low, recovering. Probably engaged in running therapy, he thought and returned to his truck. He drove the roads near her house for a while, hoping to see her. When she didn't materialize, he gave up and went home.

Chapter Twenty-Five

ANNABETH'S SUNDAY WAS unlike any she'd spent since she'd left Kansas. She and Theo made a plan to run early, before church, along the river. It was a gorgeous late-summer morning, quiet if one didn't count the sounds of birds and bugs screaming at full volume. The air was sticky from the first step, but it felt good to run anyway. Theo set a moderate pace and they ran together beside the barely flowing river. They were soon too hot and sweaty to talk much and finished gasping for breath. They walked along the water, waiting to cool down, and came across some old stone steps someone had built to access a long-gone dock. "I'm tempted to jump in," Theo said.

"You sure? It seems kind of mucky to me."

"Nah." He looked into the river again, then ran down the

steps and jumped in. The water only came to his waist. "It's great!" he claimed.

Annabeth laughed. "I don't believe you."

Theo shrugged and climbed back out, his legs and feet now coated in sandy mud.

"Yeah, okay, it wasn't quite great. It was wet, though."

"Mostly." She looked at his legs.

"Right." Then, "I guess we'd better get going so we can get cleaned up in time for church. I'll pick you up in an hour."

At first Annabeth had wanted to avoid this whole church thing, but because it meant more time in Theo's company, she'd changed her mind. Now, getting ready, she was starting to worry that she'd made a mistake. She should have just said she'd meet his family at lunch and not gone along for this big production. What if Theo's family had its own version of Aunt Janet waiting in the wings, full of questions and advice and sniffs of disapproval? Surely not. There can't be that many Janets in one summer, can there?

She dressed in a print sundress, a white cardigan, and ballet flats. Theo was dressed as she'd never seen him—a blue button-down shirt, khaki pants, and lace-up shoes. "You look beautiful," he said as she got in the car. Annabeth realized she blushed at the compliment, a reaction about as ridiculous as this whole enterprise.

"Thanks," she said. "You, too."

"I feel more cute than beautiful," he responded.

She laughed and made to clock him with her clutch.

"So, we're doing this?" he asked.

"You make it sound irresistible. Yeah, can't wait."

In a short five minutes, they were there. The church could not have been more classic New England if someone had plucked it from a tourist brochure. It had white clapboard shingles and a green roof, old wavy windows, and a small, pointed steeple. The bell in the belfry pealed a call to worship as they walked toward the entrance where people spoke friendly hellos to Theo and introduced themselves to Annabeth. By the time they took their seats in the row with his parents, Nancy and Ted, and his eleven-year-old sister Molly, they were among the few not already settled for the start of the service. Ah, yes, church. She remembered this. She and her parents attended church sporadically, but often enough that she knew the routine. The people sitting in the pews could have been transplanted from her old church: the squirming little kids, the woman who seemed to know everyone, the older man whispering instructions to the ushers. The hymns were different, though, and the quality of the choir's singing was astonishing. She turned to Theo wide-eyed after one soaring solo, and he whispered, "Professional opera singer." It wasn't like any church choir she'd ever heard.

The smiling minister took the pulpit and began with the obligatory corny joke. Everyone laughed politely because they liked her, Annabeth could tell. The sermon was about the line in the Lord's Prayer, "as we forgive those who trespass against us." The congregation was working its way through the prayer, taking it apart phrase by phrase each Sunday in order to understand it, rather than just recite it. The minister referred to a previous sermon that dealt with the concept of divine forgiveness and was now planning to devote the entire message to these "few powerful words," as she put it. There was a bit of a theological debate, she said, about whether these words meant something akin to "you must strive to forgive other people as generously and thoroughly as God is forgiving of you" or whether they were something harsher "you will only be forgiven to the extent you yourself are forgiving of others."

She explained the thinking behind both points of view but didn't tell them which she believed or what they should believe. Annabeth had never considered that a phrase as well-known and often repeated as this one would still be open to interpretation after two thousand years. She wasn't sure quite what to think herself. She mentally tucked it away for future consideration.

When the service ended, Annabeth and Theo were surrounded by his family's church friends who were eager to wish Ted happy birthday, greet Theo, and meet Annabeth. With a gentle touch, Theo maneuvered Annabeth through the door and onto the lawn where tables were set up to serve lemonade and cookies. More greetings, more small talk, more people than Annabeth had met the entire time she'd been living in Connecticut. For whatever reason, the crowd didn't oppress her. These faces seemed familiar in a way, goodwill contained in their smiles and their questions warm and welcoming. She even met one couple who'd known her parents a little. They offered their condolences and shared a story about meeting her father at the garden center and being invited to lunch on the spot. "That's when we knew he wasn't from around here," the wife said. "We were looking forward to getting to know them better. I'm so sorry for your loss."

"That sounds like my dad," Annabeth replied. "He was very of-the-moment."

"More people should be like that," said the wife, and the husband agreed.

Theo guided her toward the parking lot and after a few more conversations they were able to leave, waving to small clusters of parishioners as they drove away.

"You survived," he ventured and squeezed her hand.

"I did." Annabeth squeezed back and said, "Honestly, it

wasn't so bad. They were nice. It reminded me of going to church in Kansas."

"Yeah, they are nice. But . . . all that nice can get to me after a while—answering the same questions over and over, realizing a lot of them have known me since I was born, but I hardly know them at all."

"It is kind of like a big family, I guess."

"Yeah. And now off to the smaller family. You up for this?"

"Of course, I'm starving."

He looked at her. "Umm— I meant—more *family*."

Annabeth laughed. "I know what you meant. Yes, I'm up for it. I must have been missing all this *family* without realizing it. It isn't bothering me at all. Your parents and Molly seem great."

"They are. If you need a break, though, and whenever you want out, give me a sign, and I'll help you escape." He smiled a little uncertainly at her.

"Okay. Thanks. I will. But I won't."

Chapter Twenty-Six

THEY ARRIVED at Theo's house before his parents, but the driveway was already full of cars. "My older sister is here, and my aunt and uncle. Sorry." He inhaled as if he were about to dive off a platform. "Let's go."

Annabeth laughed at him. "Steady there, we can take it. After all, you survived dinner with my Aunt Janet. How much worse can it get?"

"That was different. She was your crazy aunt. These crazy people are mine."

Theo introduced her to his older sister Nicole, his uncle Mike and aunt Emily, none of whom seemed the least bit crazy to Annabeth. Theo's parents and little sister arrived a few minutes later and food began magically appearing on the patio table, all prepared in advance. Theo's uncle Mike had started the grill and was taking orders for hamburgers or hot dogs, while his wife Emily helped Nancy get the rest of the meal together.

"What can I do to help?" she asked.

"Hmmm." Nancy looked around. "Why don't you take that basket of buns outside? Theo, would you open the umbrella? It's going to be hot in the sun."

In a matter of minutes, they were all seated at the table. Molly had positioned herself on Annabeth's right and Theo was on the other side. From across the table, Ted looked around at his brood and said, "Well, if this isn't about the best birthday party ever. I'm so glad you all could be here. Who's up for grace today?"

No one volunteered, so after a moment Ted asked, "Annabeth, would you do the honors?"

"Dad!" Theo said. "I'll do it."

He spoke a few words about gratitude and blessing, then everyone said Amen. He squeezed Annabeth's hand under the table. Food was passed and a get-to-know-you conversation ensued. Molly barely took her eyes off Annabeth and hung on her every word.

"Are you ready for school to start, Molly?"

"Yes. No. Kind of." She seemed to be looking for the answer that would please everyone.

They all laughed. "I know what you mean. I used to love school and was always eager for a new school year, but at the same time didn't want summer to end."

"Yes!" Molly exclaimed, as if Annabeth had unearthed one of life's major discoveries.

"Are you ready for school to start?" Emily asked Annabeth.

She paused before answering. "I'm not sure I'm going back

to school right away. I haven't decided exactly what to do about school."

Silence prevailed as they waited for her to explain in more detail. Instead, Theo rescued her. "Annabeth is taking a break from school for a while. Her parents passed away last winter, so she's had to deal with—all that."

"Oh, I'm sorry," Nicole said.

Murmurs of sympathy ran around the table. Molly gazed at her, wide-eyed and sad.

"Thanks," Annabeth said.

Theo's mom smiled at her. "You are wise to take your time deciding what to do. You just keep praying about it and the answer will present itself. When it feels right, you'll know what your next steps should be."

Theo glanced at Annabeth nervously, but everyone else nodded in agreement. Molly patted her arm.

"Thank you," Annabeth said. "I hope so."

After another minute of silence, Ted spoke. "Annabeth, we have a Sunday family tradition, and I hope you will indulge me on my birthday . . ."

Theo groaned, which made Molly look worried. Nancy began, "Now, Ted, I don't know if . . ."

"Annabeth, you don't mind indulging a nerdy old guy on his birthday, do you?"

"Of course not. But who would that be?"

What on earth was he going to say that had everyone else on tenterhooks? Seeing their reaction made Annabeth wary.

"Thank you." Ted bowed. "On Sundays after church, we have a tradition of saying one thing that struck us about the sermon. Then, if we feel like it, we talk about our 'one thing' and have a little post-worship symposium of our own."

Her heart sank as quickly as Theo's face fell. He shot her a panicked look of apology.

"Who wants to begin?" Ted asked.

"Me," Molly said. "One thing that struck me about the sermon was the minister sweating—a lot."

Her comment elicited the laughter she'd intended, but Ted wasn't going to let it serve as a response. "Very clever, Miss. But what struck you about the message?"

Molly looked at the sky, thinking. "I guess that I'd better start forgiving a little bit better or God isn't going to forgive me."

"What?" Nicole seemed shocked. "*That* was the message of the sermon?"

"Yes, it was, wasn't it, Dad?" Molly looked wounded.

Turning to Nicole, Ted answered, "The sermon was about whether that is what the Lord's Prayer means when it says, 'as we forgive others.' Reverend Post didn't sum it up for us, but she did throw that interpretation out there for us to consider. I guess, Molly, that's what it means to you?"

"That's what it says," she defended herself.

"That's ridiculous," Nicole said. "No human can be as merciful and forgiving as God himself. The whole Bible is about God's unending mercy. It's not a quid-pro-quo deal. What kind of God would that be?"

"I think that human limitation is baked in the requirement," Nancy said. "I think it's more 'try all the time to be more like God in your forgiving' with the understanding that God knows we are going to fail, because he knows we are only humans. To me, it's the sincere trying he wants from us."

"But it doesn't say, that," Molly insisted. "Does it, Dad?"

Clearly, Ted was the resident biblical scholar, and Molly

was his star pupil. At the moment, Theo looked like the kid in the back waiting for the bell to ring. He squirmed in his seat.

"What do you think, Annabeth?" Ted asked.

When Nancy gasped and Theo groaned again, he looked around. "Oh! Is that wrong? I shouldn't ask Annabeth? I didn't want her to feel left out."

"Dad," Theo said. "I just don't think it's quite fair to put Annabeth on the spot like that, two hours after you met her."

"I truly did not mean to make you uncomfortable," he said to her. "I was just curious—it's what we usually talk about on Sunday, and I just wondered what you thought." He smiled at her and touched his hand to his heart. "Forgive me."

"That's all right," Annabeth replied. "I've never thought about it before, and I'm not sure yet what I think."

"Very diplomatic of you."

"Ted, darling, not every family has a Sunday lunch theological disquisition," Nancy said.

Annabeth breathed a sigh of relief, but then continued, "That's true. We didn't. But I was just imagining how my father, even though this wasn't his field, would have jumped in with both feet. I can picture him waving his arms, making his points, asking my mom to Google things on her phone to back him up. He would have been right at home."

"I'm sorry about your parents," said Nancy, and looked at her with sympathy. "You must sorely miss them."

"Yes. I do."

Ted leaned back and slapped his thighs. "He sounds like a man after my own heart. I would have loved to have known him." Then, "How did he feel about chocolate cake?"

"A huge fan." Annabeth smiled at him. "Add mint chocolate chip ice cream, and he'd say he was in 'gastronomic heaven'."

AFTER A CONVERSATION about everything but theology, Annabeth and Theo offered to clean up. At first Nancy demurred, but upon their insistence, she left the two of them alone in the kitchen while the rest of the group stayed outside to set up the croquet set, another Sunday afternoon tradition.

"I like your family," she said.

"That was some introduction."

"I wasn't kidding when I said I could see my dad doing the same thing. Maybe not about the Lord's Prayer, or anything theological, but he liked a meaty table topic."

"Ha ha."

"You know what I mean—he loved to hear about what other people were into. Especially if he could get into it, too. Always a professor. I've missed that."

"I can't say I've missed this . . ." He gestured toward the patio.

"You would," Annabeth couldn't help saying.

Theo stopped, then pulled her toward him. "I'm sorry. What a dumb thing to say."

"It's okay." She looked up at him. "It's strange. I know they weren't perfect, but at first, after they died, it seemed disloyal to think of them as they were. Every time I remembered how my dad did go on, or how my mom did not go on, I felt so guilty. I kind of transformed them in my mind into two other people—the faultless version of themselves. But it's been long enough now that I can remember them as the people they actually were. And in some ways that makes me miss them more."

He murmured his understanding.

"My dad would have loved this lunch with your family. He

would have invited them to dinner—for tomorrow probably. I kept seeing them through his eyes. Missing him, though. Really, really missing him."

She kept her head against his chest in an effort not to cry. From outside, they heard the voices of his family, then a ripple of laughter.

"I know I'm lucky," he said.

"Yes, you are."

He lifted her chin and bent down to kiss her. She was content at this moment—her first real boyfriend and his kind and loving family on such a beautiful summer day—all this, an unexpected gift after a season of so much loss.

Chapter Twenty-Seven

RUTH STOOD in the customs line behind Brian, watching with interest and concern as the agents took every single item out of his bag and discussed each one in detail. She had no idea what they might be saying, so she whispered to Brian, "Is something wrong?"

"I hope not."

After several minutes of consultation, a supervisor who spoke English arrived and began quizzing Brian about his watch, his cufflinks, his computer, his iPad. When and where did he buy them? How much did he pay for them? Where were the receipts for the things he'd bought in China?

Brian answered each question with firm confidence and declared that the only things he bought in China were food and drink he consumed on-site. This answer seemed to annoy one and all, but Brian wouldn't back down. Ruth began to worry that they'd miss their flight and people in line behind them started to mutter and complain. Still Brian was adamant. With obvious reluctance the customs agents threw Brian's possessions back into his bag and shoved the bag at him. Ruth's turn.

"Are you traveling with him?" the English speaker demanded.

"Yes. We work together." She tried for the same confident tone Brian had just employed. The process repeated itself, with the agent asking her questions about her jewelry, such as it was, and the book on Chinese gardens she'd bought for David.

"You buy this in China?" the supervisor glowered.

"Yes. The receipt is inside the book," Ruth pointed out. He looked at the receipt, clearly unhappy that the amount was insufficient to generate a fine or additional duty.

"What else you buy?"

"Just what I ate and drank," she responded.

After more gesturing and angry words, they dismissed her as roughly as they had Brian, almost throwing the heavy coffee table book at her.

"My, that was pleasant," she joked to hide her genuine fear. "I was imagining what the inside of a Chinese prison might be like."

"No, you weren't," responded Brian, without the hint of a smile. "These guys have their own rules. I never buy anything here because I never want to give them a reason to have anything to do with me. But they seem to hate that even more than the possibility of somebody sneaking contraband out of here. Pretty ironic considering that most of what's for sale is counterfeit anyway. Once again: it's a complicated place."

Ruth refrained yet again from reminding him that he had originally intended to send her here all by herself. At least they got the deal done and were on their way home. She was about to say as much when Brian spoke. "I just hope they don't find some way to screw us on that contract before our plane lands."

"What? You think that might happen?" she asked.

"I don't think it will happen, but I won't be shocked if it does. Still the wild west, or erratic east, over here. They have a long history, so we shall see."

Although he did not seem at all pleased to be stating the dismal facts, neither did he seem to be dismayed. Brian was enlightening Ruth about the reality of their situation and accepting it as somewhat beyond his control.

"We did the very best we could. I think it will be good enough, but . . ." He shrugged.

"I will be devastated if this thing falls apart. We all worked so hard. And I think we closed all the loopholes. It is an excellent contract. If it goes bad, please don't ever tell me."

Brian laughed. "Okay. I'll just show up one day with another ticket to China and let you figure it out."

"Oh no. By the time this thing goes south, or not, I will be back in Connecticut, working on other stuff. You can send some new fool to China." She shook her head in emphasis. But did she mean it? Would she come back here again with Brian to this fascinating place? She just might.

"Let's hope it doesn't come to that," he said.

The flight home was endless. This time the first-class novelty of real food, decent wine, and brand-new movies was not distracting enough to keep Ruth from longing for the flight to be over. She slept in fits and spurts until the last couple of hours, then sat upright and looked out the window, willing the California coastline to come into view. Brian followed his tried-and-true routine of melatonin, ear plugs, and eye mask, and slept most of the flight in apparent total comfort. Ruth marveled at his ability to control even his own biological clock. This deal was destined to hold, if for no other reason than the strength of Brian's will. His shrugged shoulders weren't an indication of a lack of concern. They were an acknowledgment that this might just be a step along the road. There was never any doubt that he would get his way.

As the flight crew began their pre-descent activity, Brian awakened and freshened up. She had already done all she could to repair her haggard appearance. No one would be waiting at the airport anyway. All she had to do was try to get herself back on west coast time, call David, and reenter the world she normally inhabited.

"You going to the office?" Brian asked in a cheerful voice.

She turned, stunned, to stare at him. "What?"

Brian grinned. "Just kidding. I wondered how you'd react."

"You're a crazy person, you know that?"

"I've been told."

Ruth made a face of disbelief. "Don't tell me you are going to the office?"

He just looked at her.

"Well then," she responded in a determined tone, "I hope you have a very pleasant day. Don't try to shame me into going with you. It can't be done."

"No, no. I wouldn't. But we've been away several days. What else am I going to do?"

"See the girls maybe?" she asked, incredulous.

"Of course, but they are in school right now. I'll just be distracted by wondering what happened while I was gone if I don't spend the afternoon catching up."

"I can't believe I am going to ask this question—but—you don't need me for anything, do you?"

He laughed. "Such enthusiasm. No, I don't. Get some rest and we'll hit it again tomorrow."

"What day is tomorrow again?"

"Friday."

She swallowed, then took a breath for courage. "I'll see you tomorrow. But then I need to go home. I haven't seen David in forever. I'm going to book a flight for tomorrow afternoon."

"That's fine. You deserve it."

After landing, they walked together down the ramp toward customs. Ruth was so glad to be home, she said to him, "I'm looking forward to good old American red tape."

Brian gave a rueful laugh. "You might not believe it, but the U.S. Customs guys can be as tough as the ones in China. They seem to think everybody who's been to Beijing is a smuggler to one extent or another. We should be fine, but just warning you to be prepared for them to doubt that all you bought was one book."

"You're kidding," she groaned. "Can I follow you again?"

This time the agents were too busy to spend much time on them and they were through the line in a matter of moments. They gathered their belongings and waited together for the driver Simone had booked to take them back to the city. As they waited, Ruth turned on her phone. Her inbox and voicemail box began to fill with messages.

"My gosh," she cried. "All these messages. My phone is going to melt."

"Start with the newest ones. The old ones have probably been resolved by now," Brian advised.

Her most recent voicemail, along with a number of those preceding it, was from David. She tried to listen, but the little spinning ball of doom just kept whirling its way to nowhere. "I can't get to my voicemail. This is so frustrating."

"Maybe you could get a call to go through. Or do you want to try mine? It seems to be working okay."

"Thank you. I'll give it right back."

She walked a few steps away from him to try her call. No way Brian Bishop would have a cell phone that didn't work. This time she reached David. A few minutes later she rejoined Brian and returned his phone.

"I have to go back right away, it's an emergency. I'm sorry, but I can't be at work tomorrow. I'm going inside right now to book a flight".

"I'm sorry, Ruth. Do what you need to do, but don't go back in there—hold on."

He called Simone who booked Ruth a new flight leaving in less than two hours. He picked up her bags and ran interference through the crowd, then waited at the ticket counter and made sure she had everything she needed, including the cash in his pocket when she admitted she only had forty dollars in American currency. "You can't go anywhere on forty bucks."

He walked with her toward the security line and said with sincere concern, "You'll sort it out, whatever it is. Let me know if you need anything, and I will see you when you get back. We're okay here."

"Thank you so much, Brian."

"Check in when it works—have a good flight."

"Thank you. I will. I appreciate this."

"I'm glad I could help."

She joined the line and Brian began walking toward the exit. He waited near the door and watched her clear the ID check and load her luggage onto the conveyor belt. When she made it through the body scan, she looked back at him and mouthed, "Thank you." He gestured in acknowledgment. I might actually miss him, she thought.

She collected her screened bags and looked back in his direction one last time. He hadn't moved or stopped watching her, but the expression on his face had changed. Oh! She perceived with a jolt. He was going to miss her, too.

Chapter Twenty-Eight

DAVID CIRCLED the airport parking lot for the third time after receiving the text that Ruth had landed. As he approached the baggage claim door, he finally saw Ruth waiting and pulled over to pick her up. How was it possible that he'd forgotten what she did to him? Even after lord knows how many hours on planes, wearing no makeup and rumpled clothes, she looked beautiful to him. Seeing her still made his heart leap.

"Ruthie!" He grabbed her, bags and all, into an awkward bear hug. She wriggled out of his arms long enough to set her things on the ground and hug him back.

They embraced without speaking, and then Ruth said, "How are you? I've been so worried!"

"I'm okay. Let's go. I'll catch you up on the way."

As they drove away, David took her hand and said, "What a sight for sore eyes you are!"

"I'm a sight all right. A complete zombie at this point. I can't believe I'm here. I feel like I've been on Mars."

"Yeah, me too. I kept trying to reach you, but . . ."

"I know, impossible! We couldn't use our phones, you know, and email was a disaster. It wasn't until we landed that I saw all your texts and missed calls and then my phone imploded or something." She turned fully in the seat to face him. "What's going on?"

As they drove home, David finally told Ruth the full story of Sid Day, as he had taken to calling it. Although he'd experienced it, and retold it several times, the tale still didn't sound real, even to his own ears. Ruth was floored and could only gasp and groan as the details emerged. Hearing about the gun, which David hadn't been able to tell her on the phone, caused her to burst into tears.

"My God! He tried to *kill* you?"

"I don't know. Maybe just scare me. But, yeah, the guy shot at us."

"David, I'm . . . I just can't believe it. It's only by the grace of God you are sitting here."

"Don't cry, Ruthie! It's over now. I'm fine. But also, kind of not. Hard to explain."

"Thank goodness the guys were there!" Ruth grabbed David's arm and grew even wider-eyed. "If it had just been you against Sid . . ." She closed her eyes and shuddered.

". . . might not have turned out so well." He agreed. "The guys were just great, heroic, really. I owe them."

"So do I."

Ruth released him and sat quietly, trying to put the pictures into focus. "Are they okay?

What about Annabeth?"

"The guys are all fine. Annabeth got tossed around some and she was pretty rattled. I haven't seen her since that day."

"Should we check on her? How badly was she hurt?"

"Not seriously. I'm sure she's okay. I did try to call her, and I went by there, but no one was home. She must be okay if she is out and about."

"I guess so. If she isn't in the hospital!"

"No, no, she wasn't hurt like that."

"I guess if I were a saint, I'd have the guys and Annabeth over to dinner tonight—to thank the guys and check on her— but I just want to be alone with you. Do you think that's self-ish?" Ruth asked.

He considered her question. "Maybe I should already have done that. Just not thinking all that straight, I guess. But to-night, Ruthie, please, just us."

They pulled into the driveway and David shut down the car. He turned toward her. "Like I said, I'm not quite thinking straight. Dinner with you, it's been forever since we've done that. I'm so glad you're here, you keep me headed in the right direction."

After her long journey, Ruth craved a hot shower. Refreshed and restored, she and David spent the evening touching base emotionally, reading each other's gestures, smiles, silences as best they could, their concern for each other making them less awkward than when they'd last seen each other in San Francisco. Now and then, they started talking about some-thing they'd forgotten the other one knew nothing about, but being at home together helped them reconnect. After a dinner of delivery pizza, the day drew to a close, and at long last, they spent a night together in their own bed.

Chapter Twenty-Nine

THE NEXT DAY jet-lagged Ruth awakened before the sky held even a hint of dawn. She turned to look at David, still sleeping, beside her. He was breathing regularly, one arm thrown above his head, in a posture that looked as if he hadn't a care in the world. Sleep came with a peacefulness for him that didn't quite bestow on Ruth. She wanted to put her arm around him and snuggle in, but she was afraid she might wake him, so she moved as close as she dared without touching him. She could feel his warm body, watch his chest rise and fall, even feel the beating of his heart. He was, as always, her dear David. She placed her hand on his bicep. Still sleeping, he shook it off and turned away from her.

Making as little noise as possible, Ruth got out of bed

and slipped downstairs into the dark kitchen. She fixed herself a cup of coffee and opened the back door to the garden. The still-night air was cool, a harbinger of autumn. By midmorning, it would feel like summer again, but at this hour Ruth needed the thick throw from the sofa to venture outside. The whisper of leaves in the gentle predawn breeze was the only sound. It was as dramatic and harmonic as a symphony, and in an hour would go unheard amid the cacophony of full-on morning. She curled into a chair, cradling her mug as the wind stirred her hair, and listened. Off to the east the promise of pink lay just beneath the horizon. Returning to a habit that travel had made hit or miss, she began to pray. It was a muddle of a prayer, mostly incoherent mutterings interspersed among "thank you," "help," and "now what" that were the best she could manage. She rambled on, distracted and inarticulate, until she brought the prayer to an abrupt close by saying "Amen." A hummingbird sipped from the salvia blossoms, then whirred out of sight. Ruth rose and went inside.

DAVID ALSO OBSERVED the beginning of the day. Or rather, observed Ruth observing it from the window of their bedroom. He woke up when she left their bed and couldn't go back to sleep. He glanced out the window and saw her, wrapped in layers, take a seat on the patio below. She looked cozy and content, tasting her coffee and gazing at the tree above her head. He considered getting his own coffee and joining her. They could sit side by side in silence and watch the coming dawn together. But this view of her was perfection, unmarred by any intrusion from him. He watched from above until she came inside.

He made his way downstairs and into the kitchen where she was gathering things for breakfast. "Morning," he said, and kissed the top of her head.

"Morning," she responded. "Did I wake you?"

"No, I've been awake for a while." He looked at the eggs she'd placed in a bowl.

"Sorry, there's not much here to eat. Tell me what you need, and I'll go out and get it."

"No. There are eggs and the herbs in the pots outside. I think there is a loaf of that farmer's market bread in the freezer. There's enough for now. Are you hungry?"

"Now that you asked, I think I might be."

She smiled and opened the cabinet door for one of his mugs, which she filled and handed to him. "It won't take long."

"Thanks," he said, adding milk to his cup. "Any jobs for me?"

"Keep me company and tell me what you want in your omelet."

"What are my choices?" he asked as he pulled out a stool and took a seat.

"Salt, pepper . . . ?"

"Load it up. I'll take them both, be right back."

He went outside where the sky was now more light than dark and cut a few snips of this and that from the herb pots on the patio. In a short time, she'd produced a meal—oven cinnamon toast, "vegetable" omelets, and a single apple to share, sliced and arranged in a pattern on their plates.

She took his hand and said, "Thank you, God, for this food and this family."

"Sorry, Ruthie. I've become a heathen in your absence."

"David, I just wanted to say thanks. Now eat."

He squeezed her hand and then tucked in, murmuring

in appreciation with almost every bite. As she watched him finish his breakfast, he sighed and smiled at her. "I'm the cartoon man—lost without my woman, needing only her kisses and a full belly to be content."

"I am so sorry I wasn't here for you, or even over there for you. It's awful to imagine you going through the Sid thing alone."

"I'm fine, you're here now."

"So, what's next?"

"We sit here and drink coffee. You tell me about China."

She gave him a questioning look. "And then I'll help you with—whatever needs to happen next?"

"Tell me all about your trip, Ruth," he insisted. "That's what needs to happen next."

She looked at him for a minute, then began, "China is quite a place . . ."

LATER THAT AFTERNOON he drove her to the trailer site. Although she had heard him describe what happened, she was still shocked by the damage. David told her that the insurance company had declared the structure itself a total loss after the metalsmith said it was beyond his skills to repair. Now they had to find someone to tow it away for parts and scrap. He had already cleared the interior of everything he'd deemed salvageable, but he asked Ruth to help him check one more time.

"Be careful," David told her. "I'm sure there is broken glass in here. I just want to make sure I haven't missed anything." They entered the damaged trailer.

"All I see are papers and broken furniture. Did you get your computer?"

"Yes, it's at home, trashed I'm afraid. Annabeth has us doing a few things electronically now, but I don't know if they are stored on clouds or servers or whatever. I need to ask her." They made one last round.

"I guess that's probably it, then."

From inside the truck Ruth looked back at the mess, but David stared straight ahead and started the engine.

"Even now that I've seen it, I still can't believe some guy came at you with a gun. That doesn't happen here, does it?"

"Apparently it does. Let's go."

She patted his arm. Without responding, David put the truck in gear and started down the road. "I've got a meeting with a realtor about some office space in town," he told her. "Wanna come be my lawyer?"

"Sure. But . . . you're moving into town? You don't want to get a new trailer for out here?"

"I don't know. I figure it was pretty lucky the guys happened to be there when Sid showed up. Otherwise, there's no one else around out here . . ."

Ruth had never perceived David as fearful or even cautious. "True. But there is room for all the equipment out here. And you like having green space around you. Surely nothing like this would ever happen again."

"I hope not. But it's not even about me. I can't ask Annabeth to put herself at risk like that again."

"Maybe now that the files are online, she doesn't have to go in. Maybe she works from a computer somewhere and you don't have to remake everything?"

"No, I need her to come in and I need to know she'll be safe." He was adamant.

Okay," she said, "I'll go with you."

They soon pulled into a small strip mall with a sign advertising office space on the second floor. A jovial man greeted them and showed them around the dark-paneled office with room for a couple of desks. The worn carpet was far dirtier than any soil David had ever dug and the toilet-only bathroom in the back made Ruth slightly ill. All this for a monthly rent that should have purchased a palace.

"So, what do you think?" asked the agent.

She glanced at David, who, to her amazement, seemed to be considering the place.

"It's not bad. A little pricey. What's the security here?"

"Every office has its own alarm and there are cameras at the outside entrances. The building is passkey accessible on the weekends and open to the public Monday through Friday."

"Okay, I don't think this is what I'm looking for then."

"Because of the security? Is there something we could add to make it more attractive to you?"

"I'm looking for something where I can control who I let in. All the time, even during the week."

"You could always keep the door to your office locked. There is a small safe in the wall over there."

"No. I just want to know who's coming in. I don't think this will work. Thanks for showing it to me."

He shook hands with each of them and walked them back to the parking lot. Ruth and David got in the truck. "Pretty expensive. And on the second floor without a way to control who's in the hallway. That's not at all what I want."

"To say nothing of it being so posh," Ruth said. He didn't seem to hear her.

"Maybe there are new trailer-sort-of-things that come with better locks? The one you had was pretty old."

"Yeah, maybe. I'll look into that, too."

She was determined to help him solve this problem he was obsessing about. "In the meantime, you could work from home. I'm not using the office at the moment. Why don't you set up shop in there until you figure out where you want to go?"

"Mmm. Maybe,"

They rode through the busy part of town. There were Office Space For Rent signs everywhere. "Plenty to choose from, in this recession world," she said. They drove a while longer looking for better locations.

Out of the blue, David said, "I think you're right—I should check on Annabeth. I can drop you at home and then run over there."

She felt a twinge of uneasiness. "I'll go with you. I want to see her myself. How do you think she's holding up?"

"That's why I'm going there. I need to find out. I haven't seen her since Sid Day." His voice had an impatient tone.

"Okay." Ruth looked out the window. "I guess what I literally meant was how was she the last time you saw her?"

"Pretty upset. She's kind of a shaky person, you know. If she hadn't been working for me . . . if I'd managed Sid better . . ."

"Gosh, I hope you aren't thinking that what happened was your fault. There is no way you caused Sid to go nuts. You know that, don't you?"

"Of course, not directly. But you don't know what it was like, Ruth. It was scary for me, and I'm a big, tough guy. Even the crew is still a little shook up. It was awful for Annabeth. I thought having her come work for me was going to make things better—clear out Janet and give Annabeth something useful to do so she could get a little traction in her life. This could be the thing that sends her back to square one—or worse."

"Let's go see how she's doing. If she's distraught, we'll help her. Get counseling for her, if she needs that. We'll do what her parents aren't here to do."

"No. We are definitely not her parents, and we can't be her parents. It's not like she's a child. She's an adult and we need to recognize that."

Ruth felt a stab in her gut. "Of course, David. I know we aren't her parents." She sat in wounded silence, trying to force her lungs to function normally. "I know very well that we are not anyone's parents," she said.

David groaned. "Oh, Ruthie. I'm sorry. I didn't mean— that's not what I meant . . ."

He pulled over and pivoted to face her. "I meant we can't treat Annabeth like a child. She's delicate, but not a kid." He reached for her. "Ruthie, I feel terrible."

She resisted his embrace and looked at him, tears rimming her eyes. "This thing has rattled you, too. I know you didn't mean to be cruel. I know you're only thinking of Annabeth."

Of course, he hadn't meant to be unkind. He had been merely thoughtless. And yet . . . her David had always been an absolute rock, and also, the sweetest man on earth. Especially to her. He had never forgotten to be gentle and tactful about not having children. He had never been worried about security cameras and double locks. He had never rejected an offer of her help or companionship. Annabeth wasn't the only shaky one. Something about Sid's attack seemed to have pushed him off his own foundation, pushed him into acting like someone else, someone different from the man she knew, and at this moment, someone she didn't even like all that much. Before now she would never have expected anything to tilt his axis, but this thing obviously had. He's human, she told herself. Be patient. Be the giver here. She took his hand and held it next to her chest.

"Hey—" She looked at him. "We're in this together. Just like always—you and me against the bad guys."

He touched her cheek. "Yeah." He looked out the window, then sighed and turned back to look at her with tenderness. He extracted his arm and pulled back onto the road.

"You're right, Ruthie. Let's go home."

Chapter Thirty

RUTH STOOD IN THE KITCHEN looking back and forth between the barren pantry and the enormous tower of mail teetering on the kitchen counter. David, who'd been mowing the lawn, came into the room for a glass of water and a quick hug.

"You better?" she asked.

"Yeah, I am. How are you doing?"

"I'm okay."

"I'm glad," he said. "I hate to go, but I do need to hit a job site this afternoon. Can I pick up anything?"

Ruth considered. "No. We need to make a grocery run, but I think it would take me as long to make the list as it would to just go do it."

"You sure? I can wait a little bit, or you could text me?"

She laughed. "Since when do you actually read texts? No, anyway, my thumbs would fall off. I'll go."

Ruth was determined to reestablish some sense of normalcy for them both. She wanted her house back the way it was when she lived here—groceries on hand, mail where it belonged, the kitchen clean and the laundry folded. Even more, she wanted her husband back the way he was. The thing with Sid was terrible, but David's freakout this afternoon seemed out of proportion, or off the mark in some way she couldn't quite identify. She sighed as picked up her keys and got ready to leave. House tending was easy; David mending might be hard.

They left the house at the same time, headed in opposite directions. He tapped the horn to say goodbye and watched through the rearview mirror as she drove away from him. Ah, Ruthie-belle. How had he been lucky enough to have married her? There was nothing so great about David Crawford that she should love him the way she did. Whatever imaginary guy she thought he was, far surpassed the reality of the man. The past weeks were proof positive of his inadequacies. He'd let pretty much everyone down: Ruth, Annabeth, the crew, even Sid, as complicated as it was to realize that. How could she be blind to all those failures? He was chagrined to admit that sometimes instead of building him up, the depth of Ruth's love and admiration made him feel embarrassed not only for himself, but also for her. Nobody was as great as she thought he was. How could she be such a damned fool?

He pushed those thoughts away as he headed toward the job where the guys were working. Things were returning to normal, at least out in the field. This late in the season not having his designs in order was still a nuisance, but not the catastrophe it would have been if they'd all been destroyed in the spring. Silver lining, he supposed. He would have to find a place to reorganize all that, though, as much as he'd rather not think about it. The office they'd seen earlier was a pit, and although he was not a fussy guy, he would never want to go there. And he could never ask a client—or God forbid, Annabeth—to step foot in a dump like that. The trailer may have been flimsy, but it was clean and sat out in the country where there was light and air. Maybe he should look into getting another trailer. But then it would be so vulnerable. Although one might think that Sid was done with his shenanigans, at some point soon he would be free to roam around again. A restraining order, or whatever it was James recommended, wasn't going to restrain a truly crazy man, as he'd heard Ruth say.

David grew angry with Sid all over again and smacked the steering wheel with the palm of his hand. "Damn Sid! I don't want to spend my time worrying about this crap." He pulled into the drive where there were two of his trucks and a team of guys reloading the tools they'd used on this beautiful property. David had to admire how it had turned out. This job had started as a much smaller project, but the homeowners liked the initial work so much that they asked David to implement phases two and three, originally planned for next year and the year after that. If you had money, a recession was an opportunity. Beyond the income boost, David was thrilled they'd made that decision because now, as a completed project, it was stunning. Exceptional enough to be included in Samantha's next book, if he did say so himself. Once Sam saw it, she'd work her magic and get it in some upscale design magazine, too. David didn't care about the publicity per se, but the more he became known as a designer of big, bold things, the less he'd have to make do with one-off beds of deer-resistant shrubs and daffodil bulbs.

He got out of the truck and helped the guys finish loading. Then he and Rick walked the property. "This looks great,"

David said. "It's even better than I imagined. Have the owners seen it yet?"

"No, they're not home, but I think they'll like it."

"And unlike Sid, they seem to be sane, so if they don't, they'll just tell us. But I can't imagine what they wouldn't like." David examined a few of the plants up close. "It's incredible we got this quality so late in the season."

"Overstocked, not too many projects going forward, I guess. Lotta crews laid off right now," Rick said. "The guys and I—we're grateful you keep us working."

"I'm glad we are keeping busy, too. And I'm grateful for you guys. I wouldn't have these jobs if you weren't so good."

Rick nodded his acknowledgment of the compliment. Together they returned to the waiting crew so David could thank them for a job well done.

"Not sure what we're doing Monday," David told them. "I never found the master calendar."

"Maybe Annabeth had it on her computer?" Rick asked.

David perked up. "Oh—you think so?"

"I don't know. Maybe. If not, we'll figure it out."

"I'll ask her—it'd make life easier if we still had that schedule."

Might as well run by there now, he thought. It's not too far out of the way, and you know . . . kill two birds with one stone. If she has the schedule, he'll be golden, and reminding her how important she is to him, well, to his business, might be just the lift she needed. The vague feeling of gloom he'd been experiencing dissipated the second he climbed into his truck. He gave Rick a cheerful thumbs-up and headed toward Annabeth's.

Chapter Thirty-One

ANNABETH AND THEO were giving Chip a long overdue
bath. The sweet compliant dog, willing to endure almost anything his people asked of him, detested baths and would hide
under the bed if he got scent of dog soap, dog towels, or any
item related in any way to dog cleanliness. Theo devised a ruse
of playing ball in the backyard while Annabeth gathered supplies. It was almost cruel how excited Chip got when at the
end of their ball session Theo put on the dog's collar and
leash. His tail wagging madly at the prospect of yet another
fun adventure, he was crushed when Theo led him to the front
yard and the tub full of water. Chip looked at Theo with sad
eyes. Betrayed. But he wasn't a dog who would be disobedi-
ent, so he submitted to the humiliating discomfort of getting

wet, then bubbly, then rinsed and dry. Once free of the towel and given a treat for his cooperation, he tore all over the yard, diving into the grass and rolling from one end of the property to the other.

"Well, that didn't last long," said Theo, laughing.

"At least it's clean dirt now."

"And he does smell better."

After a few minutes Chip returned, having forgiven them. After lots of pats and praise they made good on the promise of a walk. Theo caught the leash and commanded Chip to heel. A bath and a walk coming one right after the other was a lot of excitement for the old dog, but he fell into a lively step at Theo's side, looking up at him every so often in gratitude and wonder. Annabeth, on Theo's other side, had to laugh at Chip's obvious glee.

"Is he smiling?" she asked.

"With his whole body," he replied. "Good boy, right Chip?"

"Thanks for helping. I can't hold him and bathe him at the same time. My mom and I used to do it together. Wow—I don't think Chip has had an official bath since last fall."

"I'm sure he's been rained on a time or two. He was okay."

They ambled along without talking. This time of day there was almost no car traffic and the three of them were able to saunter across the breadth of the road. Without a preset destination, they allowed Chip to investigate as many shrubs and mailbox posts as he wanted. The climbing sun had warmed the day enough that Annabeth took off her running jacket and tied it around her waist.

"So, what's on your schedule for the rest of the day?" Theo asked.

"Nothing special. What about you?"

"Same. Want to go to the farmer's market and get some stuff for lunch?"

"Sure. Any interest in getting in a run?"

"Yeah. Maybe later, though. It's already getting hot and I'm hungry."

Annabeth laughed. "Imagine that. Want to turn around?"

They made a wide circle at the next intersection and headed back in the direction they'd come.

"I can't believe the cicadas are already singing this early in the day. A sign of fall, my mom used to say."

"Not ready. No way."

"When does school start for you, anyway?"

"In three weeks, but I need to get back earlier for cross-country."

Annabeth's breath caught. "When is that?"

"I'm leaving at the end of next week."

She forced herself not to groan. "I guess the cicadas are right, then. For you, summer is almost over."

"What about you? What are you going to do this fall?"

"I haven't thought about it. Work for David, I guess, until I figure out what's next."

"So, you aren't going back to school?" he asked, surprised.

"I don't know. Maybe not. Or maybe not there." She shrugged. "I haven't thought it out."

"Not for me to say, but maybe you should think about it. Doesn't the college assume you are coming back?"

"Probably. I didn't officially drop out. My coach has been emailing me, asking me to rejoin the team, but I've been ignoring him."

"Why?"

"I quit the team. There will be new, faster girls than me. I might not even be on varsity anymore."

"I bet you would."

"Maybe. I don't know . . . it's just not calling my name, I guess."

He stopped and looked at her. "What is calling you, Annabeth?"

She paused and considered, then, "Um, nothing?"

He frowned. "Seriously, I think you might get kind of bored hanging around here, working at that landscape place. I mean, I know I would."

She bristled slightly. "Yes, I know you would. But you have a whole other life at school. Cross Country, Track, and friends and classes and all that. I assume you like it?"

He nodded.

"Yeah, so for you that's a good place to be, and here, not as much. It's different for me. I don't have all kinds of warm memories and good friends waiting for me. School is just another place to be alone. So, here or there, what difference does it make?"

He looked at her with sadness. "It shouldn't be like that. You didn't connect there because of what happened, I do get that. What about another school? Someplace where you could walk on the team and sort of start over?"

"No," she said with conviction. "I'm not up for a new adventure, if that's what you mean."

"No, just a fresh start."

"I've had plenty of fresh starts in the last few months. I'm not exactly longing for another one."

Why was he pestering her? She'd been able to avoid thinking about his leaving and she didn't want to start now. Theo had been the one good thing that had happened since last fall. Why couldn't they just enjoy the remaining days of summer?

He put his hands on her shoulders, turning her to face him. "I don't mean to be bossing you around. I just worry you might get down staying here, more or less, by yourself." He inhaled. "And, okay, so I have this other idea if you don't want to go back to your old school." He paused again. "Why don't you come to mine?"

"Ha! I'd never get in. My grades were awful last year."

"I think that's pretty understandable. I know our coach would put in a good word for you. We had a couple of girls quit and he's always looking for runners."

"I'm guessing he might be looking for runners who are *fast*?"

"Yes, of course, but you were fast in high school, and you've been getting faster all summer. You just got derailed last year."

"How do you know how fast I was in high school?"

He smiled a bit sheepishly. "Race results live forever on the Internet."

"That's weird. You looked at my race results?"

"Yeah. Does that bother you?"

"No. Yes, or, kind of. Why did you do that?"

"Don't deck me, but I wanted to talk to the coach about you and I wanted to have some proof that you were good, so I spied on you. Are you upset?"

"I don't know. It's public, but it makes me feel weird for some reason. Not quite the runner I once was, anyway."

"Annabeth, would you cut yourself some slack? I know those high school times are good enough to make our team. Would you at least let me talk to the coach about you?"

She was bowled over. Theo cared enough to look up her old times and try to convince his coach to recruit her? There is no way that coach would want her, but it touched her that he would go to this trouble.

"I don't know. He'd say, 'thanks, but no thanks.' Let me think about it."

"All right. You might be surprised by what he has to say. I'm going to call him when I get back."

"Hang on, I'm still not sure. But it is very sweet of you, Theo. I forgive you for spying on me."

"Let's not say spying. Building a case."

"Hmmm. Whatever."

They dropped off Chip and headed to the farmer's market where Annabeth banned all talk of coaches and colleges for the duration of the afternoon.

Chapter Thirty-Two

WHEN IT BECAME CLEAR that she needed more than just a long weekend in Connecticut, Ruth called Brian and asked for additional time to sort things out. He agreed without a moment's hesitation, telling her to take all the time she needed. Ruth permitted herself to accept his answer at face value. Then she and David turned their attention to restoring ordinariness to the Crawford household. She paid bills, made phone calls, and in general caught up with her Connecticut life. She begged off when David asked her to accompany him on another office hunting expedition and encouraged him to enlist Rick's help instead. Despite her vague misgivings, she also encouraged him to connect with Annabeth, who'd become impossible to reach.

"I just want to be sure she's okay. I tried to call her, too," she told David.

"You called her? Why?"

"Just to check in. I'm a little worried, like you are."

He frowned, displeased.

"No need for you to take this on, Ruth. It's probably over-kill, and you have plenty to do already."

Was he peeved at her? She paused before responding.

"Okay. But I would like to know she's coping. You still haven't spoken to her—right?"

"No."

"Who else would she turn to? Her boyfriend?"

"He's just her friend, but yeah, that Theo kid might know how she is. I don't remember his last name, though." He paused to think, then said, "Can't come up with it. I'll just go by her house again." He picked up his keys and walked with purpose toward the front door. "I'll let you know what I find out. No need for both of us to worry. Just put Annabeth out of your mind."

But that was impossible after David practically ran out the door. She wished she hadn't raised the subject of Annabeth at all.

ANNABETH KNEW she was hiding out, to some degree. She was doing research on Theo's college, his team, her high school friends' colleges, and their teams. She'd been home once when David came by but didn't answer the door. She needed to sort this stuff out without David—or Theo or anyone—telling her what she ought to think or do. It never occurred to her that David would be worried. He wasn't ex-pecting her to work with the trailer trashed, so she didn't even consider getting in touch with him. The work she was doing on her own behalf was important and, unusual for her, well-organized. Instead of going along with however events transpired, she was taking the time to figure out how she'd like them to transpire. That process turned out to be time-consuming and sometimes frustrating. But she was determined to come to a decision and then get moving. All her research left Annabeth more confused than ever, though. She had ruled out a couple of schools, but still hadn't felt the "aha" that her mother had taught her would indicate she'd come up with the correct solution to a problem. Mom, she thought, I need a little help here. Whisper in my ear, okay?

She walked the sunny backyard with Chip, cutting some hydrangea blossoms to take to Theo's house tonight. She was having dinner with his family and then, in theory at least, going to help him pack for his return to school. She liked his family but wasn't so keen on the packing. Annabeth didn't want to think of Theo's leaving or the conversation she knew he would start regarding what she was going to do next. For the moment, she welcomed a little bit more time alone. She put the flowers in water, then went through the house making a half-hearted attempt to organize the clutter that seemed to appear out of nowhere. Her random thoughts bumped into each other as she loaded the dishwasher, refilled Chip's water bowl, threw a giant stack of unopened mail into the recycling bin, and then took it out to the garage. She might regret that, but if it was important, she figured somebody would bother her about it later.

After making some limited progress with the tidying, she headed for her shower. Dismayed by the piles of clothes on her bedroom floor and lack of clean towels in her bathroom, she decided she couldn't face that mess either. Her parents' bathroom was pristine, she knew, undisturbed except for the cleaning Aunt Janet had given it a few weeks ago. She quickly shed her running clothes and added them to the shorts and T-shirts on the floor. One good thing about living by myself, she thought. No one to see me or my piles of laundry. She tossed a load into the washer and headed for her parents' bath, where there would be plenty of clean towels. Maybe in the shower she could sort her thoughts and make a final decision. She promised herself she'd clean her own bathroom tomorrow.

It was a sign of how lost in thought she was that entering her mother's perfectly kept sanctuary didn't cause her to go wobbly with grief. She turned on the shower and waited for the water to get hot, noticing all the details her mother had taken care to get right—the thick fluffy towels, the grapefruit-scented soap, the row of perfume bottles arranged on the vanity—objects that put her mother close at hand. Months after she was gone, Lydia was still caring for Annabeth by leaving her this lovely space to refresh her body and soul.

Annabeth stepped into the shower and relished the warm water that washed over her. She stood still and sighed in contentment for full minutes before she reached for her mom's luxurious shampoo and began to wash her hair. Her fragmented thoughts started to order themselves into comprehensible notions, so she stayed in the shower until the water grew cool. Then she stepped on the mat and wrapped herself in one of her mom's bath sheets and let the towel absorb the dripping water from her hair. While she hadn't reached a firm decision, she had come up with a plan. By now, the clothes she'd tossed in the washer were probably clean, so she stopped by the laundry room to put them in the dryer. She dropped the bath sheet in the washer, planning to add the collection of towels from her own bathroom after she dressed. Less burdened, she started down the hallway toward her own room. She almost giggled at herself. She hardly ever went around the house undressed because she didn't feel comfortable nude. But hey, there was a first time for everything. If she couldn't be naked when she was alone in her own house, she needed actual therapy.

She shook her towel-dried hair and lifted it with her fingers to the top of her head. The late summer breeze through the open windows felt wonderful. Toned after months of running, she was also happy in her body. It felt good to be young and healthy and clean. She smiled with pleasure, half-twirled in a circle, and turned the corner that led toward her bedroom. As she did, something in the hallway caught her eye. There was a man standing at the top of the stairs. Before she could scream or make a move, some remote corner of her mind recognized David Crawford, gazing at her. This can't be happening, she thought. She froze in fear and embarrassment, too upset to look at anything but the floor in front of her. She had nothing to cover herself. There was nowhere to hide. There was only her exposed self, David, and the wide empty hallway.

She heard his breathing, perceived the force of his attention focused like a laser on the woman standing before him. She ventured a peek at him and saw in a shocking instant that he was lost. David, his mouth slightly open, his face gone slack, was in thrall to her, and not because she was fragile and needy, but because she was lovely and fine. She'd never imagined she possessed this astonishing power. Experiencing it now amazed and emboldened her. She lifted her head and gazed back, unblinking, into his eyes.

"Oh, Annabeth," he moaned. He took a step toward her. She didn't back away.

Chapter Thirty-Three

RUTH SET THE LAST of several bags of groceries on the kitchen counter. Her timing was, as always with this task, impeccable. David was elsewhere, otherwise engaged. While she unpacked the first bag, the phone rang, caller ID showing it was Sarah. "Hey! I was going to call you as soon as I finished putting away the groceries. Are you still free this afternoon?"

"Of course. I've missed you. And Hannah's dying to see you."

"I can't wait to see you guys. Come over whenever you want."

"We'll be there in fifteen minutes. Can I pick anything up for you?"

Ruth laughed. "No, I bought every single thing there is to buy at Stop and Shop. Just come over."

She turned on the oven to preheat and unloaded the bags as quickly as she could. Then, she cut up a roll of slice-and-bake chocolate chip cookie dough and placed the pieces on a baking sheet. Hannah loved baking cookies, but making a batch from scratch with her was more of a flour festival than Ruth wanted to undertake this afternoon. Wearing an apron and eating the cookies warm from the oven was what counted as baking for Hannah, and today that was just fine with Ruth, too. It was also fine with Ruth, truth be told, that David wasn't home yet. He was not one to hang out with the girls in the kitchen. Ruth had missed Sarah and Hannah almost as much as she'd missed David. The frequency of their check-in texts had diminished when she went radio silent in China, and now, they needed to catch up. And sweet Hannah! It seemed forever since Ruth had held Hannah or seen her little round face.

"Knock, knock. We're here." Sarah called at the kitchen door.

"Aunt Ruthie!" Hannah burst into the room. She ran toward her with her arms upraised. Ruth picked her up and snuggled her. "I missed you, sweet girl."

Then, Hannah saw the cookie dough on the baking sheets. "Cookies! I want to help." She wriggled out of Ruth's arms.

"Put on your apron."

Hannah ran to the bottom drawer Ruth had dedicated to her niece. In it were a few cooking utensils, an over-loved Barbie, a box of crayons with a drawing tablet, and a child-sized apron, personalized with Hannah across the front. She pulled out the apron and had Sarah tie it in the back for her. Then she dragged her step stool from the corner of the kitchen and placed it next to the counter where the cookies were waiting.

"Shall we put them in the oven?" Ruth asked.

"Yes. I help you."

"Okay, hand me the trays and I'll slide them in. Be careful, all right?"

With powerful concentration and two hands, Hannah carefully lifted each tray and passed it to Ruth. Once they were placed in the oven, she let Hannah set the timer. "Now we just wait until they are done."

Hannah watched the cookies bake for all of thirty seconds before she hopped down and pulled Barbie from the drawer. While she and Barbie went on another adventure in the living room, Sarah and Ruth sat down at the kitchen table.

"She's grown a foot."

"I can't believe how much she's changed since she turned three. The baby is pretty much gone, and she is all little girl now. I'm having a blast with her. We have actual conversations."

Ruth smiled at her niece in the other room, babbling away to herself and Barbie. "I've missed her so much. And you. How are you feeling?" She glanced at Sarah's middle.

"Good, feeling good." Sarah smiled and moved right on. "How are you?"

"Good, actually. The work is interesting. My client seems to like me . . ."

"Imagine that."

"Ha! China was so crazy I can't even begin to tell you, and of course, San Francisco is gorgeous. I don't see as much of it as I'd like. Our offices have great views though."

"So, how long will you be out there?"

"I don't know. Sometimes I'm not sure why I'm even there at all because a lot of what I do I could do from here, but Brian, the boss, likes to be able to talk in person. He still travels all over the world to have one-on-one meetings. I guess he's kind of old school. I like him. He's a workaholic, but also a good guy. He expects a lot from all of us, but you know, it's the classic case of successful people expecting even more of themselves."

"I'm glad you're happy. I miss you, though."

"Come see me. You've never been, right?"

"No, never. I'd love to go. But *you* are my overnight babysitter. I don't know what I'd do with Hannah. She isn't quite old enough for a trip like that."

Ruth thought for a moment. "Do any of her preschool teachers ever do overnights?"

"I don't know. I never needed to know before. I'll ask Mark if he could manage it if we made it a weekend. But I'd like to stay longer than forty-eight hours."

Ruth checked the timer while they both pondered other possibilities.

"Hey," Sarah said, "What about Annabeth? The girl who helps David? She seems very sweet, and so cute. She's alone now, right? Maybe she would want the company."

"Maybe." Annabeth was very sweet. And if Sarah thought of her as a reliable babysitter . . . she'd been crazy to worry. "I don't know how much experience she has with kids, but she might be available. She's not working at the moment with the trailer in pieces and headed to a junkyard somewhere."

"Good grief! How is David?"

"He's okay. Mostly. It does seem to have knocked him for a loop, though."

"I would think. That man who did it must be a lunatic. Over landscaping?"

"I know. There was more going on with him than we

realized. He was under investigation for securities fraud, also losing a lot of money, I guess, but still . . . insane. I think he spent time in jail."

"You mean he's out now?"

"I don't know, but I'm guessing he has the means to make bail. I haven't heard."

"That's kind of scary. Do you think he'll come back?"

"To do what? He already wrecked everything."

The timer on the oven rang and Hannah came flying into the kitchen. "The cookies are done; the cookies are done! Let me help!"

"I'll just take them out of the oven, honey. You can help me put them on the plate when they cool down a little bit."

"Why don't we get some milk, Hannah, while we wait?" Sarah said.

Together they poured milk into three glasses. Hannah climbed into one of the chairs and sat watching the cookies across the room. "I think they are cool now," she said.

"Let's see." Ruth tested one, even though she knew it was still hot. "Not quite. We have to wait a little bit longer, so we don't get burned." Hannah's legs swung back and forth, and she began singing an invented song about bunnies . . . or something. Sarah and Ruth tried not to laugh out loud.

Ah, yes, this! thought Ruth. Treasure this . . . the sound of Hannah's voice, the smell of these cookies, sunlight streaming through the window, cold white milk in these untouched glasses . . . this room, right now, is perfect and holy. Thank you, God.

Chapter Thirty-Four

RUTH SPENT the rest of the afternoon taking care of other household things David lacked the time and inclination to address. She put the pantry and fridge back in order and prepped a three-course, home-cooked dinner. With her to-do list completed by six, she took a shower, poured herself a glass of wine, and went out to the patio to wait for David. When he hadn't arrived by seven, she texted him: "How's it going? There is real food in the house. What time do you think you'll be home?"

She received no reply. At seven forty-five, she decided to start cooking so it wouldn't be too late when they sat down to eat. She called and left him a voicemail at eight-thirty and then started to worry. It's been dark for a while, she thought. Where on earth is he? She'd lost her appetite by nine.

She fixed David a plate and put it in the microwave, then packed the rest of the dinner into plastic containers and put them in the refrigerator. She poured herself another glass of wine and went to her window seat to watch for his headlights. "Don't think it, don't think it," she told herself. Don't think what? That he'd been in an accident? That Sid had come back? That something unimaginable had happened? He wasn't home at midnight or two a.m., and Ruth's panic escalated. She hoped it was ridiculous, but she called the hospital to see if he'd been admitted. No one by that name. As the sun rose, she decided it was not unreasonable to go to the site of the old trailer. Heart thumping, she tore down the empty road to find nothing. No truck, no crew, nothing at all. She drove back home detouring by the places she thought he could be—the diner in town, the parking lot of the reservoir where they hiked—nothing. She would not drive by Annabeth's. He couldn't possibly be there.

She kept texting and calling him as the day wore on, but he still didn't respond. Ruth found Rick's number and called him. Not wanting to worry him or embarrass herself, she casually asked if David was free to talk.

"He's not with us," Rick said. "I haven't seen him today, but I wasn't expecting to. If he stops by, I'll tell him you called."

"Thanks. His phone is probably turned off. Nothing urgent. I'll talk to him later."

She spent the day calling his cell and driving through town and pacing and praying. She checked the hospital again. Nothing, thank goodness. Feeling ill by now, she got back in the car and this time forced herself to drive by Annabeth's. His truck wasn't there, as she'd assured herself it wouldn't be. At the trailer site, the grower's lot—no sign of him. She decided that if he wasn't home by ten that night, she would call the police. By then it would have been more than twenty-four hours since she'd seen him, and she'd be able to file a missing persons' report, God forbid. How on earth was this happening?

The stranger who shuffled home after dark that night was some shadow of David, almost unrecognizable. He resembled David but had gone completely blank. He just shook his head and refused to say a word when Ruth ran to greet him. She put her hand on his shoulder and asked, "Are you all right, honey?"

He grabbed her hand, squeezed it hard, and walked away.

"I don't feel well," he said as he left the room. "I'll sleep in the guest room tonight."

"What kind of not feeling well? Should I call the doctor? Do you need some medicine?" She followed him down the hall.

"No doctor, no medicine. Just, let it be Ruth."

He kept walking and went into the guest room, locking the door. She wanted to follow him, pound on the door until he opened it, but his hollowed-out demeanor frightened her. Okay, okay, leave him alone. He'll be better tomorrow, and we'll sort this out.

Of course it was another night of no sleep for Ruth. She was up and waiting when he appeared in the kitchen the next morning.

"David, I am so worried about you. What happened? Where were you? Are you hurt?"

His eyes looked as if he hadn't slept either. He shuffled around the room without looking at her.

"No, not really. Ruth, it's so hard to explain." He gripped the edge of the countertop, keeping his back to her. "I've driven all the way to Essex trying to figure it out, but I can't even explain it to myself, let alone to you, so please, don't keep asking me."

"What? I've got to ask you. This is way too mysterious for me."

"It is for me too. When I know, I promise I will tell you. But for now, I . . . I need to be alone to think and—get things right." He looked out the window and then back at the floor. "You probably should go on back to California. I'm so embarrassed to be . . . like this, whatever this is."

"No. What a terrible idea. We do this together."

Ruth came out of her chair and stood next to him. She tried to put her arm around him, but he stepped outside of her embrace. She fought back the sudden urge to vomit in the sink.

"No, this isn't something we can do together. I have to handle this by myself."

"Handle what? David, you aren't making sense."

She stepped into his line of vision. She had to make him see her, his Ruthie, the person he'd loved for years. "I'm not leaving."

He ran his hands through his disheveled hair.

"Okay, then I'll find someplace to go, and you can stay here. But we can't be in the same house right now."

Now she was crying. "No! I don't understand. You're scaring me. You can't have thought this through!"

"Thought it through? No, of course I haven't thought it through. I'm trying to tell you I'm barely thinking at all! I don't know if this is the only solution or completely crazy, but I can't stand you looking at me like, like, like I'm a mental patient or a total loser. I can't stand what I see in your eyes. Your *empathy*, your, your perfectly perfect perfection is only making it worse!"

She shrank back in wounded silence. Is this how he thought of her? For how long? Had he been secretly hating her for years? That wasn't possible. He couldn't have lied so many times telling her he loved her. He couldn't have held her and laughed with her and made love to her so many times secretly detesting her. Their whole life together couldn't have been a sham. She would have known.

"You didn't mean that. I know you."

"I'm sorry," he said. "I don't know what I mean. But—but that's why we have to be apart. I can't be fair to you right now, Ruth, and if I'm awful to you, I'll just prove to both of us what a horrible person I am for doing, or not doing, whatever the hell this is." He stopped, closed his eyes. "Please. Please go back to California until I get it together. For me. For us."

AND SO, SHE DID. No part of Ruth's mind could follow a path from Point A (life before Sid Day) to Point B (this expulsion). That a single traumatic event would cause him to have a breakdown? David? Lots of people endured terrible crises without deciding to wreck their lives, most of them weaker and less grounded than David. What if he liked having her gone? What if he would be relieved because he'd stopped loving her before any of this? She was ill at the thought. Maybe he'll come to his senses. Maybe leaving him alone is the right thing to do. But then again, the person making that suggestion is talking like a lunatic. Her instincts told her to stay, but in the end her pride forced her out the door.

As her plane took off, Ruth prayed for guidance, for some reason to hope. David was wrong about one thing: she would never think he was a loser. She knew she'd be the one losing someone wonderful and something precious if they didn't get this thing figured out. She could leave his side for a little while, but no way was she giving up on her life with him, a life she loved as much as she loved David himself. The flight went on forever. Her mind and stomach churning, she couldn't eat or rest. She had no interest in trying to spot Brian's building as the plane circled the city. Marin County in the distance held little charm for her today. She thought of Maeve and her beautiful house and kind ways. Was this how it was for her when she and Brian broke up? No, Maeve was the one who left Brian, so she'd endured a different kind of torture. And then survived, and surmounted it, and was now thriving, or at least seemed to be. But Maeve's story will not be my story. David and I are staying together. Period.

When the plane landed, she collected her bags and revived her phone. Right on cue, it began to fill with texts from Brian, Bernard, Sarah. Nothing from David. It was her habit to text him the descending plane emoji when she landed, but she hesitated about whether to do so now. "Don't expect a response and you can handle it," she told herself, then decided she couldn't risk it and dropped the phone into her tote. The driver Bernard had booked was waiting for her. Re-entry begins, she thought. Work, please fill my brain.

Chapter Thirty-Five

ANNABETH PUT the last suitcase in the trunk of her car and called for Chip. He trotted over as quickly as his ancient legs would carry him and climbed into the back seat, panting with anticipation. "You do love a ride, don't you, buddy? I'm sorry we haven't been doing that much lately, but that's about to change."

She opened the driver's door and gazed back at her parents' house. Never hers, nor full of fond memories as a childhood home would be, the house didn't have time to acquire a place in her heart before it became a place of sadness and then of a single earth-shattering event. No question that under different circumstances she could have loved this place as much as her parents did, but not now. And because not now, not ever. Her father's office untouched, her mother's books still on the shelves, the house remained more of a sorting project than a home. "I can't love you," she told the house aloud. Sad-eyed windows stared back at her. "Someone else will, though. You'll be okay."

With that she got in, started the engine, and pointed the car toward the street. "And we're heading out, Chip." The dog looked at her from the backseat, then sighed and lay down. In a few minutes they were in front of Theo's house where his mother was working in the garden.

"Hi, Mrs. Comstock."

"Hello, Annabeth. What a pleasant surprise. I haven't seen you in a while. Are you over your flu?"

"Yes, thank you."

Nancy rose from her gardening cushion and removed her gloves. The beds where she'd been working looked perfect to Annabeth, full of blooms and, now that she knew how to recognize some of them, absent of the weeds that filled the beds at her own house.

"Oh good. Summer's almost over. You must be getting ready to go back to school—packing, planning, all those fun things."

"Probably not so much as I should be."

"Theo's been packing all morning, but he'll be happy for such a wonderful interruption." She smiled at Annabeth. "Why don't we go get him?"

She smiled back and asked, "Do you mind if I put my dog in your backyard? It's fenced, right? He'll get too hot in the car. I had to bring him with me today—I hope that's okay?"

"Of course. He can come in the house if you'd like." She walked over to Annabeth's car. "Hello there, fellow!" She scratched the dog behind his ears, causing Chip to thwack the car seat with his exuberant tail. "We always used to have dogs but are in between pets right now. Molly is begging for a Great Dane. Can you imagine? Somehow, I can't. So, we're negotiating. Let's bring him in. What's his name?"

"Chip."

Annabeth got him out of the car, and they all went inside. Mrs. Comstock proclaimed Chip a darling old thing and called Theo to come downstairs for a visitor, or two. He bounded down the stairs and after hesitating for a moment, burst into a big grin.

"Hey! I thought we were running later—did I mess up?"

"No, I'm not ready to run now either. But—do you want to take a walk?"

"Sure. Be back soon, Mom. Chip, good to see you, too, buddy."

Outside the door, he put his arm around Annabeth's shoulders and squeezed them. "I've missed you. Been kinda worried about you. You feeling better?"

"Better. Didn't mean to worry you. I just wasn't feeling great. But, yeah, I'm better now."

They walked along the road until it ended on a narrow path next to an old stone wall. The path continued for several hundred feet and then opened onto a meadow that someone mowed but never seemed to use. Once there, he grabbed her hand and pulled her toward him. He held her tightly, then bent to kiss her. She turned so that he kissed her cheek.

"Uh-oh," he said. "What's wrong? Are you contagious or something?" He grinned, joking.

"Ha. No, I don't think so. I just need to talk to you."

His face fell. "That sounds way worse than being contagious."

"I'm going away for a bit. I just can't stay here. It isn't you or anything about us, but I have to go back to Kansas and handle some stuff."

"What kind of stuff? School stuff? Aunt Janet stuff?"

She bent down to pluck a flower and avoid meeting his eyes and the look of dismay she'd caught on his face. He waited for her to straighten, but instead of stopping to face him, she kept walking. In two long steps, he caught up with her.

"What stuff?" he asked again.

"Stuff . . . I can't do here. I know that's pretty vague and kind of dramatic, but I have to go." She threw up her hands. "It's impossible to explain, so I guess you have to just trust me. As it is, you're leaving in a few days and I should be figuring out school, so we wouldn't be seeing each other anyway. I hope you don't think I'm trying to be all mysterious, but I'm driving to Kansas with Chip today and I just couldn't leave without seeing you."

"You're driving to Kansas by yourself?"

"No, with Chip."

He gave her a look. "Okay, with no other humans, just your dog?"

"Yeah, we did it already in the other direction. Chip is great company, and he will keep away any bad guys." She thought a moment. "Strangers. He loves me."

"Smart dog. Me, too."

Her heart flipped. He'd never said that before. Every fiber of her being wanted to say, "Me too. I love you, too." A week ago, she would have. Now she couldn't possibly make that declaration. If she loved Theo, as she thought she did, how could she have let what happened with David transpire? All she could do was to retake his hand and hope that gesture conveyed her affection.

He went on in a more urgent tone. "Okay, I've got an idea. Why don't you give me a day to get my school stuff together and send it on and I'll come with you. I could fly back before cross-country starts. It would be a blast to take a road trip together."

She smiled at him. "That is tempting. But I need to do this alone, and anyway—I'm going to stay with Aunt Janet when I get there, so . . ."

"Why are you doing that?"

"It's free, and some of the things I have to take care of involve her, so that's what we decided. Plus, Chip loves her, and she loves him. She's nice to him."

"Not always so nice to you." He looked at her skeptically.

"She and I have been talking more and I'm not as scared of her as I used to be. She's not the easiest person on Earth to be around, but she is okay if she has a job to do. I'll be all right. And I don't think I'll be there too long."

Theo picked up a stick and took a thwack at some weeds. "I can't say this news is exactly making my day. It seems kind of sudden."

"Yeah, well, it kind of is."

"Okay, don't shoot me, but I have something else I wanted to tell you, too. I was going to tell you after our run." He took in a deep breath. "So, you know I mentioned I would get in touch with my coach about you?"

Her eyes widened. "Yes. And remember how I said, that was nice of you, but I hadn't decided? And that there was no way that was going to work?"

He was so excited to share his news he stepped in her path and jogged backward to look at her while he talked. "Yeah, I remember that, but I figured I'd just see if he thought there would be any chance for a spot for you on the girls' team. He looked up your old times and said he thought there probably was. I told him I'd been running with you and that I thought you'd fit right in. He can blue card your application and help you transfer at semester, if you want to come."

She looked into his happy, eager face and for a moment almost allowed herself to believe the plan would work. It sounded hopeful, something to look forward to. But no, she couldn't begin a new life until she dealt with the consequences of the old one.

"No, no way. I'd never get in. My application would just embarrass both of us."

"Your high school grades were good enough to get into your old school. You could explain what happened and you know, start over. At a new place. And we'd be there together. It'd be great. Everyone will love you and you would like my friends." He grinned. "They are all just like me."

Despite her dismay, she laughed. "That supposed to entice me? Oh, Theo. I know you mean well, but the timing isn't right and, honestly, I don't even know if I ever want to go back to school."

He looked at her and cocked his head to one side, his smile sliding from his face. "You are kind of a hard person to figure out sometimes. I thought you'd be annoyed for a minute and then excited."

"I'm going to Kansas."

"But will you think about this?"

"Yes, sure, I will think about it. It's just that I've resolved to do this trip and stick with a decision that *I've* made, not do what somebody tells me I want or should want or must do or must feel." Her voice caught and tears started to form. She angrily swept them away. "Arghh! I'm not crying today."

They stood in silence. "You are such a good guy, Theo. I like you and— I might even love you, too," she allowed. "But I am going to Kansas today."

She turned around and started back the way they'd come. They walked the whole way without speaking. When they reached his house, they mimicked a casual goodbye in front of his mother who delivered a treat-filled Chip back to Annabeth. She asked Theo to walk her to the car. He helped Chip get in, then faced her.

"I'm sorry if I screwed this up. You know I care a lot about you."

She put her hand on his chest. "If anybody screwed things up, it's me. You are so great. Someday I hope to be able to explain it to you. Do you trust me?"

"I guess I have to."

She felt her whole body sag.

"Annabeth, I do," he said. "I do."

She kept her tears at bay as she got back in her car and kissed Theo goodbye through the open window. When she made the turn that took her off his street, she could hold them back any longer and broke into sobs so intense they forced her to stop the car. She cried off and on as she drove for miles without even seeing her surroundings, only attending to the route when her unexpectedly useful phone sang out directions. Chip dozed in the back seat as they moved west through the heavy traffic on the interstate. The suburban towns blended one into the next, all of them looking more or less the same until, after a while, there began to be open space between them. The suburbs became actual towns with some measure of distinction and Annabeth started to take note of their features, wondering if she could live in one of them. Could I just stop here, get some kind of job, maybe change my name, like a heroine in a novel? A part of her was very tempted to do exactly that, but the larger part, the part that was impelling her forward toward deeper healing, shook off her romantic childishness. "Been a baby long enough. Just keep going. There are sane people waiting for you in Kansas." Aunt Janet? Sane? "We're going to stay with Aunt Janet, Chip. Can you believe that?" Chip wagged his tail once. "I guess you're not feeling it yet, buddy. I guess I'm not quite feeling it either. We'll have to stick together."

Aunt Janet had been calling her from time to time all summer, but of course Annabeth rarely picked up the phone or called her aunt back. She believed Janet's bossy disapproval was the last thing she needed and knew it was the last thing she wanted. But the day after David's appearance, Aunt Janet called again, and Annabeth answered.

"My God, you're alive!" Janet shouted into the phone. "I thought about calling the FBI, but then I thought about what a bunch of crooks they are, so I didn't. Where on Earth have you been?"

"Right here, just not answering my phone, I guess," she answered blandly. "You know me."

"I suppose I do. But you know, Miss Just-Who-I-Am, that's rather rude. And if your mother were still alive, she'd no doubt be telling you that. More like your father in that regard. He did the same thing."

Annabeth was pleased to hear that. "He did? I never noticed."

"Of course you didn't." She paused. "Did you and your very helpful *landscape designer* friend get any of that mess sorted out?"

She hesitated only briefly before she somehow answered in a steady voice, "No, we didn't make much progress on that."

"Just as I suspected. Eager to be the hero, that one, but not the most reliable was my guess."

"I think you might be right about that."

When Janet didn't respond, Annabeth realized that being told she was right, by Annabeth no less, may have shocked Aunt Janet into momentary silence.

"So. Then what are you going to do about getting that place sorted out? I offered before and I'll offer again right now to come out there and finish the job."

"Okay, sure, that's fine."

Again, Aunt Janet was shocked into silence. "So, when should we do this? When does school start for you?"

"I don't know."

"Good grief, it's August. Don't you think you ought to find out? Do I need to do that too?" Janet was back in form.

"Aunt Janet, the truth is, I am not sure if or when I am going back to school. I am not sure what's next for me. I'm just a little, uh, unsettled right now. I know you are not ever like that, but as you so often say, sometimes my dad was. I guess I'm more like him than I am like my mom, or you. I'm sorry. I know it's driving you crazy, but . . ."

"It's Just-Who-I-Am," Janet said.

"Annoying little pain, aren't I?"

"Yes. Yes, you most definitely are. But you're my niece, and I know I can be kind of an annoying little pain myself, so . . ."

". . . big pain." Annabeth interrupted.

"Ha! Right then. Okay, big pain, but we are family and that's just how that works. I can be there tomorrow."

Annabeth looked around the room where she was sitting and said slowly, deciding in that moment, "No. I want to get out of here. Can I come to you instead?"

"Of course. But we can't do that cleaning out from here, you know."

"I know. We can do that anytime. I just want to take a trip. Is that okay?"

"Yes, you know it is."

"Do you still have tomatoes?"

"Yes! What kind of a gardener do you think I am? Oh—*Mr. Landscaper's* tomatoes not doing so well, are they?"

"I have no idea. I just remember eating tomatoes still warm from the sun in your backyard and I hope we can do that again."

Janet paused, then said, "We can."

Annabeth was remembering a summer when she was about eight years old. Her parents were away at a conference, and she was staying with Aunt Janet, who was just as bossy and scary back then. Her house wasn't stocked with many toys, so Annabeth spent her time reading or helping in the garden. Janet wasn't about to let even a kid get by on make-work garden projects. Annabeth had to weed and water and rake and mulch. It seemed like drudgery until the day Janet pointed out that the tomatoes were ripe enough to pick. Together they chose the reddest of the bunch and sat down on the back porch with the fruit in a basket between them. Janet told her to choose the best one and eat it like an apple. She can still remember the warmth of that tomato in her hand, the sweet taste of it and the juice running down her chin. That specific moment defined the summer for her. She wonders if Janet remembers it, too.

"Annabeth?"

"Yes, Aunt Janet?"

"Take your blasted phone. And get a car charger. And answer the damn thing now and then."

"I will! Okay, gonna pack now. See you soon, Aunt Janet."

"Do not go silent on me."

"No, I won't. I promise. I'll see you in a few days."

"Goodnight, Knucklehead."

"Goodnight."

ANNABETH GLANCED in the rearview mirror at Chip. Going back to Kansas, despite how it might look to an outsider, was not some safe return to the nest. She had no home there anymore, her friends were gone, and Aunt Janet's tongue would be as sharp as ever. She might regret this. Annabeth expected to wonder forever about the encounter with David. Had her subconscious brought it on? Had she somehow conveyed a message she didn't quite intend? Or, even worse, had she wanted something she couldn't admit she desired? The power she felt that day came as such a shock. It terrified her to remember again how it felt. All she had to do was be young and pretty and present. Have other women always known they had this weapon? So potent, so certain, it was a power that proved to be as irresistible to her as her availability was to him. But the after-effect was awful, sickening. She avoided meeting her own eyes in the rearview mirror. Thinking now about what she allowed to happen filled her with shame. In an instant she'd forgotten everything her mother taught her to cherish—her value as a woman apart from sex, the need to set and hold moral standards, the obligation to consider the effect of her actions on others. It was hideous, the impulse that threw all that aside to please, no, to control a man, and it arose not from passion or even attraction, but instead from curiosity: what would happen . . . if she just let it? Well, now she knew. It was way too easy to toss a bomb in somebody else's life. She shuddered and shook her head to erase the images of that day. But there was no way to erase what had happened. Somehow, she had to put this whole mess in the past, stop churning in place, and move forward into a lie where this was only a part of who she was and the event that defined her.

In time she will feel that she has mostly succeeded in this goal, but now and then, when she least expects it, some fragment of that summer will catch her unaware and hit her like a wave. She will smell salt air or hear a song from that season and think, oh my god, who was that girl? How could she let this thing happen? Why didn't she say no the moment he stepped toward her? Or a moment later, or the moment after that? She will try to pinpoint the instant when she could have prevented the depth of the shame she feels now.

It will take time, but one day she will be able to tell herself that she was human after all, that desire was complicated, that the current between David and herself couldn't be so easily defined. One day she will be ablet to answer without regret, "It was you, Annabeth, a grieving orphan, searching for the parents she'd lost, longing to be held. It was you, Annabeth, thrilled to be seen as a grown woman in a man's eyes, even as that woman was making a mistake.

Each time she returns to this question, the answer will become a little clearer, slowing her to see a little better who she'd needed to be then and who she has become, a girl moving ever closer to forgiveness.

Chapter Thirty-Six

DAVID DROVE to the old trailer site, where he knew Rick and the crew were doing busy work because he had left them no clear instructions. He found them washing trucks, sharpening tools, and tidying the yard where the equipment was stored. The scene felt familiar, and after the turmoil of the past few days, its normalcy was welcome. This, he knew how to do. This, in fact, he did very well.

"Hey Boss," Rick called. "Good to see you."

"Hey Rick." He left his turmoil in the truck and joined the guys, thanking them for getting on top of the maintenance work, no one's favorite part of the job. "Sorry I kind of left you hanging. I've been dealing with insurance people, the police, it's been a nightmare."

"That's okay. We just got to it. What's up next? Everything here is pretty much ready to go."

"Yeah, I see that. We don't have a next thing ready to go, unfortunately. I was in the middle of finalizing plans for a couple of small jobs when Sid happened. I haven't finished them yet."

Rick looked crestfallen. "We can help. I can't draw pretty pictures like you can, but I know the green stuff pretty well. How far along are you? Can we talk about plant material yet?"

"To be honest, I don't remember, and I can't find the old plans. I am not sure they were rescued from the mess. I have a terrible feeling I'm back to square one on both of those designs."

Rick looked at the ground and shifted his weight. "Okay. Then, maybe you and I should go back and do site visits, take measurements and start over."

"I guess so. I've been all wrapped up in this other stuff— just not exactly moving in a straight line. Maybe I needed you to remind me to get my ass in gear."

Rick grinned back at him and said, "All right. These trucks are way too clean at the moment. Let's get 'em dirty."

While David's inner enthusiasm was not quite as heartfelt as his words implied, he was glad for some direction. It was a fresh kick in his gut that Sid's rampage had destroyed these plans, too, leaving David no choice but to start over. With so few people commissioning landscape projects these days and so many landscapers hungry for work, he'd lose these clients if he didn't get moving. And he did want to get moving, didn't he? What else could possibly both distract and settle him?

His famed (according to Ruth, anyway) talent for compartmentalizing kicked in and off he and Rick went, first to one location, then the next, taking photos, measurements, and re-familiarizing themselves with both settings. A few hours later, they returned to Rick's truck. The guys had gone home.

"Okay, boss, so you gonna draw tonight? I can start on the materials list tomorrow if you want."

"Um, not sure I can finish both plans tonight. I'll have to see how it goes. I think I have what I need from the sites, but I still haven't found the case with my drafting tools. I guess that's gone."

"I'll make a run." Rick pulled out his phone, ready to create a list. "What else?"

"My notes—which I'm guessing are gone, too." David thought for a minute. "Maybe Annabeth had already scanned the designs and has them on her laptop?"

Rick made a face. "Nah. She didn't do that. That's a dead end."

"Probably, but I should check. I could run over there and ask her—might save you a trip."

"I don't think she did that." Rick paused, and then said, "But we can call her right now and save *you* the trip."

"No, nope. You know she never answers her phone."

"It's after seven, Boss. She's a kid—probably out somewhere. Maybe with her boyfriend."

"People keep calling him her boyfriend, but he's not, he's just a friend." David was indignant at the suggestion.

"Okay, whatever, but she doesn't have the plans, I'd bet my truck. I'll make a supply run, and you go home and start thinking. In the morning, we can probably get a lot done."

They spent a few minutes completing a list of the necessary supplies. When they'd finished, David thanked Rick and said, "I think that's it. Just to be sure, though, I think I'll run the list by Annabeth and let you know if we forgot anything."

Rick gave David a searching look, then said, "We didn't

forget anything. And Annabeth wouldn't know anyway. You go home and start planning." He waited a minute before adding, "You know, the guys and I—and you, too—need the work. Let's not lose these jobs."

Although David was taken aback by the boldest statement Rick had ever made, he just said, "Yeah. You're right. We won't lose 'em."

BUT JUST TO BE SURE, David made another run past Annabeth's house. Rick was probably right, she wouldn't have anything at home, but he told himself it was worth checking.

He drove past her dark house, then turned around and pulled into the driveway. Her car was gone, but he approached the front door anyway. No answer. Maybe try the back door. But no, the porch was empty, and no one responded to his knock on that door either. He tried the handle, which he hadn't expected to be locked. He needed to talk to her, about so many things. Sighing, frustrated, he returned to his truck. As he engaged the ignition, he saw someone walking up the driveway carrying a flashlight. David shut off the truck and got out.

"Hi," he said, "Can I help you?"

"No, I don't think so," a woman's voice replied. "Can I help you?"

"Ah, no, I don't think so. I was looking for Annabeth, but I guess I missed her."

The woman had reached him by now and put out her hand. "I'm Cindy, Annabeth's next-door neighbor. I don't believe we've met?"

David shook her hand. "I'm David Crawford. I know Annabeth from work. Actually, she works for me."

"I heard about what happened. Horrible."

"Yeah, it is. We're trying to get things put back together now. I was going to ask Annabeth about some papers we lost in the ruckus."

The woman looked at him quizzically. "I may have misunderstood, but she asked me to bring in her mail. She said she'd be gone for a while and the hold didn't start until Monday." Cindy laughed. "She was very proud that she'd remembered to stop the mail. I guess that's a new thing for her. Such a sweet girl."

"Yes, she's great. I didn't know she was going away?"

"Huh. Maybe she left a message you didn't get? I'd think if she remembered to stop the mail, she'd remember to tell you. But you know kids—it seems to take a long time for them to tick all the boxes. At least it did mine."

"She probably did. I'll check it out."

He looked toward the house. "Or maybe she left a note inside. Want me to take the mail in for you?"

A tiny frown furrowed her brow. "No, thanks. I've got it." Then, with finality, "It was nice to meet you, Mr. Crawford. Have a lovely evening."

She made no move toward the house. David raised his hand in an awkward goodbye. "Yes, nice to meet you, too," he said. He walked back to his truck. She waited in the driveway and watched him leave.

David drove home in a state of confused annoyance. Where the heck was that girl? She'd said nothing about going anywhere. She never went anywhere. After the last time they were together, he couldn't imagine she would just leave, no communication at all. Seeing his own dark house was a fresh reminder that Ruth was also gone. He dreaded going inside the empty house, but it was his own fault it was empty, so he climbed out of the truck and trudged into the kitchen. He switched on some lights, opened the fridge, and pulled out some leftovers from the last dinner Ruth cooked. He popped them in the microwave and grabbed a beer. Looking around, he noticed that Ruth hadn't tidied the kitchen before she left. "How did things get this screwed up?" When dinner was warm, he sat down and pulled out his phone. No calls or texts from either Ruth or Annabeth. Hesitating, he called Annabeth's number and hoped against hope she might pick up. He hung up when the voicemail kicked in. How could she just disappear without a word? Ten minutes later he tried her phone again. He paced and drank more beer. Where was she? He forgot all about landscape plans, Rick, the crew, even Ruth. He had no space to think about anything but absent Annabeth.

Chapter Thirty-Seven

RUTH ENTERED the office to a chorus of greetings. "Hey, welcome back!" "Glad you're back!" "It's Ruth!"

"I see you managed to locate the car and driver without too much trouble," Bernard said.

"I did. Thank you, Bernard. I very much appreciated them. Once again, I have to ask: What would I do without you?"

"Once again, I have to reply: I have no idea." But he grinned at her and gestured toward the conference room. "Still early in the day here in God's country, Ms. Connecticut."

"How wonderful," she answered in a monotone. "Might there still be coffee hot somewhere?"

"Your wish is my command," said Bernard, as he left to get her a cup.

Ruth had prepared herself for a struggle not to let any of them see her inner turmoil, but her mood upon arriving at the office was far better than she'd expected. She felt welcome. When did that happen? She had grown to like it here, to like the people here. This modern, glistening tower, so different from her cozy house, had somehow become warm and familiar, a transformation she would never have predicted.

When she opened the door to the conference room, Brian gave her a broad smile. "Ruth, how was your trip home?"

She offered a bland, "Fine, thanks," in response.

He gave her a brief questioning look, then came forward and took the heavy briefcase from her. He put it next to an empty chair beside his own. "Have a seat. We were just sharing some unexpected good news." He nodded to one of the young men at the table. "Malcolm, you want to tell them the latest?"

Malcolm eagerly told the group that the proposed purchase of a large Connecticut property that Ruth and Malcolm had been working on was now officially executed at a better price than they'd expected. Brian nodded around the table at each of them in turn, smiling and giving everyone the thumbs up.

"You guys did a terrific job. Kudos and thanks."

Ruth had worked on the wording of that contract, but hadn't given it a thought the past few days. It was Malcolm who'd done the hard bargaining. But when she attempted to deflect the credit to him, Brian was having none of it. "It's the team's success. Everyone is equally important and that's good for the whole firm."

After a couple more minutes of celebration he said, "That's great, everyone. Now, if you'll excuse me, I'm due on a conference call in five. Ruth, I'll need you on this one, too. In my office."

The mini party broke up and Ruth spent the next several hours racing from one conversation to another without a moment to take a breather, or barely even a bathroom break. When the day wound down, she was spent. What a schizophrenic day, she thought as she gathered her things to head back to her hotel.

Brian popped his head into her office. "What a day, huh?"

"It was pretty crazy. I'm shot." She began walking toward the elevator with him.

"Thanks for the work today. It's good to have you back—not the same around here without you. Everyone noticed."

"I missed all of you, too."

"You did?"

"Yes, I didn't realize how much until I got back here."

"I'm glad. On another note—I hope everything went better than just 'fine' at home?"

"Thank you, Brian. Ummm. Things at home are a little tricky right now. A wild story, getting wilder."

"Yeah? In what way?" The elevator doors opened, and he said, "I'll ride down with you."

The doors closed. "So, tricky how?" he asked.

"Not really talk-it-over-with-the-client kind of tricky . . ."

". . . friend."

"Yes, okay . . . if it were, you'd definitely be the client-friend I'd confide in. I'll just say that the encounter my husband had with that crazy man seems to have thrown him so off-kilter that he's almost another person. I am not trained in the ways of trauma, but if it can do this to David—the most grounded guy ever—it's a miracle anyone else gets through it at all. I'm totally flummoxed about why. I'm pretty sure you can't un-flummox me, Brian, much as I'd love for you to do that."

He waited for her to say more. Ruth was tempted to con-fide in him. His expression conveyed sincere concern and she knew he was capable of keeping a confidence. But this was a boundary she wouldn't cross; the topic was too personal and too fraught. She was also tempted to hear what a man might have to say about David's irrational behavior, especially some-one as smart and worldly as Brian. It took real effort on her part to resist unloading the whole thing on him.

When after several floors she didn't speak, he said, "I've been spared that particular kind of trauma, thank God, but I do know a little bit about how events can capsize a stable guy. I went wobbly after the divorce. I guess getting a divorce you don't want is a kind of trauma? I was off my game for quite a while after it finally sunk in that I couldn't get Maeve to change her mind."

"It must have been awful." Ruth's stomach dropped at the sudden mention of the D-word. She and David were not in di-vorce territory by any means. She shuddered as she dispelled the thought. Then she put her hand on Brian's arm and said, "It's a kind offer, and I appreciate it, but I can't imagine what you could do. Thanks for caring, though. It means a lot."

The doors opened and they walked through the lobby to-gether. At the exit to the building he said, "I hope things get sorted out, Ruthie."

"They will. I just have to trust that they will." She pointed toward the sky. "You know, turn it over like we are told to do."

"Yes. Why do we always wait to do that until all else fails?"

"Slow learners, I guess."

They went their separate ways. The exhausting day, a meal

of room service pasta, and too much of a bottle of red wine worked their soporific ways on Ruth. Although she wouldn't have predicted she'd sleep for five minutes, she fell asleep fully clothed on a still-made bed, her face unwashed, her phone at the bottom of her bag.

SHE AWAKENED to the morning gray, for a moment confused by her surroundings. The blackout of the night began to lift, however, and the reasons for her current state of disarray came rushing toward her. She groaned and reached for a pillow to cover her face. A moment later she willed herself upright and rummaged in her purse for her phone, which was out of power. She managed not to chuck the useless thing in the trash and instead found the charger and plugged it in. Then she headed to the bathroom where a shower, toothbrush, and healthy layer of concealer made her feel another day was, in fact, possible. She dressed and went to the lobby for the coffee she knew she'd find there, then hopped into a taxi and went to the office.

Bernard raised his eyebrows when he saw her. "Looks like I'm a day late to buy that Revlon stock."

"Ha ha," Ruth replied. "I'm hoping it's your turn to make coffee this morning."

"It isn't, as you well know. But because I am an exemplary human being, I will jump the queue and spare both of us your feeble efforts."

"You are a dream come true, Bernard. I can't thank you enough." Then, "Is he in?"

"How long have you been out, Sleeping Beauty? Of course he's in. I'll be back in a minute."

"Thanks—bring it to Brian's office, do you mind?"

Bernard proceeded to the coffee station. She knocked on Brian's door and waited for his invitation to come in.

"Hi. Good to see you this morning. I need to catch you up on a few things. Have a seat."

Ruth sat and then accepted the coffee that Bernard had produced.

"Shall we get started?"

Within a few minutes they were elbow-deep in documents and laptops, making phone calls, working comfortably and efficiently side by side. Before Ruth realized it, they'd again worked through an entire day.

"I'm headed up to Marin tonight to have dinner with Maeve and the girls. First day of school tomorrow. Want to come with me?"

"Brian, what a nice invitation, but it sounds like a family night. Tell Maeve thanks and that I would love a rain check."

"You're family. We'd all love to see you."

"That is very kind of you, but I think you guys should pack the backpacks and sign the permission slips without me."

"That just proves how much we need a lawyer there. I'd never have thought to sign the permission slips."

Ruth laughed. "Yeah, sure. Maeve will be all over it."

"She'll appreciate the backup, then. You know I'm just going to keep asking until you say yes." He bestowed an I-know-I'm-impossible-but-also-irresistible smile on her.

He doesn't have to try so hard, she thought. I like being with him. And Maeve and the girls. What else would I do tonight anyway? Order room service and click through television options looking for some mindless way to kill time? Being the fifth wheel with the Bishop family sounded way better than that.

"Okay. I'll stay out of the way, do the dishes, or whatever, while you guys do your thing."

"Great. Head out in about twenty minutes?"

"Yes, sounds good. You are a very persistent host."

"I'm a very persistent person. As you know."

MAEVE GREETED THEM in the driveway. The girls came running, excited to see their dad and show him their back-to-school goods. It was a similar scene to Ruth's own childhood and one she'd always imagined having as a mom herself. But she was so practiced at deflecting any stab of longing that she experienced this scene as merely a glancing blow. Some things that must be endured can only be endured by ignoring them: denial, the most essential survival skill.

Maeve and Ruth trailed Brian and the girls into the house. She gave Ruth a quick hug and told her how glad she was that Ruth was there. She poured them each a glass of wine and led them to the terrace with the heart-stopping view. Brian, Lily, and Emma came out to join them.

"Cool stuff," he said. "Way better than when I was a kid."

"Most of it was not invented when you were a kid," Maeve said.

"True." Brian grinned. "Did you say I'm grilling tonight?"

"I did."

"All right—who wants what?"

With an ease that did make her feel like family, they included Ruth in the dinner prep and conversation about school, soccer, and carpool. It was once again a revelation to observe the non-office Brian. Not exactly a different person, because office Brian was as confident and cheerful as this guy. It was more as if his incredible drive for business success morphed into an even stronger desire to *win* fatherhood. As far as she could tell, no other contender came close. When Maeve announced "bedtime", Ruth insisted on clearing the table and loading the dishwasher. Alone in the kitchen she was ashamed to realize she envied Maeve the life she'd always pictured for herself—a mom and a dad and a couple of kids, doing normal family things like picking out school supplies, adding color-coded events to a refrigerator calendar. How could Maeve not want this every night? Was being Brian's wife so bad? Ruth stopped herself from imagining herself in Maeve's place. She was already someone's wife, as depressing as it was to acknowledge the sorry state of her own marriage.

She opened the terrace door and walked out into the chilly night. Looking up at the sky she prayed yet again for her own house full of family. Tonight, the prayer felt hollow, a rote and pointless recitation. Maybe what she wanted was just not meant to be. Maybe it was time to kill her improbable dream once and for all. Maybe she was destined to be an aunt, a family friend, not a mother. She never allowed these fatalistic thoughts. Their timing was terrible; she couldn't succumb to them here. When she heard Brian and Maeve return to the kitchen, she willed herself to get it together so she could paste on a smile and go back in the house.

"Thanks so much for cleaning up, Ruth. The kitchen looks better than when I do it," Maeve said.

"My pleasure. Thank you for dinner," she said, then glanced at her watch. It was hard to stay now that she'd perceived all this as a fantastical dream.

"We should get going," Brian said. "It's a school night for the grown-ups too."

Ruth and Maeve made a promise to get together, and then, she and Brian got back in his car.

"It was fun having you here. I hope you can tell how much we all like you."

"You are all wonderful."

"You're a family favorite."

"And you're one of my favorite families."

"Glad to hear that," he said, "Because we all love you."

She didn't respond. What did that mean? When after a pause Brian raised a work matter they'd need to take care of tomorrow, Ruth was only half in the conversation. She was flustered and gratified by what he'd said—who doesn't want to hear they are loved? Should she have responded, "I love — you—or all of you—, too."? Now that the opportunity to reply had passed, she decided it was better she hadn't said anything.

Chapter Thirty-Eight

DAVID'S FRAME OF MIND had not improved. He let Rick down by not even thinking about the lost plans overnight. He seemed to remember that what he'd drawn before had been better than the new ones he hastily put together the next morning, but he couldn't be sure. He didn't much care. He told himself the plans were just outlines and subject to change on-site, but the truth was he felt no real interest in these jobs, or even whether they went forward.

He met Rick at the site of the old trailer and showed him the new designs. Not being familiar with the originals, just having something on paper seemed to lift Rick's spirits. "Great, you gonna show these to the clients today?"

"I'll see if I can get ahold of them. If not today, then by the end of the week."

"Hmm. Okay. So, until then, what do you want us to do? We're all caught up, pretty much."

"Just the mowing jobs for now. Tell the guys I'll pay them for forty hours this week anyway. Next week, we'll have to see."

Rick hesitated, then said, "All right then. Let me know as soon as you know anything, okay?"

"Yeah, sure. Gonna try those clients now."

"Good luck," said Rick, as he left to join the crew.

Both clients agreed to move forward. David didn't tell them that the plans had changed. They wouldn't remember anyway, most likely. They were non-gardeners who trusted him to give them a pretty piece of property.

He dialed Rick and told him the good news. "We'll place the materials order tomorrow. I'll need your help putting it together, and then we'll get going. Looks like we are in business for a little while longer, my friend."

"Glad to hear it. Really glad to hear it," Rick said.

But that was tomorrow's work. He'd done everything he needed to do today. Might as well drive by Annabeth's and see if there were any signs of her—or the old plans. The neighbor didn't say how long she'd be gone. Yeah, good idea to check again before they placed that order. He got in the truck and left, feeling hopeful, but Annabeth's house was still empty, and he didn't think he should just hang out, what with that unfriendly neighbor keeping an eye on the place. Man, where was that girl?

As he got back in the truck his phone rang. Concentrating so hard on summoning Annabeth, he was sure she was the one calling and picked up without looking.

"Hey," he said with relief.

"Hey," said a male voice. "We're supposed to be meeting?"

"We are? Who is this?"

"James. Remember me? Your lawyer?"

David groaned. "I try not to sometimes."

"Yes, I know. But we did say we'd meet today about your lawsuit against Sid?"

"I completely forgot. Yeah, okay, it needs to be today, I guess?"

"We should get going. I hear Sid's in pretty bad straits financially and you'll want to be in line already if he declares bankruptcy. Come over and let's get started. I was under the impression you wanted to be reimbursed for the losses your insurance won't cover?"

"I do. Yeah, of course. I'll be there in a few. Sorry I forgot."

Pretty much the last thing he wanted to do right now was meet with James. David knew he was a good lawyer from all the past praise Ruth had heaped on him. He also knew James was the rainmaker for the law firm, and as a friend and a colleague of Ruth's, he'd be particularly relentless in getting whatever could be won from Sid. But the prospect of spending an afternoon answering the detailed questions he'd fire David's way was most unappealing. To his surprise, James was thorough without being obnoxious, and by the end of their meeting about his legal options, David was more in the moment than he'd been in a while.

"Nice to have you back, man," said James, as they walked toward the parking lot.

"I'm back. Just figuring out where everything and everyone went and trying to get the business going again. This was more disruptive, a bigger pain than I anticipated. Without the trailer—and also, apparently Annabeth who has disappeared off the face of the earth—it's been a slow re-start."

"I can imagine. That's why we're going to sue him. To make

you whole. If we are lucky, his insurance company will settle, and you'll get your money sooner rather than later. Getting paid might take a while, as I am sure Ruth told you."

David said nothing for a moment. "Ruth and I haven't talked about a lawsuit. She's very busy—thanks to you."

"Not my fault. Blame the client, not me."

"No, I know. I just meant since you *gave* her the client. That client. In California. Remember?"

"Yes, of course I do. She's blowing them away, by the way, but you knew she would. Bishop is supposed to be a decent guy. If she asked, I bet he'd let her come to Connecticut and give you a hand for a few days."

"She did already, but things were still too screwed up for us to know what to do about everything. She went back a few days ago."

David cast a sideways glance at James. Had Ruth told him about the mess they were in? James looked none the wiser and carried on.

"Okay—maybe now that things have started moving again, you could go out there? Rick can more than run the place. No offense."

"Thanks, James," David clapped him on the back, "I can always count on you."

"I just meant, you give him directions, then he works like a madman until every last thing is done. Everybody needs a Rick. Makes you look good, doesn't he?" He laughed.

"He sure does. But we're not at that point yet. And anyway, going to California—it isn't for me, that place. We tried a weekend out there and it didn't click."

James nodded. "Sure, I get that. Not everybody loves spending time with a wonderful woman in a gorgeous setting with all those great restaurants. Takes a special guy to put up with *that*." He laughed again. "But you will figure it out. I'll let you know when I hear back from Sid's lawyer. Maybe it will be short and sweet."

"Hope so."

David walked back to his truck, his mind a fresh mish-mash of thoughts about Ruth, Annabeth, Sid, Rick, and James. What a mess. He was not used to being forced to think through tangles. Mostly events just rolled along—Rick un-stoppable, supporting him; Ruthie amazing, loving him; Annabeth sweet, needing him; James being a jerk much of the time, but helpful in his own arrogant way. Sid, just a gray blob in his consciousness. Finding out Sid was in real financial trouble made this guy less of a blob, though, and he wished he didn't know that fact. If Sid were truly desperate, maybe that was why he went nuts, but the last thing David wanted to add to this mix was sympathy for Sid. "That guy tried to shoot you—and Annabeth," he reminded himself. "Don't get too choked up about him."

He had enough people to get choked up about and was trying to take care of all of them. He'd paid the crew for the days they couldn't work and was determined to keep them employed through this recession. He'd told himself that he sent Ruth away as a kindness, to spare her pain. But the truth was more complicated than that. He sent her away for him-self—too—because he couldn't bear for her to know how much less of a man he was than she thought him to be. And of course there was the betrayal, the unforgivable lapse, the one thing he'd never be able to tell her. By not telling her, was he in fact lying to her? No, no, he was protecting her. And how could he explain the incomprehensible to himself, let alone to her? The burden of this major, terrible screw-up had to be his to bear. He couldn't risk being with Ruth until he'd pushed his misdeed so far beneath his consciousness that he had in effect erased it. Someday it would no longer be an obstacle between them. But that day wasn't here yet.

And Annabeth. Oh, man, Annabeth. He'd intended to rescue her—from loneliness, from Aunt Janet, from her parent-less drifting. The least he owed his deceased friends was his focused attention on their daughter. That had been his intention. He was only trying to do the right thing! But somehow, over the past weeks his concern for her had become something selfish and low, and he lost his way. How was that even possible? He was supposed to be the guy in the white hat. Had he turned out instead to be some kind of creep? He just had to find Annabeth and then find the words to explain himself. Until that happened, he would have to learn to live with the silence of his shame, his own frailty, his unspeakable desire, all the things that made him unworthy to call himself Ruth's husband, not good enough for anyone who loved him, let alone himself.

Chapter Thirty-Nine

DAYS OF STEADFAST DEVOTION to work served as an effective distraction that somehow carried Ruth through to the weekend. The fact that she hadn't broken down shocked her. Be grateful, she thought. Here I am, no clue what's happening with David, and yet I'm putting one foot in front of the other, about to go out the door, looking for all the world like a fully functioning human being. She'd rented a car to drive to Muir Woods, a beautiful place Maeve could not believe Ruth hadn't yet seen. "Do you like to hike?" Maeve asked her on the phone the day after the family dinner.

"Yes, David and I go pretty often, but it's been a while."

"Want to join my hiking group on Saturday morning? It's a fitness/social group, not for hardcore climbers. We are headed up to Muir Woods. Please come. If you haven't been there yet, the scenery alone is worth it."

They firmed up plans for when and where to meet, and now Ruth was driving away from the city, looking forward to the further distractions of physical exertion and Maeve's company. She parked her car and met Maeve and her group at the base of the trail. After introductions, the women broke into pairs to hike the smaller paths. She and Maeve peeled off, walking side by side. The scenery was magnificent and this early in the morning the trails weren't yet clogged by families with young children. Maeve was once again the amiable tour guide, pointing out hidden vistas from narrow trails that skirted the main routes. The whole area was pleasantly scented with a tree unfamiliar to Ruth. Eucalyptus maybe? Or a western fir tree of some sort? David would know, she started to think, then shut down the thought. Just enjoy it, she chided herself. It doesn't matter what it's called.

"Brian and I used to run here before the girls were born. Not side by side, you know, we are talking about Brian here, but we'd reconnect along the way, then go out for breakfast. That was usually our only time alone together all week, so I loved those Sunday mornings." Maeve smiled at the memory. Maybe she harbored more regret over the break-up than she liked to admit?

"Does he still run?" Ruth asked. "I've never heard him mention it."

"No, I think he works out at the gym before he goes to work."

"*Before* he goes to work? You mean at three-thirty in the morning?"

Maeve laughed, then said, "Yes, that sounds about right.

And now he goes to church fairly often. That was not something he did much when we were together. He went when he was a kid, but later lost interest and stopped going — until we got divorced, I guess."

They'd reached the peak of a ridge with a view of a wooded valley below.

"This is more than worth the climb," Ruth said. It felt good to be taxing her body, even better to be rewarded with this vista for her efforts.

"I once ran into Brian at his church, oddly enough."

"That's kind of wild. At Grace Episcopal?"

"Yes, I think so. A big cathedral kind of place?"

"That's it. Small world!"

They trekked a long way in one direction, then at Maeve's suggestion, headed back on a different trail. The conversation turned to travel and restaurants, and before they knew it, they were back where they started. They chatted a bit with the other women finishing their hikes, and then left for a breakfast place Maeve knew. The restaurant was in a cabin and run by young people with lots of ink and piercings.

"The food here is delicious," Maeve said, "especially the California scramble."

"Is the coffee as good as it smells?"

"Heaven."

They chatted while they waited for their order, and when their food lived up to its advanced billing, Ruth said, "I'm definitely coming back."

"Yes. Bring your husband next time he's in town. He'd love it, I bet."

Ruth hesitated. "I never know when he's going to make it. I may not be able to wait that long." She glanced into her now empty cup, then signaled to the server for a refill.

"The fact is, Maeve, and I do not want to get into all the details, but things are pretty unsettled between my husband and me right now. I must say that is a sentence I never thought I'd utter, but . . . some stuff has happened, and we've been apart, and we are not doing a great job of sorting it all out. So, I don't know. I don't know when he'll next be here or when I'll next be there."

Maeve listened to Ruth with a surprised, but also sympathetic expression. She touched Ruth's arm before she spoke. "I'm sorry to hear that, Ruth. That's rough. Of course I don't know what's happening, but I know feeling unsettled like that is awful. Belly ache all the time . . ."

"Yes, usually. Although I managed to eat this morning well enough, thanks to you. But you are right. I'm kind of half queasy and spend a lot of time trying to keep so busy I can't think."

"I'm sure Brian is helpful on that front." Maeve smiled.

Ruth smiled back. "Why, yes, he is. But right now, I am glad for that. I want my brain to be fully occupied with thoughts other than the hamster-wheel-of-worry I can spend hours spinning."

"Yes. I remember that, too. It is just awful. But eventually it gets better."

"It sounds like it got better because you guys decided to break up. We are nowhere near that—and we won't be. I mean, it seems like it was the right thing for you two, but, but not for us."

"Good. I think. I mean I don't know why you're having trouble. If he's hitting you or an addict or some other horrible thing, then we need to have a different conversation."

"No, no nothing like that. It's hard to explain because I guess I don't really know myself. There was a freak incident

at work, and it upset him more than I would have expected."
She paused. "Then he kind of checked out. That's not like him.
He's the competent, down-to-earth guy in the pickup com-
mercial. Also, I haven't been there to help much. Actually, we
haven't even talked in over a week."

"Oh no!" Maeve said.

"I don't call because I don't know what to say," Ruth continued. "And he might not pick up. So we are at a stand-off, or
something, I guess."

Maeve paused before she spoke again. "I'm not the expert
on keeping marriages intact, obviously, but I do think you
have to start talking to each other. Things aren't going to get
better all by themselves."

"No, I know, but I'm at such a loss. All I can do is pray
about it. And hope whatever sent us in opposite directions
goes away."

"Hmm. Just hope and pray? You sure you want things to
get better? Forgive me, Ruth, but that sounds like pretty passive behavior."

"Does it? Doesn't feel passive to me. You haven't heard
me pray. I'm dying inside, and I have no idea what to do, but
I know I can't fix it by myself. Ugh. I don't want to talk about
this anymore. Sorry I didn't mean to drag you along. I know
you only want to help, but I'm done talking now."

Each of them sat lost in her own thoughts. Ruth already regretted sharing this news with Maeve, who she should have
known would have a different perspective from her own. She
wished she could retract her words and go back to talking
about the food. The quiet at their table began to feel awkward.

Maeve broke the silence. "Do you mind if I say one more
thing?"

"No, of course not."

"Living in limbo is not sustainable for very long. You either need to risk it—reach out to him and keep trying—or face the fact that if you can't take the risk, you might not want the relationship as much as you are telling yourself. But you're the one inside your head. Only you can make that call."

Ruth nodded, then finished the last of her coffee. They waited while the server left the check. Ruth grabbed it and put her hand atop Maeve's. "I owe you. I had no idea I would drop this on you this morning. I'll think about what you said. I promise next time we'll just trek and eat. No sob stories."

Maeve shook her head. "No apologies necessary. I'm glad you brought it up and hope I didn't overstep. Next time we'll talk or not, whatever you want. I'm around if you need me— to walk or drink wine or compare stories of baffling husbands. It stinks what you are going through. I'll help if I can."

They hugged good-bye and went their separate ways. Alone, Ruth was plagued by a new worry. What if Maeve told Brian? No, she wouldn't do that, would she? If only she could rewind the clock and just spend a lovely morning with a friend without drama or revelations. She vowed that between the two of them this topic would never surface again.

Chapter Forty

THE NEXT DAY, feeling fragile as glass, Ruth resolved to get herself to church, any church. She dressed and began walking toward the nearest steeple, maybe a church she'd visited before. Its bells were ringing, and its doors were open, so she went inside. Oh, yes, she had been here before—it was Brian's church. She slipped into a spot in a back pew behind a large column so if he showed up, he wouldn't see her. The sanctuary was dark and quiet. Congregants filtered in, some chatting with acquaintances, others, like Ruth, silently sliding into their chosen spots. As much as she missed her little Connecticut colonial church, it was a relief to be anonymous here. Better not come back too often.

The sermon was based on one of Ruth's favorite scriptures,

the story of the prodigal son. The minister, she could tell, loved it as much as she did. "If you could only read one parable to explain Christianity," he said, "this is the one to read. It's the very depiction of God's grace." He closed his sermon by saying, "My prayer for you, my prayer for myself, is to become, in all circumstances, the loving father in the story."

Ruth felt tears filling her eyes and was grateful for the pillar that gave her cover while she wiped them away. As those around her filed out, she pondered the passage. Could any human do what that father did? The son told his own father to drop dead so the son could get his inheritance. And the father, counter to everything his culture taught him, gave it to him. Then years later, when the rotten son had spent it all, the father raced down the road to welcome the filthy wastrel back home. Who but God himself was capable of that kind of love? She searched her own heart and wondered if she had the depth of love or faith to be that forgiving. Despite the minister's prayer for them, it seemed almost impossible to summon that much grace.

She waited until the sanctuary was empty before she rose to leave. As she exited the church, she saw Brian standing just outside the door. "Ruth? I thought I saw you in there. I had about decided I was wrong. He looked at her closely and asked, "You okay?"

"Yes, I seem to cry in church almost every Sunday. I do not know why."

"Maybe because you pay attention."

"Maybe. But I'd like to get through one Sunday without ruining my mascara."

"You look pretty good to me." He pulled out a linen handkerchief. "But, here, take this."

Of course, it was starched and ironed, Ruth noted, monogrammed with two intertwined Bs, and about to be ruined by her mascara.

"Any chance you want to have breakfast at my spot again?"

"Yes, I would like that."

Bumping into Brian had forced her to lose focus on the sermon, but now she wanted to talk about it. As they took a table near the back of the restaurant, she asked him, "So what did you think of today's message?"

He looked eager to answer. Leaning forward, he said with enthusiasm, "I love that story. So much in there. Every time I hear it, I identify with a different character."

"Who were you today?"

"Definitely the prodigal. I've spent a lot of time and energy chasing after things that mean nothing. I'm better, but I can still get caught up in the wrong stuff."

They ordered breakfast, then Brian asked, "What about you? Who were you today?"

She tilted her head and considered. "I suppose the older brother, all annoyed about his father not appreciating him enough, giving all the love to his rascally brother." She stirred her coffee and reflected again as she took a sip. "But I also harbor unrealistic aspirations to become the father."

Brian looked impressed. "Worthy goal, that."

"Yes. My thinking is that it might not be possible for mere mortals."

"My thinking is when it comes to parents and their kids, it's easier. Otherwise, it's almost impossible without a lot of extra help. But you've read stories about people who forgive their child's murderer, for heaven's sake. Husbands who forgive unfaithful wives. Wives who forgive husbands who gamble away every cent. Those stories seem genuine. I just don't know how they ever happen without some serious divine assistance. We human creatures are a lowly bunch."

"Most of us. At least this creature . . ." She pointed to herself. "I don't even know how good I am at trying."

"Then you've got a problem." He was serious. "The trying is essential. The trying, it seems to me, is probably all we can manage on our own. But without the trying, forgiving is impossible. It takes human intention and divine intervention, both."

She rested her cheek on her fist and considered his words. "Yes, I think you are right."

"Okay. Church ended half an hour ago. Let's talk about something lighter—like work," he said brightly.

She checked to make sure he was kidding, then laughed. "Oh yeah, let's definitely do that."

"You don't sound all that enthused, I must say. Fine, then. What would you like to discuss?"

"The lovely day I spent with Maeve, maybe? She introduced me to some wonderful hiking trails and a fantastic restaurant."

"Yes, her old hippie place. It's good. She told me you guys went there. She mentioned that you were dealing with some stuff back home. No specifics. Anything I can do?"

Ruth did not believe Maeve had left out the specifics, going by the look on Brian's face. "No thank you. It's personal. I'll figure it out."

"I am sure you will. But you know I'll help if I can."

"Thanks, Brian. I appreciate that."

Maeve had probably shared her secrets thinking that it would be good for Brian to have an inkling of the strain Ruth was under. Still, she wished Brian didn't know. What could he do? Recommend that she leave David? No way she wanted to hear that. Look at her with pity? She'd rather he never looked at her again. Since he'd designated her beloved by the family, maybe he was only offering to hold her hand, figuratively. Or literally. Something felt . . . risky. . . about that.

They spoke of other things as they finished their breakfast. Brian paid the check and said, "I need to stop by the office and grab something, then drive up for the girls. How is work these days? Is there anything we should be doing differently?"

"No, work is fine. Great, even. I haven't quite reached the state of every-second-of-work-rocks nirvana that you've achieved, but it's good."

"Good," he said. "If it ever isn't, I want to know."

He'd turned out to be so different from who at first she thought he was. Not the maniacal master of the universe James described, and she therefore was inclined to see. He was in fact a good person, a kind person. She guessed that everyone is misrepresented by his or her first impression at least to some extent. That day she met him, Ruth would not have guessed how much she'd come to like the man.

Ruth declined Brian's offer of a lift to the office. "I'm not going there," she announced. They said good-bye and went their separate ways. She strolled through the neighborhood and down the hill toward Union Square. Mid-Sunday morning was one of the rare times she enjoyed going there—too early for the tourist mobs but late enough that the evening's partiers had moved along. The bay sparkled in the distance, and one could read the architecture of this unique city. She'd taken so little advantage of its cultural offerings. Like Muir Woods outside of town, the museums and galleries were just names on a map to her. When she arrived at the Museum of Modern Art, she went inside. On this pretty Sunday morning, she had little competition for the exhibitions. She wandered around the building, not bothering to pick up a printed guide. For once she had no interest in packing her brain full of facts and analysis. She just wanted to look.

Although much of the art was weird and left her cold, some of it was stunning. She was overwhelmed by the beauty of Joan Mitchell's *"Bracket"* and stopped to stare for several minutes. No one hurried her along or jostled her out of position. She simply stood before the piece and enjoyed it. She had no idea what message, if any, the artist had intended to convey through those colors and that intense pattern, but the notion that came to Ruth was hope. The painting was just swirls and blobs and colors in one sense, but in another, by putting those precise swirls and blobs and colors on the canvas, the artist had created an experience that was much more than its physical components. It had a character, an emotion, a message in the disorder that spoke to her. Ruth, not inclined to take kindly to messes of any kind, was surprised that this piece affected her in a visceral and positive way. She resisted the urge to interpret her response, instead just allowed it to be. After a time, she moved on to other work, but when nothing else compared, she left the museum.

The streets were now filling with people and threatening to destroy the joy she'd caught from the painting, so she hailed a cab for the ride to her hotel. By closing her eyes, she could preserve her mood a little longer. The driver was not a talker, thank goodness, so her trick worked. She just nodded as she walked past the doorman she knew and made a beeline for her little room. Oh God, I want to do the right thing. Tell me what to do.

A thought that canceled all others: Call him.

Good grief, I am losing my mind. The voice of God? But even if it wasn't from God, it was from somewhere beyond her conscious thoughts. Despite the message of the sermon and the feeling from the painting, the idea of calling David again was just too scary, too humiliating. What if he didn't answer? What if he did?

Ruth. You cannot even push the buttons on a phone and less than three hours ago you were imagining yourself running down the road to wrap a ruined loved one in forgiveness. If you can't muster the courage to make a phone call—it's hopeless.

Her heart pounding, barely breathing, she dialed David's number and waited. It rang once, twice, five times, then she heard a message, "This subscriber's voicemail box is full. Please try your call again later." Argh. She threw her phone across the room and said out loud, "God! If you were going to tell me to call him, couldn't you at least have told him to answer the phone?"

Chapter Forty-One

DAVID LEFT THE APPLE STORE with a brand-new phone. His old one had disappeared. Somehow it had survived Sid, but now was nowhere to be found. The new phone looked cool, seemed easy enough to use, but was full of features he knew he would never try. He was disappointed to learn that his old voicemails were not recoverable. Nothing to be done about that. He'd managed to get through the last of the pre-autumn planting without a functioning phone, and now that they were winding down, he wouldn't need those old messages. His first call on the new phone was to Rick. "Hey. I'm officially a techie. I got an iPhone."

"Ha! Don't think that makes you a techie exactly. But that is good news. Congratulations. Does your truck have Bluetooth? You could talk on the phone while you're driving."

"What? I have no idea. Sometime, you'll have to tell me about that." Maybe he would learn how to use this thing, take the class the Apple kid told him about. Even as he thought it, he knew he never would. "Anyway, you guys good to go today? What's the breakdown looking like?"

They sorted through who would do what. It was easier to get things done when they could speak in real-time, David had to admit. He felt upbeat, almost optimistic. An iPhone could do that?

It was a gorgeous early autumn day, done as only Connecticut can do. The air was crisp and the light sharp and clear. Orange and red leaves stood out against a crystal blue sky so pure it made one ache a little. This was David's favorite time of year. The hardest of the hard work was done and he wasn't yet stuck inside or out snowplowing in the wee hours. He knew whether the season had been a boom or bust, and in this particular year of the downturn, after Sid, and everything else, he was relieved to see that he'd still turned a modest profit.

When Ruth decided to take the position in California, they'd both kind of assumed she'd be back by fall. But she must have fallen in love with the place, because even before they went radio silent, she said not one word about when she'd return on a full-time basis. James said she was thriving on the gig and the client was thrilled with her, so all was going to roll along as it had been for the past few months. That was how it was, he guessed. She was always a self-sufficient person and David was not one to tell his wife where she needed to be. He could be self-sufficient, too. Once it would have been unimaginable that they would not be speaking, and yet here they were. He was almost used to it. Strangely, the longer the silence went on, the more normal it seemed. Hard to know exactly what to say at the beginning, now it was hard to imagine them speaking at all. And yet—that's B.S., he thought. I miss her so much. I have majorly screwed up.

He drove around without a specific destination, thinking about this insane summer and wondering how in the world things got so far off track, and if they would ever get right again. If Ruthie were here, she'd tell him to pray about it. "Talk to God," she used to say to him. "It might take a while, but eventually, you will get a clear sense of what you need to do." That was fine for her. She and God seemed to be good buddies, but David and the Big Guy were not on such friendly terms. David believed, kind of, in the idea of God, but it wasn't an idea he thought about much. And even if God existed, David doubted he would be interested in hearing from him now. What would he say anyway? "Hey, remember me? It's been a while. If you're what they say you are, you already know I have made a mess of things. Guess you know what went down with Annabeth, an actual sin, I guess you would say, and the way I totally ruined things with Ruth, the person I made all those promises to. If you can clue me in on what to do now, I'd appreciate it. If you feel like meeting me halfway, giving me some direction, great. Thanks." That was not going to work.

That prayer was not going to work because it was false, a veneer of virtuous word covering is egotism. He's good at this trick now, deceiving himself about what he's doing and why he's doing it. In service to his self-image and public persona as the Good David, he is skilled at pretending not to know what lies beneath his noble gestures. The prayer is a lie because the last thing he wants is for God or anyone else to reveal the truth about the person who uttered it. It's so familiar, this performance, like all the times he stole glances at Annabeth, or drove by her house or sat too long in her driveway, telling himself he was just checking on her; like all the times he caught himself wondering what she was doing, pretending he was only concerned for her welfare. He got so good at it he was surprised when he found himself inside her house, then reaching for her that day. His delusional thinking allowed him to maintain his good guy façade quite well. It was almost impossible to break the habit of fooling himself even as he feels the pull of another force drawing him toward the truth: that he is no hero, that he stopped being the stalwart husband, the trustworthy friend some time ago, and hadn't even noticed.

The best he could hope for now is that maybe one day he will possess the courage to recognize the flawed and shadowed face in the cracked mirror as his own. And that maybe at last when he sees who he truly is, he will find the strength to ask for forgiveness.

Chapter Forty-Two

RUTH KNOCKED on Brian's door and waited for his invitation to come in.

"Hey there. I was going to find to you in a minute. Your timing is perfect." He was almost ebullient.

"Is it? What were you going to see me about?"

He stood and raised his arms in the symbol for a touchdown. "They finally closed."

"Who closed?"

"The Chinese buyers. I almost gave up a dozen times, but the funds were wired today. So, congratulations. And thank you. Could not have done it without you."

He came out from behind his desk and seemed about ready to give her a hug that he transformed mid-motion into a high-five. Ruth slapped his hand.

"I had given up, I must confess. Do you think they'll actually comply with all the terms?"

"I have my doubts, but there's no chance of that without the signed documents and the transfer, so one can hope. I don't think they'd be particularly eager to face a lawsuit in U.S. court. Fingers crossed."

She held up a hand with crossed fingers. "Yes, let's hope so. At least the process was good for developing patience. Not always my strong suit," she said.

"Nor mine. On this deal it was either be patient or let them win. No way we were going to let that happen."

She smiled. "No, of course not."

He sat back down. "So, what's up?"

She took a breath and began. "Actually, the timing on this might be as good as it's going to get. I've decided I need to go back to Connecticut permanently."

His happiness drained away. He said nothing, waiting for her to continue.

"It's time I went back home—to the firm, to my real life. This has been wonderful, and I wouldn't trade a second of it for the world. I just need to go."

He tapped into his unending supply of energy and began speaking with confidence. "There is another deal about to fire up that is perfect for you, Ruth. Now that we have this one under our belts, we'll avoid some of our past mistakes. It could be fun. Back to Beijing and some fisheye soup?"

Again, she smiled. "Beijing, Connecticut? Wasn't that the original idea? Gosh, that is tempting, but I need to go home. We have another young partner who's single and would love this opportunity. He can take my place."

Brian continued as if he hadn't heard her. "Let's say this

instead—you go home, but this time for longer—take as much time as you need. Then we'll re-evaluate."

"I appreciate that, Brian, but I have to decline. I need to re-inhabit my real life."

"This isn't your real life?"

She knew he would try to convince her to stay, but she hadn't quite expected this full-court press.

"Yes, in many ways, and it was great. You, Maeve, the work, this place—all better than I expected. But," and she took a deep breath, "I also have a marriage. It was foolish to think I could just leave that on autopilot this long." She placed both palms down on her lap. "I'm not getting into all that with you."

He hadn't been listening and picked up where he left off. "One more idea, just hold on a sec: your husband could come here. I believe it snows in Connecticut, right? Probably not a busy time for landscapers. We'll get you out of that hotel and into an apartment. That might even be fun for you guys?"

Ruth wondered how many suggestions she'd have to rebuff.

"He's not the biggest fan of California, to tell you the truth. He still has work in the winter and he's not much of a city guy. He's not going to do that. But it's a generous offer. Thank you."

He appeared to have reached the end of his list. They sat in silence. Brian shuffled some papers on his desk, then looked up at her and said, "This is probably a mistake, but . . ."

No, don't, she thought. Please don't.

He plunged in headfirst. ". . . your husband is a fool," he pronounced. "If you were my wife, I'd never have done what he did. I would have moved heaven and earth to be with you."

Don't say it, please don't say it, she thought.

"I wouldn't give a damn about busy cities or anything else at all." He spoke with a passion that demanded a response.

"You don't even know him. You don't know what he has or hasn't done."

"I don't know him, but I have observed what he has and hasn't done because I recognized it—the same thing I did to Maeve—a terrible mistake. No, I have to fault your husband in this."

Tears welled in Ruth's eyes. "Right. And I don't want to make that same mistake either. I made a promise, to David, which I don't even know if I can keep. And you are making it harder for me."

"Maybe I mean to make it harder. God forgive me, I should be encouraging you to go back and try. But maybe I am giving you another option—to open your eyes to see another possibility, something better, what you deserve. Here." He looked her in the eye. "With us."

He paused, took a breath, and said, "With me."

Chapter Forty-Three

BRIAN'S WORDS TOOK up residence in her head, playing on loop every hour she was awake. She heard them, but she wouldn't allow them to penetrate her heart. The next day she booked her flight home and began to work through her leave-taking tasks.

She called Maeve and asked to meet for lunch. Although she didn't expect Maeve to be enthusiastic about her plan, she hoped she would understand why Ruth had come to this decision. Midway through her explanation, though, Ruth read Maeve's tight lips and downcast eyes as disapproval beyond Ruth's persuasive ability to change. She cut her explanation short.

"Ruth, are you sure? You and David have agreed you are both all in?"

Ruth wouldn't tell Maeve that she still hadn't spoken to David.

"Hard for us to be all in when we're living three thousand miles apart, isn't it? That's exactly why I'm going home. This isn't a problem we can solve over the phone."

"No, I guess not," Maeve replied. "I hope it can be solved. I just want what's best for you."

Ruth thanked her, then spent the rest of the lunch steering the conversation toward other topics of little significance to either of them. She doubted she was the only one who was relieved when it came time to pay the check. They hugged each other good-bye with genuine affection and mostly-meant promises to keep in touch, Ruth already mourning the loss of a friendship that would never reach full flower.

She spent the rest of the afternoon packing her personal items and sending her work papers on their way via FedEx. She had booked a red-eye and, through Bernard, secured a prescription for a bottle of Ambien.

"Don't ask," he said on the phone.

"Thank you, Bernard. Gosh, I'm going to miss you."

"Yes, you will. But you will think of me every time you need something done and there is no one around to do it."

She laughed. "Yes, I will. I hope you know how much I have appreciated everything you've done. Do you ever come to New York? We could have dinner in the city, or you could come up to Connecticut."

"Good lord! I do not think I'd be interested in petting any cows or whatever it is you people do in the country. But I do go to New York from time to time. I'll let you buy me dinner next time I'm there."

"Wonderful! Please do call me. I would love it so much."

"As would I."

"Till then, I guess. Bye, Bernard."

"Till then. Goodbye, Ruth."

She called the bellman to help her load her luggage into the car Bernard had arranged, one last kindness on both his and Brian's part. She bid goodbye to her hotel's favorites and headed to the airport. What was she feeling? Not regret, but a bittersweetness about the ending of this chapter. But her decision was made and that was that. It was time to embrace the future. And what of that future? What she wanted was a reset, a return to the place she and David had been before this strange summer. But that was magical thinking. They'd allowed themselves to become a little lazy, then distracted, then otherwise engaged. After pushing the thought from her mind for weeks, Ruth now knew for a fact that she'd forever lost some part of David. It made her sick to her stomach. It made her even sicker to admit that she, too, was at fault. She'd allowed her work, her desire to please Brian, her dedication to team and success and tidiness and a good night's sleep— and ultimately her pride—to keep her from even picking up the phone. How hard had she tried, really, to keep them connected? She had taken her marriage and David's constant adoration for granted, but she forgot to adore him back. That mutual adoration had been the core of their marriage. How could they have been so careless to let it slip away? Where had it gone? She had a good idea where his adoration went. She could barely stand to contemplate it. To know, though, the how and the when, the terrible details, was more than she could bear. Her vows, her faith, demanded that she forgive him and, somehow, she must find a way to do that. If she had to forgive him for more than just a vague awareness of his "elsewhere" state of mind, it might be impossible. To have images and specifics . . . oh no, that would be unendurable.

She prayed, "Forgive me for being so careless. Give me the strength to forgive David for wandering off, but please do not force me to know more than that. Lead him back to me, my David. And then, please stay right by our side. We are going to need you." She prayed, and tried not to cry, almost the entire flight back to JFK.

When they landed, she did her best to pull herself together in the ladies' room and made her way to the luggage carousel. Like everyone around her, she turned on her phone and watched the incoming messages load. Her phone indicated one new voicemail from a number she didn't recognize. She tapped the button to hear it. She was startled to hear David's familiar voice say, "Hey Ruthie. It's me. I got a new iPhone now, new number, so call me back when you can. I miss you." An intake of breath, and then, "I am so sorry."

PART THREE

Winter 2009

Chapter Forty-Four

ANNABETH HESITATED before pushing the Christmas card she was sending to the Crawfords through the mailbox slot. She wrote in order to close that chapter as best she knew, and even now was second guessing what she'd said, a message she'd pretty much memorized after rewriting it so many times:

Dear Ruth and David,

I've been thinking about you both. I am sorry
I flaked out on you and left without saying
good-bye. It was a messed-up summer and I just
had to get away to get myself sorted out, which
I more or less have done. Am doing. I've been living
with Aunt Janet. Can you believe it? She's still a

corker, as she would say, but she doesn't bother me so much anymore. She actually is a good person— she just doesn't want anyone to know that.

I'm sort of back in school. I took freshman math at the community college. It was a class I blew last year, but I'm getting an A this time—which will help when I apply for school next year. I might even go back to running if everything works out. Theo keeps trying to get me to apply to his school. I guess we'll see.

The house in Connecticut will soon be on the market. Aunt Janet is driving the real estate agent nuts. Surprise! It seems we are certain to lose money, according to the agent, a fact Aunt Janet refuses to accept, so you can imagine how those conversations go. But, all in all, I wanted you to know that things here are better, even good.
I hope they are with you, too.

Merry Christmas,

Annabeth

Done, then. Wise or foolish, the card was on its way. She turned her back to the mailbox, stretched, and began to jog down the road. It was her favorite time of day. She loved running at dusk under the vast prairie sky as it turned from pale blue to the vibrant colors of a winter sunset, crimson and navy and gold. She picked up speed through Aunt Janet's residential neighborhood and ran into the farmland that surrounded the town. Before long she was running down country lanes lined with barbed-wire fences that bordered harvested wheat fields. The houses out here were few and far between, yellow lights in their windows warm and welcoming in the distance. Only one car slowly passed. No other runners were out to-night. She was alone as she found her pace, her breath show-ing in the chill, field-scented air.

As it grew darker, she recalled her mother's advice, "Take a flashlight. Something might happen to you." But Annabeth did not have a flashlight. Many things had already happened to her that her mother's love could not have prevented, her worry and warnings notwithstanding. A flashlight wouldn't have done much good. Annabeth remembered now her moth-er's words on another occasion. It was the state cross-coun-try championship, and a large crowd of exuberantly cheering parents lined the four-mile course through the wooded hills. Somehow amidst the din, Annabeth could hear one specific voice, that of her quiet and reserved mother. There she was, calling directly to her daughter, her voice audible in the midst of the cacophony: "You're looking strong! Keep it up! You've got this, Annabeth!"

And so, it seemed, she did. She'd come out on the other side of something she still didn't quite understand. There were many questions she might never be able to answer—why her parents died, what drove Sid crazy, how things with David went so wrong, and why that day she didn't resist being a part of that wrong. Although she may never have the answers to those questions, she knew for a fact that she did have this. Annabeth Brady had become the resilient young woman her parents raised her to be.

She flew through the darkness alone, her hair in the wind, her feet on solid ground, racing toward the future she had chosen.

Chapter Forty-Five

RUTH STIRRED A POT OF CHILI and peered through the window at the snow just starting to fall. The temperature was predicted to drop into the teens before morning, making this the first cold night of the season. She turned to the day's mail on the counter and noticed a few early Christmas cards. Their arrival made the usual sorting more pleasant: junk mail into the recycle, one stack of David's mail, one of Ruth's, one for mail addressed to both of them that she would open and then pass along to him. She opened the Christmas cards as she came to them, then placed them atop David's pile. When she was almost finished, she came across a red envelope with no return address, postmarked Lawrence, Kansas, hand addressed to "Mr. and Mrs. David Crawford." She stared long at the card, then placed it unopened at the bottom of David's pile. When she'd finished sorting everything, she picked up David's stack and carried it into the office where he was working.

"Today's news," she said as she placed it on his desk.

"Thanks," he said, glancing up at her. "Almost done here. Is that chili? It smells amazing and I'm starving."

"Yes. It's just about ready. The cornbread needs a little more time. I might get a glass of wine. Do you want one?"

"In a minute. I'll just go through this stuff and call it a day." He closed his laptop and turned to the mail in front of him.

Ruth perched on the edge of the chair opposite his desk and watched him go through his own sorting process. He put the business correspondence in a stack to deal with later, tossed most of the rest, and then turned his attention to the cards. He didn't bother to read the letters or notes, just glanced at the photos. When he got to Mark and Sarah's card, he held it up and said, "That Hannah is just a showstopper, isn't she?"

"Beautiful. And next year there'll be a new little face on their card."

"Yep, another heartbreaker in the making," David said.

When he came to the red envelope, Ruth saw him turn it over to look for a return address, then raise his eyebrows at her in a question. She shrugged. He looked at the postmark. She saw a wave of comprehension pass over his features before he blanched and swallowed. He looked up at her, then back at the card, deciding something. After a moment he, too, shrugged and tossed it unopened in the trash. Their eyes met again. She nodded in the direction of his desk, the mail, the wastebasket.

"Are you done with all that, then?"

He held her gaze and said, "Yes, Ruth, all done."

Together they went into the kitchen where he poured each

of them a glass of wine. They sat down at the table and, as usual, Ruth said grace. In the days before last summer, they would have held hands while she prayed. Tonight, they ate, side by side, surrounded by a careful stillness so intense it was a presence at the table. They will not talk about their separation, or the pain they'd endured. Annabeth's name will never be mentioned. Ruth will never speak of the other man she loves. They will not raise the hope they still share for a child.

For now, this is how they exist. Watching their words and guarding their hearts, they tiptoe cautiously, separately, through the altered landscape of their lives. Ruth prays and believes that one day they will find each other on the road to forgiveness. She trusts that, in time, all this hurt will be redeemed, then transformed into something better than they'd ever had before.

ACKNOWLEDGMENTS

To begin at the beginning, thank you to my parents for filling our house with lots of love and many books. I learned to treasure the world of words because of you. I love you and miss you, but you know that.

Thank you to editors Natalie Hanemann, who taught me how to structure a novel, and Eleonora Masala, who made this book better in every way. All the mistakes that remain are mine. Thank you to everyone at Westport Writers Workshop, instructors and fellow students, who taught me so much about the process of writing and publishing. What a wonderful, talented community of writers you are!

Thank you to my first readers: Amanda, Caroline, Irma, Clay, Marie, and Steven. Your wise counsel and kind encouragement kept me going. Thank you to others who must go unnamed and who saw promise in the book when I was sure I had taken leave of my senses. Huge shout out to friends and colleagues who cheered me on: my Wednesday morning book group (get it?), my Thursday evening book group, my Sunday morning book group (again!), law school and law firm friends, other Westport and Kansas City friends, and fellow writer Scott McCandless, who has a book inside him that I hope he will write one day.

ACKNOWLEDGMENTS

The road to publication had a few potholes. I am grateful to everyone on that road who believed in the book and moved the project forward. I am especially grateful to my talented agent, Jaclyn Gilbert of Driftless Literary, who came into my life at just the right time and gave the book all the enthusiasm and support an author could want. Thank you to the team at Meryl Moss Media and Meridian Editions, especially Meryl herself, who had faith in me from the first time we met. Thank you to Monique, Camryn, Erin, JeriAnn, Gerri, and John (and any others I don't know yet!) Working with all of you has been a delight.

Thank you to my dearest ones, my family. Amanda, writer of extraordinary talent, thank you for reading, rereading, offering insight, holding my hand, and understanding so well the ups and downs of a writer's life. I loved sharing this process with you and quite literally could not have done it without you. To Clay, thank you for your early reading and for providing me with insight from a male's perspective. Thank you for your hugs and heartfelt peptalks. Thank you, Nick, Cassidy, Thea, Simon, and little Rory for cheering me on and bringing me so much happiness. Thea, you too will be a published author one day, maybe sooner than you think!

Finally, thank you Steven, for over forty years of a shared journey that took us places we never could have imagined. Thank you for reading and discussing sections of the book a million times and for telling me over and over, "It's good. Trust me. It's really good!" Thank you for your unwavering belief in me, and for your unending love.

DIANE PARRISH is originally from the Midwest and now lives with her husband and their elderly Corgi in Connecticut, where they raised their two children. Her essays and short fiction have appeared in various literary journals and magazines. *Something Better* is her first novel.